THE WITCH'S JOURNEY

Praise for Keith Miller's Novels

The Book of Flying

"Original in concept, elegant in language, funny, cruel, and tender." Ursula K. Le Guin

"[Miller's] writing balances power and delicacy, delivering sudden glimpses of beauty … This is a book that you can't wait to finish but read slowly, to make it last." *The Bloomsbury Review*

"Haunting, surprising … an extraordinary debut novel." *The Baltimore Sun*

The Book on Fire

"One of the most beautifully written books I've ever read; a triumph of style, a hymn to the senses." *Vector Magazine*

"Miller has sculpted a work that is a story, poetry, humor and verbal beauty … A must read for any book lover, *The Book on Fire* is another masterpiece." *Fast Forward*

"Gritty, surreal, intoxicating, full of wisdoms and madnesses, and always a terrible beauty deranging the senses." Ian Watson, BSFA Award–winning author of *The Embedding*

The Sins of Angels

"A compelling, genre-bending novel … Highly recommended for readers seeking a sometimes dark but always beautiful adventure." *Huffington Post*

"This novel will hold you under a fantastic spell." Christopher Barzak, Crawford Award–winning author of *One for Sorrow*

"A masterful fusion of literary modes and the mark of a great talent. Miller wields his pen like no one else." Simon Strantzas, Shirley Jackson Award–winning author of *Burnt Black Suns*

THE WITCH'S JOURNEY

KEITH MILLER

Elsewhen Press

CONTENTS

I

THE KEY

In her dreams things shifted. At night, while the demons ranted beyond the shutters and the townspeople cowered indoors muttering prayers, Mira dreamed, and when she woke things were changed. Tangerines still rolling across the tiles among fragments of blue-glazed pottery. Or the eastward windows open and the carpet soaked with rain. Once she woke to hear her mother screaming, and she hurried into the kitchen. Her mother was standing before a vase of jasmine, and Mira thought she'd cut herself. But then she saw her mother's face flickering as though underwater and realized the flowers were on fire—each tiny bloom within a nimbus of flame. Still in her dream state, she was able to quench the fire somehow; she didn't know how. And the flowers, astonishingly, were untouched, though an odor like burnt sugar lingered. But the broken crockery and cracked mirrors and fallen icons could not be mended.

Her mother had learned that things went easier if Mira was out of the house—the soup didn't boil over, the iron didn't scorch—so the girl spent her days wandering in the town or, more often, along the river, hair like a blown flame, scavenging in the flotsam or sitting on an upturned crate looking out at the far shore. The river brought gifts—cat skull, snail shell, driftglass—and these she stashed under her bed, taking them out to look at by candlelight if the shrieking demons kept her awake.

She was always angry. Well, perhaps angry was the wrong word. But there was always something like a little irksome tickle in her mind or under her nails or under her ribs, which she could never quite reach and could only scratch by yelling or breaking something or refusing to scrub the floor. Her aunts, when they came over to drink tea and gossip, said it was a phase, she'd outgrow it, but she knew they whispered it was the red hair, and that made her furious. She heard them muttering, heard the words "witchery," "possession." So she'd stomp out, slam the door, and run down through the winding streets to the shore to see what the river had brought.

At the shore it was quiet.

The waves seethed and sometimes a crow cried, and that was all.

Her companions were the maimed cats, who likewise picked through the flotsam, but they were not searching for the same things.

* * *

The morning of her thirteenth birthday, Mira woke from a dream that the house was hurtling down a steep slope; that she stood at the open window gripping the sill, wind in her face, peering like a navigator into the darkness while the curtains snapped like pennants about her ears. There was no telling what lay in the depths, or even if there was an end to the plummet.

She woke gasping, clutching the counterpane, relieved to find her bed stable, horizontal. But as she lay there panting, she realized something was wrong. The light was askew or her bed had moved or something. Sitting up, she saw that her bedroom was unchanged. Maybe she'd just slept too late. Only when she walked into the living room and pulled open the curtains did she see what had happened: the house was backward, as if some enormous hand had reached from the sky and plucked it up and turned it round and set it down again. The front door now opened onto the disheveled backyard; beyond it was the brick wall of the neighboring house, laundry flapping from a line off the balcony.

She turned and walked through the kitchen and out the back door—what had been the back door. Bending, she examined the corner where the bottom step joined the pavement. There was no sign the house had been uprooted: the mortar was unblemished and a little moss grew in the crevices. She looked up at the house and put a hand in her hair, tugging through the tangles. Then she shrugged and walked down to the river.

The gray clouds swept low across the rooftops, churning slowly, and the wind tasted of steel. The church spire was smudged by mist, as was the stone Sentinel north of the town, so they might have been giants standing there, heads in the sky. The town seemed emptied of people—not a light on, not a lullaby or a leaf of smoke. It must be very early, she thought. Dawn, or soon after. But she couldn't shake the notion that the light was more like twilight. Or not twilight exactly, but some other light. The light before a storm ...

The shore was deserted of cats. Kicking a crate over, she sat watching the water. She could hear, beneath the caress of the waves, pebbles grinding.

"It's my birthday," she said aloud. Her voice sounded strangely flat. "It's my birthday," she said again, and as she spoke a wave rushed up and simmered around her ankles, rattling the stones. When the wave subsided, something glinted among the washed pebbles. Before the water rose again, she darted forward and plucked up the glinting thing and stood ankleted in foam, looking at it.

It was a key. A little gold key—one of the old kind, with a four-lobed hole in the grip and a delicate, complicated bit. She turned it between finger and thumb.

* * *

When she got back to the house, her mother was shouting and her father, still in his pajamas, was sitting on the kitchen steps, forehead propped on his fingertips, and all the neighbors were standing around. Some were sipping tea; the men were smoking. Two men crouched at the base of what had been the back wall, examining the join.

"Witch girl!" a neighbor woman screamed as Mira walked up to the house. The other neighbors turned to stare. Mira stared back. She wasn't afraid anymore.

She went up to her mother and opened her hand. "Look," she said. "The river brought me a birthday present."

Her mother snatched the key and flung it down the street. In the sudden silence, they all heard it ringing erratically as it tumbled along the cobblestones.

"I wish you'd never been born!" her mother screamed.

Mira turned and walked down the street. She bent and picked up the key and kept walking, clutching it tightly, not looking back. At the river, she sat on the crate once more. She didn't think she could go back home. Not for a while.

She was terrified, but also titillated.

Where did the power come from? She certainly didn't summon it. And she had no control over it. But as she sat watching the churn of the current, she realized she knew: it came from the same place as the anger; the source of that irksome tickle. Releasing the anger felt so good, though it also frightened her.

She opened her fist and plucked up the key. The shape was printed into her palm. A gold key. What door did it open? As she turned the key between finger and thumb, pondering, movement caught her eye. A cat was picking its way toward her, stepping carefully through the broken glass and tangled nets. Mira knew all the cats in the town, even the strays. This wasn't a stray, though— it was old Mrs. Zaccaroth's silver cat. She didn't know its name. It seldom came down to the shore, and when it did it kept to itself. But this morning the cat tiptoed up to Mira and sat beside her, curling its tail precisely around its front paws. It looked up at her with its disparate eyes—one blue as a rainstorm, the other gold— then blinked and looked out across the water. It wore a necklace of snail shells.

"Good morning, cat," Mira said. "Would you like to see my birthday present?" She held out the key and the cat touched its nose to the ornate wards, whiskers tickling her wrist. Then it turned and walked off the way it had come, tail waving queries. It looked back once, blinked, and walked on, so Mira followed.

The cat led her along the shore to where the pebbles ended in raw, scored cliffs. It wound up the steep path, through the tough riverside bracken. Mira clambered up the path behind the cat until, out of breath, she stood before the house at the edge of the cliffs—a haphazard, dilapidated structure, scoured bone white by sun and storm. A stone wall surrounded the house, and over this wall trembled the branch of a pomegranate tree. When Mira was younger she'd climbed the wall, intending to steal a pomegranate, but Mrs. Zaccaroth had come out of the house and thrown a bottle, missing her fingers by an inch.

Most mornings, Mrs. Zaccaroth walked to the market, a sailcloth shopping bag over one arm, an ancient handbag over the other. On these excursions she wore a tattered finery that, more than anything else, set her apart from the other women: purple velvet dresses with buttons of moonstone, rainbow-beaded skirts, tasseled shawls embroidered with peacocks and elephants, black heels with brass buckles, tooled leather belts, and a fantastic assortment of hats. Wide-brimmed straw hats with trailing ribbons, hats with ostrich feathers like gaudy moth antennae, hats adorned with outsize fruit, short-brimmed leather caps. Beneath the hats, strands of white hair twisted in the breeze. She bought small quantities of dozens of items—turmeric and cinnamon, cashews and hazelnuts, dates and dried quinces—bargaining viciously over a penny or two, and always a little fish or a poor cut of meat. When she was done, she'd turn and walk slowly back through the town, muttering, eyes shrouded under her hat brim, to her cliffside house.

When Mira was six or seven, she'd seen two boys, on the outskirts of the town, throw stones at Mrs. Zaccaroth. One hit her on the rump; the other knocked her pointed black hat into the dust. She didn't turn to scold them; didn't even look at them. She just picked up her hat and smacked it free of dust and put it on and kept walking. But the next day one of the boys fell from a mango tree and broke his arm, and that very afternoon the other boy took ill with scarlet fever and was in bed for a month. After that there was no more stone throwing.

Mira had asked her mother about Mrs. Zaccaroth once. "Was she ever married?" she asked. It was suppertime. They were eating a stew of fish and potatoes.

Her mother clicked her tongue. "That kind never get the men," she said.

"Well," her father said, "that's not strictly true."

"What do you mean?" Mira asked.

Her father chewed carefully, then tongued forth a fishbone and examined it. "She was considered very attractive when she was younger," he said.

"Attractiveness has nothing to do with it," her mother said. "Nothing to do with it at all, if you can't keep the scandals away. More stew, Mira?" she asked, with an air of finality.

* * *

The cat bounded to the top of the wall, paused a moment, tail waving, and dropped soundlessly into the garden. Mira stood before the iron door. To her right, a chain emerged from a chink in the stone, its last link a brass loop. She put her finger in the loop and tugged.

For a minute there was no sound save for the river splintering against the rocks far below. She was about to tug again when she heard footsteps. And a moment later, with a gnashing of drawn bolts and unleashed chains, the door swung open.

Mira took a step back. The woman before her was not the dowdy personage who shuffled along the cobblestones, peering sidelong from beneath the brims of her outlandish hats. This figure wore a lilac housedress trimmed with lace at the hem and cuffs. She was bareheaded, her white hair flickering and lifting about her head as though electrified. She stood straight and looked at Mira with steady eyes the color of the river at dawn: a pale gray-green. The cat braided itself about her bare feet, tail lingering on the curve.

"Mira, isn't it?" Mrs. Zaccaroth said. "Yes. I've been expecting you. Come in."

She stood aside, and Mira, despite the cold droplet that seemed to slide from nape to tailbone, stepped across the threshold. The garden was prettier than she'd expected: overlapping patchwork beds of flowers and herbs where bees scrabbled and butterflies swung. She could smell lavender and rosemary, but there were other, nameless scents, some rather pungent; unpleasant, even. Rosebushes made an arbor over the doorway and crimson petals carpeted the doorstep.

Once they were inside the house, Mrs. Zaccaroth closed the door and stood in front of it, looking at Mira. It was not a kind face. Her eyes were sharp, her lips parched. It was a face that concealed—only the eyes betrayed emotion, and that sparsely.

"Now, what have you brought?" she asked, and her voice as well was parched, pinched, prickly.

Mira opened her hand. Mrs. Zaccaroth leaned forward, looked at the key for a moment, and straightened. She glanced out the window to the far shore and something passed across her eyes. Sadness, perhaps, but freighted with a certain hunger. She looked back at Mira. The emotion, whatever it was, had been rinsed away. It was hard to return that cold, sharp stare.

"It's a present from the river," Mira said. "It's my birthday."

Mrs. Zaccaroth pursed her lips, then nodded, once. "Take a seat," she said. "I'll make tea." She went through a door, and Mira looked around the room. It was much like the parlor of her own house, with a round rag rug, doilies on the sofa and the high-backed armchairs, a glass-topped coffee table. But the walls were a rich plum, and on the mantel, where her mother kept painted porcelain angels, lay a dozen crystals and polished spheres on little wooden pedestals: amethyst, rose quartz, lapis lazuli ... Other names surfaced—tourmaline, carnelian—but she could not be sure. Some of the crystals gave her an uncanny feeling—the slightly queasy sensation she got when she looked into mirrors. She had learned to avoid reflections. Going to the window, she quenched her gaze on the horizon.

She was still standing there when Mrs. Zaccaroth returned with a tray containing a teapot, two cups and saucers, a silver pitcher of cream, a bowl of sugar, and a plate of chocolates like tiny jewel boxes, topped with gold foil or crimson beads or crushed pistachios. "Try a truffle," she said.

Mira leaned over the plate. "They're so pretty!" she exclaimed.

"I have too much time on my hands," said Mrs. Zaccaroth. "Still, it's important that things are beautiful. Or so I feel."

The truffle Mira selected had a shard of green glass embedded in it. She touched her tongue to the glass. Sweet, hot mint. Vapor smarted in her sinuses.

She nibbled, crunching the mint glass, the chocolate silky on her tongue. Her eyes widened.

"Preserved ginger," Mrs. Zaccaroth told her. She poured the tea. "I enjoy combining flavors and textures. Cream?"

"Yes, please," Mira mumbled around her mouthful of chocolate.

"Sugar?"

"Just one."

Mrs. Zaccaroth took a chocolate, nibbled, and leaned back, eyes closed. When she opened them, she smiled at Mira for the first time. "Smoked eel and cayenne," she said. "Now. Tell me what's been happening." Cradling her teacup, she looked over the rim with her pale eyes.

So Mira told her about the strange power of her dreams, about the jasmine on fire and falling picture frames and shattering vases, and finally about the house—picked up, turned around, set back down, without so much as a rustle, without a stone dislodged, and even the moss still in place where the steps met the cobbles. She looked down into the brown circle of tea, which wobbled slightly with her heartbeats. "I don't know where it comes from," she said. "And I can't seem to stop it."

"Have you tried?"

"Yes, of course. I've prayed and prayed. I tried staying awake, but I always fall asleep eventually. The priest comes over and cleanses the house, but it doesn't help, the dreams still come." Her lower lip quivered, but it felt good to be saying it, to be telling someone at last. Someone who wouldn't mutter a prayer or sketch crosses in the air or laugh at her, but who just watched her, listening.

"What do they say it is?" Mrs. Zaccaroth asked.

"Well … the possession. You know—I'm a witch girl, all that."

"And is that what you believe?"

"I guess. I haven't really thought about it. I mean, about what to call it. I know it's … it's not like what they think it is."

"What do you mean?" Mrs. Zaccaroth leaned forward slightly.

"I mean, it's—" She stopped, then started again, more slowly. "They think it comes from outside, I guess. But I think … I think it's *inside*. It's always been there, maybe, and it has to come out one way or another. Like steam, you know, in a teakettle."

"Yes," Mrs. Zaccaroth said. She set down her cup. "Yes, I do know." The cat jumped onto her lap and knocked at her knuckles with its skull. Mrs. Zaccaroth ran a finger backward through its fur and the cat collapsed, droning. She took a fold of the skin at its nape and rubbed it between finger and thumb, then scratched its chin with a stained fingernail. "This is Mr. Mugwort, by the way," she said.

"So is it true?" Mira asked impatiently.

"True?" Mrs. Zaccaroth looked up. "What do you mean by that?"

"Are ... am ... are you a witch, then? Is it true, about the powers?"

"Of course," Mrs. Zaccaroth said tersely, almost curtly. Then she sighed. "Yes, of course it is," she said more gently.

"So all the stories—magic and fairies and ... and all that?" Something surged inside her and the tea jostled so she had to set the cup down.

"Magic. Fairies." The corners of Mrs. Zaccaroth's eyes crinkled slightly. "Well, yes and no. From the inside it looks quite different. But I too was a girl once, though longer ago than you might suppose."

"Did things happen to you as well, when you were a girl?" Mira asked.

Mrs. Zaccaroth nodded. "They did indeed. They did indeed. But I was not quite so fortunate as you. In my day it was not considered seemly for a young girl to wander out of doors, alone. So I had no escape, do you see? The steam stayed in the kettle, to borrow your image. Eventually they had me committed."

"Put in prison, you mean?"

"No, no. Much worse. They shut me in a ... well, in a type of asylum. A place for girls like me. Like us. They thought I was possessed, naturally. It was a terrible place. Essentially we were left to fend for ourselves. Some of the inmates were violent." She paused and shook her head. "The less said about that place the better. But I do not regret the experience, because I met a woman inside who told me what I was. Her name was Sister Agate. She was my first teacher. And she arranged for my release—she had contacts on the outside. This was in the city far to the north. Eventually, with the help of Sister Agate's friends, I made my way south along the river to this town. Where I have remained."

"Why didn't Sister Agate get herself out?" Mira asked.

"Oh, she could have, of course. But she was ... it was her task, you might say. To help those like me. Like us."

"Did you have other teachers?"

"I did."

"Here?"

"Yes. This was the house of Mrs. Chalaban, who was my tutor

for several years. Few in the town would remember her—she died while she was still quite young."

"Of what?"

"Oh, there are dangers, Mira. Make no mistake. There are dangers. Ours is a lonely, tormented life, beset with peril."

"So you had a tutor," Mira said slowly. "Did Mrs. Cha …"

"Chalaban."

"Did she have other students?"

"No. I was the only one."

"And have you ever been a tutor for someone?"

Mrs. Zaccaroth looked out the window. She was silent for so long Mira thought she wasn't going to answer, but finally she nodded, though she didn't turn. "Yes," she said softly. "Yes, I had a student once. Only one."

"What was her name?"

But this time Mrs. Zaccaroth didn't answer, and Mira felt she couldn't ask again. She took the key out of her pocket and held it by the shaft, turning it. "So, do you know why the river gave me the key?"

"Well … I suppose it's not a secret." Mrs. Zaccaroth turned back from the window, her gaze following a beat behind. Still, she seemed to hesitate for a moment. Then she said, "It is the key to the door to the other side."

"The other side? The other side of what?"

"Of this." She moved her hand in a quarter circle, palm up, taking in Mira, the teapot, the cat, the river.

"What do you *mean*?" Mira asked, lifting her hands and letting them fall into her lap.

"Just that things are not, perhaps, quite as they seem."

"I think I'm beginning to understand that."

"Have another truffle, and I'll see if I can explain."

Mira selected a chocolate ("Pistachio and pomegranate," Mrs. Zaccaroth murmured) and nibbled at it. She looked expectantly at Mrs. Zaccaroth, who was staring out the window again.

"Perhaps the best way is to show you," Mrs. Zaccaroth said. She tipped Mr. Mugwort from her lap, and he grumbled and yawned and walked over to a ribbon of sunlight on the rug. "Hand me my reticule there," she said. Her large black-leather handbag lay against the leg of the sofa. Mira passed it across the table, and Mrs. Zaccaroth snapped open the clasp and rummaged inside. She pulled out an aged oval handmirror. Specks of gilt still clung to its frame. Moving around the table to the sofa, she sat beside Mira and handed her the mirror. "Look into it," she said, "and tell me what you see."

Mira held the mirror before her, using both hands so it wouldn't shake. The glass was corroded, her face a phantom. "It's too cloudy," she said.

"Yes," Mrs. Zaccaroth said. "Now, keep looking." Leaning forward, she breathed onto the glass.

Mira watched the oval of condensation diminish from the edges in. At first there was no change, but then, though she sat perfectly still, she saw shadows stirring within the glass. Involuntarily, she glanced behind her. But Mrs. Zaccaroth, as if from a long way away, called her back. "Look, child," she said, and Mira lowered her eyes to the mirror once more.

Like a curtain evaporating, the surface cleared and she was climbing stairs in darkness. At the top of the stairs a door stood ajar, a shaving of light beneath it. Looking across the threshold, she saw a woman standing at a window: a tall woman in a garment that seemed fashioned of shadows, her hair a storm cloud. One narrow, pale hand lay on the windowsill. And as Mira watched, she turned.

Mira dropped the mirror, which shattered against the edge of the table. The splinters leaped against her ankles. "No!" she cried. She stood and swayed, staring down at the triangles of glass, within which reflections still flitted like moths. Then she stumbled past Mrs. Zaccaroth to the door, clawing at the air as if fighting brambles.

"Mira!" Mrs. Zaccaroth called, but she was already out of the house, running along the flagged path, out the garden door, and then scrambling sideways, clutching at bracken, scraping her knees, down to the river.

She pulled the key from her pocket and looked at it. Then: "Take it back!" she shouted. "I don't want it! I don't want *any* of it!" And she hurled the key as far as she could into the waves. Before it entered the water, she had already turned and was rushing up the stony beach, into the town, back to her house, which was still turned the wrong way.

* * *

That afternoon the priest came. He was short and his belly swelled his robe. He ate the dry cake Mira's mother set out, fluffing his beard to dislodge the crumbs. His eyes flickered over to Mira, returned to her mother's face. Leaning toward her mother, he said, "They are growing stronger. The Elias child was taken last evening.

You heard?" Mira's mother shook her head. The priest rummaged in his beard and nodded. "She was fetching a plaything from the street, something she'd forgotten. Shortly after nightfall. She was taken a few steps from the door, her mother told me. Yes, they are growing in number and are becoming bolder."

Mira's mother clicked her tongue twice and crossed herself. "Evil times."

"We must repent," the priest said. "Now, tell me of the difficulties in your house."

So Mira's mother told him about the pots and porcelain angels broken, the icons shattered. The scorched shirts, the burnt casseroles. She told him about Mira's brother, Paulus, who had been taken by the demons.

"Mira was with him that evening," she said. "It was soon after he'd been accepted as an altar boy."

The priest nodded. "I remember."

And finally she told him what had happened that morning. The house plucked up and set down backward, without a rustle, without a sound. When she finished, the priest took off his hat and held it in his lap, gazing into the greasy hollow as if hoping to find a solution there. He put it back on and looked at Mira. For a minute he watched her from beneath heavy lids. Then he asked, "When do the transgressions occur? Morning? Evening?"

"When I'm asleep," she told him. She leaned forward, elbows poking into her thighs. She'd promised herself she would really do it this time—take it seriously, follow the instructions, to get rid of the magic once and for all. "They're like dreams," she told him. "Like dreams, but they come true. When I wake up, things are changed."

"Mmm," the priest said. He immersed his whole hand in his beard and scratched there. "Hmm," he said. "And have you been in communication with demons? With beings not of this world?"

Mira remembered the woman in the glass, turning toward her. She shook her head. "Not in communication, no."

"Do you pray?"

"Sometimes."

"You must pray," he said. "I will instruct you."

Then, like a doctor who has heard the patient out, he moved abruptly into action. From his battered satchel he took a censer, a Bible, and a small bottle filled with yellowish liquid. While Mira's mother fetched a coal from the kitchen, he opened the Bible, holding it a few inches from his nose, drawing his finger down the columns. Finally he found the passage and handed the book to Mira. "Read," he commanded, tapping a page. "This verse only. When you reach the end, repeat." So she read the verse, stumbling over the words at first, then more fluently, reading it over and over while the priest placed the coal in the censer and blew up the smoke and meandered around the room and then through the house, swinging the censer into every corner, under the beds, into the closets, and across the tables, filling the rooms with fragrant fog. Returning, he set the censer on the table. He picked up the bottle and dabbed thick yellow oil onto Mira's forehead, beside each ear, at the corners of her mouth, on the nape of her neck. The oil ran alongside her nose, tickly, but she kept chanting the verse, pinching the bottoms of her thighs to force herself to sit still.

At last the priest sat back with a great "Uff!" and indicated that she should cease her recitation. He passed the bottle to Mira's mother. "You will use this in the evening," he said, "before she goes to bed. And you"—he turned to Mira—"you will recite the verse twelve times before you sleep. Do not eat anything in the hours after sundown. Drink only water after dark. Sleep on your left side. There is some protection in facing the east. And remember, keep your thoughts turned always, always toward the light."

* * *

So she did it. She followed the priest's instructions honestly and precisely. With her father's help, she moved the bed so it lay catty-corner in the room, the ends facing north–south. She did not eat after sunset, and drank only a glass of water. She sat still while her mother applied the oil. She recited the verse a dozen times, lingering over each word, focusing, as she knelt beside the bed, eyes closed, facing east.

But even as she finished the recitation, as she released the last word from her tongue, she recalled the vision within Mrs. Zaccaroth's corroded handmirror, the turning figure at the window with her storm-cloud hair and dress of shifting shadows. "No!" she said aloud, opening her eyes to the patchwork bedspread, the dingy walls, the icon of the Virgin askew on its nail. For a long time she lay staring into the darkness. The demons ranted through the cobbled streets, calling, scrabbling at windows.

* * *

When Mira was eleven, her mother, exasperated by her tantrums, had taught her to embroider. Mira had immediately taken to the art—she loved the thick threads, like a tangled rainbow stuffed into a cotton bag; she loved the plump pink-leather pincushion and the grownup feeling of slipping on a thimble; she loved being able to actually make something, and something *pretty* at that. And, as her mother had anticipated, the concentration, the slow dance of hand and eye, quieted her mind. So, for a month or two, she spent her afternoons on the sofa sewing, and her parents were delighted to have her tame for a while.

Paulus was nine. He was a small boy with enormous eyes and hair as dark and soft as charcoal. He didn't have Mira's tickly anger—when their mother asked him to tidy up his toys or turn off the light because it was time to sleep, he did so without a word. Sometimes Mira hated him so much for his gentle, wide-eyed compliance that she'd put a pinecone under his sheets or hide his favorite toy. But, though he cried, he was never angry for long.

A quiet Sunday afternoon. Mira's mother was clattering in the kitchen and her father was snoring softly in his chair. Mira was sitting on the couch in a wedge of sunlight, bent over her embroidery hoop.

Paulus came in and sat beside her, nibbling a sesame cookie. "Can you teach me?" he asked after a while.

"You're too little," Mira said, rather shortly. She was embroidering an emerald frog on yellow linen. At last she blew out a breath and looked up. "Why are you still wearing your robe?" she asked. Because of his sweet compliance and his ability to learn Bible verses, Paulus had been chosen to be an altar boy. He came home from the catechism one Tuesday with his own white robe embroidered with thick gold crosses. Mira, though irked he'd been chosen, was enraptured by the embroidery, and she had taken the robe on her lap and run her fingers over the voluptuous tussocks of gold.

"Mother said I could. Will you come play with me?"

Mira shook her head. "I want to finish this while it's still light."

"Can you help me with my verses then?"

Mira shrugged.

Paulus recited the verses in his clear small voice. "Was that right?"

Mira nodded absently, tying off a knot. She rummaged in the bag and pulled out a slender skein of black thread. Licking the end, she twisted it to a damp spike and, holding her breath, held it up to poke through the needle.

"Now will you come play with me?"

"I told you I need to do this first." She tilted the hoop. "See, I'm trying to finish the eyes, and they're fiddly."

"All right."

She bent to the circle of linen, angling the needle in through the back. Did frogs have round pupils? she wondered. Or were they barred like those of goats?

Only when her mother called them for supper did she realize dusk had fallen. Dusk had fallen and the back door was open.

They found his footprints the next morning, in the soil beside the bay laurel.

* * *

After the priest came, nothing happened for three nights in a row. Mira woke with no recollection of her dreams, into the quiet morning sounds of her mother's spoon clinking in her teacup and the clatter of her father's newspaper as he folded back a page. She didn't go down to the river but stayed at the house, helping her mother peel potatoes and snap beans, beating the living room carpet, hanging out the laundry. Her mother said nothing about the change in her behavior, but the first night, after she'd applied the oil, she called Mira to sit beside her on the sofa and combed out her shocking hair, folding it into two plaits and securing them with ribbons. When she was finished, she took Mira's cheeks between her palms and nodded. Seeing her mother's face up close, Mira noticed for the first time the thumbprints of shadow beneath each eye and the minute jigsaw of wrinkles at their outer corners.

She even went to church on the second day, something she hadn't done for months. She put on her good dress and cramped black shoes and walked with her mother and father down the cobblestone main street, past the empty market square and the row of shuttered shops.

Beyond the little harbor where the moored boats rocked, thirty steps rose. The lowest ten were slick and striped with river weed combed and recombed by the waves. Then came ten that were soaked when the rains swelled the river. The highest ten tasted the river only in the heaviest storms. At the top of the steps was the church, the tallest structure in the town, with walls of black rock and a spire like a chip out of the blue. The riverward door was locked; parishioners entered through the great west-facing doors, which the priest hauled open on Sunday mornings, ushering the townspeople in from sunshine to take their seats in urine-scented gloom.

Mira's mother liked them to sit near the front, close enough that Mira could see the crescents of sweat spreading on the priest's cassock. High on the walls icons hung, so faded and veiled in cobwebs that no one could say any longer which saints they depicted. Mira would sometimes cloudread creatures in the corroded icons: a girl with a fish tail; an ogre formed of rocks, head in his hands; a gleeful demon seizing a child—though she knew demons were not permitted in here: the priest told them, every Sunday, that this place of shadows and cobwebs was a sanctuary, the abode of the light.

Mira hated going to church. She hated the starched collar and itchy stockings and painful shoes she had to wear, even on the hottest days. She hated the musty smell and the slightly sticky wood of the pews and she hated listening to the droning priest, whose voice seemed pitched to put people to sleep (which it did—by the end of the mass, snores rose here and there, sometimes snuffed with an ugly gargle by a poked elbow). She hated the rituals: standing and raising her arms and making the sign of the cross on her breast and kneeling with her forehead on the sticky, stinky pew in front of her. Though occasionally, as the priest muttered, as she lifted her arms, she had a curious sensation that there was something almost right; if a phrase were changed and the angle of her arms adjusted slightly, she felt, the ritual might shift into power, into magic.

The priest performed his labors at an altar on a dais, flanked by two boys in their white gowns. The boys were supposed to be solemn, but they fidgeted and one always picked his nose, trying to disguise it as a scratch. When she was younger, Mira had wanted to become an altar boy—being up front seemed more fun than sitting in the pews—but her mother had slapped her when she mentioned it at the dinner table, and only clicked her tongue and looked away when Mira asked why.

At the back of the dais a curtain of bloodred velvet hung from iron hoops. From time to time during the mass the priest would slip behind the curtain, emerging with the platters of communion bread or the fuming censer. Since she was tiny, Mira had longed to know what lay behind the curtain. She imagined a little parlor, with a comfy sofa and a painted tea set on an inlaid table, where the priest could hide away, tuck up his feet, and read and sip a nice cup of tea whenever he felt like it. Or perhaps it was a cozy library, bookshelves floor to ceiling, and a ladder to reach the highest shelves.

One Sunday three years ago, as the priest was droning away interminably at the lectern, Mira felt the curtain begin to move. She had been gazing down at her filthy bitten fingernails, wondering what lay behind the curtain, and she felt the iron hoops slide; felt the rich velvet begin to fold. She looked up.

The priest ceased droning, frowned, and turned. The curtain was slowly sliding along its rod. He looked sharply at the altar boys, first left, then right. The boys were equally baffled. Before it got far enough to reveal whatever it concealed, the priest leaped to the curtain, robe writhing about his hairy calves, and ducked his head behind it, but no one was there. He yanked the curtain closed and, muttering, moved to the altar once more. But before he started in on the droning, he scanned the congregation. His hooded eyes alighted on Mira, who was biting her lip, trying to quench her giggles.

The next day the priest visited their house, and from then on, to Mira's delight, she was permitted to skip church if she chose, and she spent Sunday mornings down at the river shore with the cats.

This Sunday, though, nothing happened. The priest kept a wary eye on her, and she made a sincere attempt to focus on the service. The priest's voice was so boring, however, that she found her mind wandering back to Mrs. Zaccaroth's house; to the mineral spheres arranged on the mantel, to the truffles and tea and the rustle of the river below her parlor window. Though she was in fact closer to the river in this church, the stone walls were too thick to admit any sound. She prayed, murmuring along with the congregation. She knelt and stood and knelt again, palms pressed to her chest. She took the communion bread on her tongue and told herself she could taste the transformation, though what she tasted were weevils.

II

IN THE WITCH'S HOUSE

The next morning, Mira woke from a dream of great beauty and violence. Dawn had sketched a faint line around the curtains. She tugged a corner aside and looked out into the grainy sky, waiting for her heartbeat to settle. Her mouth was dry. It had been one of the big dreams, a dream of transformation, but when she tiptoed apprehensively into the living room she failed to spot any change. She couldn't understand it: there were no broken bowls or shattered mirrors, nothing was burning. It must be working, she thought. The power was diminished. Shrugging, she put the teakettle on. When her mother got up, Mira was sipping tea and murmuring over the Bible.

The fish cart came with the morning catch, and Mira went out to choose the fish. The fisherboy, Tolly, lived in a shack on the northern outskirts of the town. He was an orphan: his mother had died of the ash fever when he was nine and his father had drowned in a storm two years later. The boat drifted to shore, and Tolly had righted it and stepped a new mast and sewed two bedsheets to serve as a sail. Painstakingly, he mended the spare net hanging in the rafters. And a fortnight after the storm, he set out on the river at dawn, and by midmorning was knocking on doors, seven silver fish in an oblong rushwork basket. Later he saved enough to buy a cart.

Mira knew Tolly's story—everyone knew his story, and the housewives treated him kindly and gave him a little extra for his wares—but she didn't like him. He was overeager, with a sideways snaggletooth grin, and he was too skinny and he stank of dried sweat and fish and he couldn't meet her eyes for more than a moment, ducking his head and blushing and fiddling with the fish. The soft tails of his hair were burnt gold, eyes bloodshot blue in his smudged face.

Tolly was the only other person who came to the stony beach— sometimes when she went down in the morning he'd be there laying out a net, his craft bobbing at anchor. He said it was quieter than the harbor, but she knew he came because of her and she teased him. Teased him about his frayed shirts and his mumble and his fish stink, and he'd blush under his tan and bend to his knots.

This morning Tolly seemed even more flustered and awkward than usual. His hands trembled as he sorted through the fish, and he handed her three, refusing to take the coins.

"What is it?" she asked. "What is it, Tolly?"

But his glance was fearful, and he shook his head, gripped the cart handle, and set off almost at a trot down the street, the cartwheels making an unsteady drumbeat on the cobblestones. Mira watched him go. The rumors must have reached him. Now even the orphaned fisherboy was afraid of the witch girl.

Mira helped her mother scale the fish and made a little salad of cucumbers and tomatoes and white cheese while her mother fried them. Her father came out of the bedroom while they were setting the table. They ate in silence, Mira in a strange emotional limbo of relief that the dream hadn't altered anything, mingled with despair that she'd snuffed the magic. But as she teased the white flesh off the skeleton, something glinted. Lifting the flat ribs, she pulled free a small gold object and looked at it.

"What is it?" her father asked.

"A key," she said. Then she stood and pushed back her chair and walked out of the house, ignoring her mother's calls.

* * *

She made her way down to the shore and sat on an upturned crate, the key in her hand. The shore was deserted this morning, silent. The spun filaments of sunlight flourished and perished in the long, twisting pour.

Ever changing, ever the same, the river originated in mystery and ended in mystery. According to some, it had its birth far to the south, in mountains so lofty their peaks were smothered by clouds, and foundered far to the north, in a sea so vast its other shore was buried beyond the horizon. But many said the river had no beginning or end; or, rather, that all places along the river were both beginning and end, for it circled the earth. It was beholden to the sky and the wind, and also to the turmoil beneath its surface. It carried in its passage life and death. Mira greeted it every morning, this ancient, blithe, fickle creature; had learned to read the moods on its face: unruly or placid, playful or grim.

"What am I supposed to do?" she asked the river, turning the key between finger and thumb. "Tell me what to do." But it offered no answer, unless its relentless northward thrust was itself a reply.

After a while, she stood and made her way up the path to Mrs.

Zaccaroth's cliffside perch. She reached for the bellpull, but before she touched it the door swung open.

"Come in," Mrs. Zaccaroth said. She seemed slightly out of breath, and peered behind Mira as if to confirm no one had followed her.

In the parlor, tea was already laid out, two cups, a feather of steam curling from the pot. A dozen chocolates lay on a silver plate. Mr. Mugwort snored on the sofa. He grunted and tucked his head deeper into the cranny between his paws when Mira scratched between his shoulder blades. She watched the steam drifting from the spout, and all of a sudden something shattered inside her. At first she tried to keep the tears in, biting her lower lip and squinting, but Mrs. Zaccaroth looked up from pouring the tea and said, "It's all right, my dear. Go ahead and cry."

So Mira sat there sobbing, tears dripping through her fingers, while Mrs. Zaccaroth added sugar and cream and stirred.

"All right," she said, handing Mira the cup. "Enough. Drink your tea and tell me what happened."

Mira tried to swallow her sobs, but they wouldn't go down. Finally she held her breath and forced them into submission. "I tried so hard," she whispered. Her voice was scarred, scraped. "I did everything they said. I recited the verse and my mother did the oil and I prayed, I really prayed, you know—I wasn't just saying the words. Yesterday I even went to church. And I thought it was working. I thought I'd killed it; killed the magic. And then last night I had a dream again, one of the big dreams, and this morning ..." She pulled the key out of her pocket and flung it onto the table, where it banged against the sugar bowl and clattered to a halt. "I tried to give it back. I threw it into the river, but it returned to me." And she told Mrs. Zaccaroth about the fish Tolly had brought.

Mrs. Zaccaroth nodded. "Things are more desperate than I thought."

"But what does it all *mean*?" Mira cried, so forcefully she woke Mr. Mugwort, who grumbled and turned his disparate eyes on her for a second before going back to sleep.

"That I can't tell you," Mrs. Zaccaroth said.

"But you ... you had teachers, people who helped you. That sister—Sister Agate—and the woman who lived here ..."

"Yes."

"So will you—" Mira fidgeted with a button on her dress, suddenly embarrassed. "I need help," she said, looking up at Mrs. Zaccaroth, lips twisted by the struggle to keep from crying again.

"Will you teach me? Like Mrs. Chalaban taught you? Like you taught your student? Please?"

Mrs. Zaccaroth smiled at her. "Of course," she said. "But you had to ask. I was waiting for you to ask."

"Oh, thank you," Mira said. "Thank you. So now will you tell me? What does it all mean? Why did the key come to me?"

"The first lesson," Mrs. Zaccaroth said sharply, "is that I mean what I say. When I said I couldn't tell you, that was the truth."

"So is there nothing I can do?" Mira wailed.

"Calm yourself, child. What I can do is teach you to control and use your power. This is not a short or a simple process. Only when you have those tools in your possession will you be able to make the journey."

"Journey?" Mira looked at her.

"Becoming a witch always involves a journey—a journey that includes certain stepping stones, certain waystations, though those will manifest differently for each girl. Make no mistake—the journey is not easy. Many stray from the path or lose their way. Many abandon it altogether. And those who persist may find the destination unsatisfactory or horrifying. But I believe this is your task, Mira. The key was given to you; you must take the adventure that comes or be forever unfulfilled."

Baffled, Mira ducked her head to her tea. "All right," she said.

"Now, there's something you haven't told me about," Mrs. Zaccaroth said. "I think we'd better start there."

Mira was mystified. "I told you about my dreams."

"Not your dreams."

"What then?"

"The mirror. What did you see in my handmirror before you ran out the door?"

"Oh." Looking down, she saw she'd left chocolate fingerprints on her dress, and she sucked her forefinger. She couldn't suppress a shiver. "What I always see. A dark staircase. A woman in a dress made of shadows, standing at a window. She turns toward me. I've seen her face before, in dreams, in mirrors, sometimes in the shadows on the river. I keep seeing it."

"What else do you see?" Mrs. Zaccaroth asked.

"Thin fingers sometimes, reaching for me. A ruined town with bones in the streets. A clock with no hands. Sometimes a high room, and I'm looking down across shadowy cobblestones to a dark river. Maybe from the same window. I don't know." She tapped a fingernail into her wrist bone to quell the queasiness.

"And what do you feel, seeing those images?"

"I'm always scared. Well … tingly scared, you know? Like I want to turn away but I can't."

"And yet you always turn away."

"No. The dream stops. I wake up, and my heart's going." She pressed a palm to her breastbone.

"And have you ever entered that landscape when you were awake?"

"No. Not until your magic mirror. I'm sorry I broke it."

Mrs. Zaccaroth shook her head. "The mirror was not magic."

"But—"

"The mirror was an ordinary handmirror, though it was very old. Just as these stones are ordinary stones." She went to the shelf where the spheres stood and lifted one down. It was the color of twilight, filled with crazings and imperfections so the center roiled like storm clouds as she turned the globe. Mira could feel something snagging at her mind as she gazed at it, and swiftly lifted her eyes.

"Smoky quartz," said Mrs. Zaccaroth. "The color is caused by radiation deep within the earth. It has little value as a jewel; however, it is peerless as a tool for gazing into the beyond."

"But I thought you said the stones weren't magic."

"Nor are they. The magic, as you term it, is within yourself. The stones and the mirror are tools. They can—if you know how to use them, and if you have innate power—free your mind to see beyond the present moment, beyond this flimsy tissue that is the world we inhabit."

Mira found she was gripping the arms of her chair and concentrated on relaxing her fingers. "So there's … there's another world?" she said, and even as she said it many things seemed to settle into place.

"There is."

"Where is it?"

"Ah. That is a question no person may answer. Whether it is behind or beside or beneath this world, none can say. What we know is this: it is bound to this world as your mind is bound to your eyes, as your shadow is bound to your soles, as the interior of this orb is bound to its surface. They are inextricable."

"And someone can get there?"

"You can, as you have seen, peer into it—*scry* is the old term— though defining what you see there is tricky. But to go there in person—to walk in that land—is another matter entirely."

"It is possible, though?"

"It can be done. It has been done." Mrs. Zaccaroth rubbed a thumb over the stone. "You must understand, Mira, that this world is not what it seems. It is, in fact, our creation. This room, the crystals, Mr. Mugwort here are things we are creating together, you and I. And if you possess both power and knowledge, you can make certain changes."

She held the orb in the palm of her hand and it became, in succession, flame, coin, feather, and then a sphere of smoky quartz once more, though the cloudy interior seemed to churn a moment before solidifying.

Mira pressed her palms together. "Teach me!" she cried.

Mrs. Zaccaroth stood and set the quartz sphere back on its stand. "Come," she said, smoothing her dress. "We'll start with cooking."

"Cooking?" said Mira, dismayed, trailing her into the kitchen. "I know how to *cook*."

"All witches start with cooking," Mrs. Zaccaroth said. "The skills involved permeate every aspect of our lives."

The kitchen was enormous, as large as the parlor. From the ceiling hung bundles of dried herbs and roots. One whole wall was filled with shelves. On most were little corked bottles, the glass bubbled like fossilized foam. All were labeled in spiky copperplate. They contained liquids and powders the colors of inks and flamingos, gooseberries and apple mangos, olives and full moons. On the highest shelf, nudging the ceiling, lay a massive cookbook the color of a tortoise, its spine warped and stained.

The wall opposite held a long window at Mira's eye level and, at the height of her lower ribs, a polished marble counter, in which was a sink with a long-spouted brass faucet. The third wall held a stove with four gas burners. Copper-bottomed vessels of all sizes hung from hooks above. From a pottery urn sprouted whisks and spatulas and wooden spoons.

Mrs. Zaccaroth took two aprons from a hook on the door and held one out to Mira. It was dark green, embroidered with orange crabs and crayfish. Mrs. Zaccaroth's was pale blue, embroidered with herbs and flowers. She took down a pair of saucepans and, from a cupboard, two paper sacks and a wooden box, and set them in a row on the counter.

"First we'll temper the chocolate," she said.

"Temper?"

"Chocolate is a fickle creature. It won't stand rough treatment, and in order to achieve perfection you must temper it." She filled one saucepan a third full of water and set the other on top of it. Mira saw they were designed to nest.

Mrs. Zaccaroth handed one of the paper sacks to Mira. It held chunks of chocolate so dark it was almost black, like fragrant fragments of dusty obsidian.

"How much?" asked Mira.

"That's up to you."

Mira dropped a handful of chunks into the pan.

"Now sugar." She nudged the second paper sack forward.

Mira looked at her expectantly. "Do you have a measuring cup?" she asked.

"Measuring cups are like erasers for artists," said Mrs. Zaccaroth. She raised her spoon. "Death!" she exclaimed shrilly. "How will you learn to trust your instincts if you use a measuring cup?"

"Oh, but—"

"Pour. And as you pour, taste the finished chocolates. In your mind."

So Mira did as she was told, tipping out a hillock of the amber crystals. After a minute the chocolate began to melt. "Stir," Mrs. Zaccaroth said. "Loose wrist. Looser. Yes."

When the mixture was ready, Mrs. Zaccaroth instructed Mira to pour two-thirds of it onto the marble island. "Tempering is a delicate process," she said. "You must stay relaxed but alert. Too little and the crystals won't form. Too much and it will all be crystals."

Plucking a pair of ebony spatulas from the urn, she showed Mira how to spade up and turn the chocolate on the marble with steady, even sweeps. "Watch," she said. "This is where the magic happens. You can see it changing. You can sense it changing." She handed Mira the spatulas. Spading up the chocolate, smoothing it out on the marble, was intensely satisfying, and she realized Mrs. Zaccaroth was right: she could feel the chocolate transforming under her ministrations.

"Good," said Mrs. Zaccaroth. She handed Mira a knife. "Now, dip this into the chocolate and let the blade rest over the edge of the counter. In a few minutes we'll know if we've succeeded."

When Mira had dipped the blade, Mrs. Zaccaroth gestured to the wall of bottles. "So," she said. "You have the matrix. Time to create a ganache for the centers. The containers are labeled."

Mira walked over to the wall and peered at Mrs. Zaccaroth's taut, elegant handwriting. Tamarind, lemon peel, cinnamon, mace, crushed pearl, vanilla, cardamom pod, honey ant, opium, musk, gold leaf ... There were many she had never heard of.

"Isn't opium a drug?" she asked cautiously.

"Yes. As are sugar and coffee and ginger and nutmeg. Eat a spoonful of nutmeg and you'll have nightmares for three days. Did you know that?"

Mira shook her head.

"A well-crafted chocolate is first and foremost a mind-altering drug. Remember this."

Mira chose what she hoped was an adventurous combination of cumin and licorice root, and Mrs. Zaccaroth showed her how to create a ganache with cream and some of the chocolate mixture.

Then they went to examine the blade. "Not bad," said Mrs. Zaccaroth. She turned the blade to the light. "Not too bad. You could have gone a moment or two longer, but this satin surface is what we're after." She tapped the chocolate with a stained fingernail.

She showed Mira how to pour the chocolate into shaped trays and then pour it out again, leaving shells. They filled those with ganache and covered the bases with more chocolate, smoothing with a spatula. Mrs. Zaccaroth smiled—more gently this time, Mira thought—and said, "We'll let those cool. Come."

Beside the front door, stairs twisted to a room perched atop the house proper. The entire riverward wall was a window, in front of which lay a dusty-rose, scroll-edged fainting couch where Mr. Mugwort slumbered. The other walls of the room, floor to ceiling, were bookshelves, and more books lay stacked at the head of the couch. On the tallest stack rested a teacup.

Mrs. Zaccaroth spread her hands. "I call it my aerie," she said.

Mira had never seen so many books gathered in one place. They were of all sizes, in various states of disrepair. Some were as big as the Bible at home and, like it, had chipped leather bindings. Snake-tongued bookmarks dangled from their pages. But there were also ordinary paperbacks and jacketed hardbacks and books missing most or all of their covers, so the folds and stitchery showed.

"The sun is not good for the bindings," Mrs. Zaccaroth said. "But the light is good for my old eyes, so I keep them up here."

"All we have at home is the Bible," Mira said, moving to a shelf.

"Then you have already entered into the mysteries, if your ears and eyes were open. But it is not enough to read a single book. It is dangerous, in fact."

Mira murmured the titles: "*Recipes for a Rainy Day, Grandmother's Chants, Nowhere Tales, Faery Stories for the Dreaming Girl-Child, The Indigo Treasury of Fairytales, The Forgotten Children's Rhymes.*" She tipped down a plump purple volume entitled *Vapors from the Cauldron*. On the cover, green smoke from an embossed pot oozed like river froth through the silver letters.

"Why all the fairytales and nursery rhymes?" Mira asked.

"It took me many years to gather these books from the attics and blanket chests of the town, from beneath beds, from backyard sheds." Mrs. Zaccaroth touched the book she held, tracing the tendrils of smoke with a finger. "There's a story about a captive princess in this book that gave me restless nights for a week," she said. "Why fairytales? Why indeed? Others have traveled the journey before you. For those who possess the power, fairytales are travel books, travel diaries."

"I don't understand."

"Neither do I. Nevertheless, it is the truth."

"Are there books of spells here?"

Mrs. Zaccaroth looked out the window. "Spells," she murmured.

"You know," Mira pursued. "Potions and …"

"The potions, as you call them, I make in my kitchen. And speaking of potions, let's see how your truffles came out."

So they went back down. Mira tipped the finished truffles onto a tray. They had slumped a bit, and a few had pockmarks where the chocolate hadn't entirely filled the mold, and the chocolate was slightly streaky. She added a pinch of "crushed jade beetle," which made an iridescent glitter on the surface, and stuck a shard of brittle rose petal into each.

"I wish they were prettier," she murmured, and Mrs. Zaccaroth nodded.

"Prettiness is one facet," she said, "and by no means the least important." She plucked a truffle from the platter and took a nibble. An illegible expression spasmed across her features. She swallowed and lifted her eyebrows at Mira.

"What is it?" Mira asked.

"Try one."

So Mira bit into a truffle. She held it in her mouth for a moment, looking wildly around for somewhere to spit it out. Then she just swallowed it. She leaned back with her palm over her lips.

"Tell me about it," Mrs. Zaccaroth said.

"That was awful."

"Yes. Describe it."

"Too sweet. And too much of … what was that?"

"Cumin."

"Cumin. And the cumin didn't go at all with the licorice somehow. And it was too squashy."

"Good. You could have tempered a little longer, as I said. And yes. Delicacy. Balance. Important qualities to bear in mind. And I would mention one more: contrast."

"I'll try to remember," Mira said.

"I'll see you tomorrow, then. Mornings are a good time for learning."

* * *

So began Mira's months of tutelage, though she could scarcely have articulated what she was learning. She left her house every day after breakfast and trotted down to the river, where she sat on an upturned crate and cleansed her gaze on the current. Sometimes she'd toss a stone or two into the water, sometimes put a scrap of driftglass or a lightning stone into her pocket to clink against the gold key. Then she'd walk along the shore and up to the witch's house.

The first thing they did every day was cook. They made chocolates and sweetmeats, breads and tarts, and Mira learned to work with paper-thin sheets of pastry, to blanch almonds and caramelize sugar and chop walnuts with her fingertips turned in, knuckles to the blade. She learned to make sage-and-onion bread and flaky brioche and delicate soups of long-simmered bones, the broth clarified with eggshells.

Midmorning, they went out into the garden and strolled among the haphazard beds. Mrs. Zaccaroth pointed out vervain and orris and loosestrife, camphire and borage and cinquefoil. One corner of the garden was corralled by a thin brass chain, from which dangled a plaque incised with a skull and crossbones.

"Poisons," Mrs. Zaccaroth said. "Henbane, hemlock, hellebore, spurge," she chanted. "Monkshood, wormwood, belladonna, briony."

Mira bent over the chain. "But there's oleander here," she said. "And isn't that periwinkle? We have that in our yard."

"Yes. Many of the common flowers are poisonous. But the old name of periwinkle is sorcerer's violet. It has many uses; one is indeed to protect the home. For magical purposes, however, you must pluck it in silence on the ninth day of the moon, after twelve hours of fasting, wearing undyed linen."

"Are you a murderer then?" Mira asked.

Mrs. Zaccaroth smiled. "No, child. Certain poisons in small quantities have healing properties, just as certain common spices in large quantities are poisonous. Now come." And she led Mira over to the spearmint plants ("Superb against headaches") and taught her to pluck only the second row of leaves from each stem, from which she would extract a dewdrop of flavor as pure and potent as a flame.

Mira learned the names of the herbs, learned when to pick the leaves of this plant, the buds of that, the pods of another. At night she held her fingers to her nostrils and inhaled the day's braided odors: jasmine, laurel, rosemary, mint, charcoal, chocolate, river slime …

Once the day's cooking was done, if there was no work to do in the garden, Mrs. Zaccaroth would change out of her housedress and take her sailcloth shopping bag from a hook behind the kitchen door and walk down to the market.

"Why do you wear those clothes?" Mira asked one day as Mrs. Zaccaroth headed out the door.

"What clothes?" She was wearing a dark-green gown with hawthorn berries embroidered around the hem, a yellow belt, and a hat of magenta leather. Her ancient handbag was over one forearm, the shopping bag over the other.

"You know." Mira waved a hand. "With all the colors, and the belts and the hats."

"Why, child!" Mrs. Zaccaroth seemed taken aback. "Is it not customary to dress up for an outing?"

"Well, yes, but—" And she found she couldn't go on, couldn't explain what she meant.

While Mrs. Zaccaroth shopped, Mira made herself a cup of tea, placed two chocolates on the saucer, and went up to the aerie to read. She received no direction, so she read at random, choosing books at whim. It was delicious to go back into the fairytales, which her mother and aunts had told her as bedtime stories—into the forests with the foundlings, to encounter the dragons and wolves and giants. The tales were both denser and more enigmatic than she remembered. And she noticed now—for the first time, it seemed—the magic within them: the charms and incantations, the witches and wizards, who were often peripheral, though they were just as often key to the story. She sighed at their endings, for the satisfaction of a tale that came neatly together or the successful slaying of the beast or, more rarely, for sadness. These last she loved most of all: the sad tales, or those whose endings were bittersweet. The fairytale books were also the prettiest, objects as gorgeous as Mrs. Zaccaroth's jewel-box truffles. She savored the leather covers, shiny with rubbed beeswax, and the gold edges to the pages and the letters chiseled into the heavy paper. She loved turning a page and encountering the flimsy sheet of tissue paper with a grizzle-bearded wizard or a chained djinn seeming to shift slightly beneath it. She revealed those drawings slowly, peeling back the tissue, reading the line of text beneath it. The books smelled of salt and cedar, grass and honey and tobacco. Sometimes as she read, Mr. Mugwort joined her, turning a ritual three times before settling on her toes or in her lap and droning for a while, then snoring and fidgeting.

The Dry Land

In a town along the river, a brother and sister lived with their father. Their mother had died, and in time their father married again. The new wife was young and was not pleased to spend her days tending to two children, and so she locked herself away in her bedroom. The brother and sister, forced to spend the hours by themselves, grew closer than ordinary siblings. They invented elaborate games and crafted imaginary countries complete with maps and ballads and histories, and they created a private language only they could understand, which they used to tell each other secrets.

The stepmother had been with them a year when hard times fell upon the land. The father lost his work at the mill and was forced to scavenge in the streets for a living. Slowly, the family began to starve.

The stepmother called the father into the bedroom one afternoon and told him that there was not enough food for all four of them. One of the children would have to go. He must choose, she told him, which child to keep and which to send away. Heartbroken, and unwilling to make the choice, the father cast lots and the ill chance fell upon his daughter. So he called her to him and put her in his little boat with a heel of bread, and with a kiss and a tear sent her on her way.

Now there was enough food on the table, but the brother was filled with sorrow and could not eat. He loved his sister more than anything in the world, and so he determined to go after her. One day, when his father was out scavenging the streets for food and his stepmother had locked herself in her bedroom, the boy took the washtub from the laundry and a long-handled wooden spoon from a crock in the kitchen, and carried them down to the river. Getting into the washtub, he rowed it away from shore with the spoon, and soon had left behind his house and the town and everything he had known.

For many days the boy traveled northward with the current, past towns and fields and orchards. And he asked all he met if they had seen his sister. "She has curly brown hair," he told them, "and eyes like stars and a mole in her neck like a clove. When she laughs it's like rain on the roof tiles."

He asked the fish if they had seen her under the water, but the fish said, "No, she is not down here." He asked the birds if they had seen her, but they said, "No, we have not seen her from the air." He asked the water rats if they had seen her, but they said, "No, we have not seen her along the shore." And the boy began to despair and imagined he would never see his sister again.

Weeping, he shipped his wooden-spoon oar and let the river carry his washtub boat where it wanted. After a while, the currents wafted his craft to shore, and it rocked there among the rushes. Evening fell, and still the boy wept. And as he sat thus in sorrow, he heard a voice: "Why do you weep?"

Looking up, the boy saw sitting on the shore a black cat with eyes that glimmered like embers in the dusk. Swallowing his tears, he told his story. "Have you seen my sister?" he asked. "She has curly brown hair and eyes like stars and a mole in her neck like a clove. When she laughs it's like rain on the roof tiles."

The cat blinked. "Yes, I have seen your sister," he said.

"Oh! Tell me where she is then!" the boy exclaimed.

"Before I tell you where she is, I must warn you that there is no turning back," the black cat said. "So, are you certain you want to know?"

"Yes, of course. She's the only one I can tell my secrets to."

"Well then," said the cat, "you must row across the river to the other side. There you will find what you seek."

Thanking the cat, the boy pushed off from shore and with the wooden spoon paddled his washtub to the far side. And it seemed to him as he rowed that the twilight had ceased to advance; a few faint stars glimmered in the sky, but it grew no darker.

The far shore was barren of tree or flower: a land of stones and bones and dust. But on a hill some distance from the river, the boy saw a single light in a window. So he pulled his makeshift boat up onto the stones and walked to the light.

In a cottage in that dry land, his sister sat at a window, a candle burning beside her. The boy knocked, and she opened the door, and then there were kisses and tears of joy. But after the embraces, she held her brother at arm's length.

"You should not have searched for me," she told him. "You have come too far, as I did. There is no return from this land."

"Yes, that's what the cat told me," he said. "There is no return. But even though there is no return, the river goes on. Come, I'll show you."

So the girl blew out the candle and took her brother's hand and he led her down to his washtub boat. They got in—there was just room for two in that vessel—and he pushed off from the dry shore and the river tugged at the little craft, twisting it and turning it, and soon they were far from land, carried by the currents. And some say they are on the river still. And others say they eventually came to their house again, but from the southern side, and there they were reunited with their father. This time, however, he did not choose between his children but instead sent the stepmother away.

* * *

Two things happened when Mira began reading. First, her dreams shifted, turning iridescent as a sunbird's throat. They shimmered and brightened, and she woke in the mornings feeling she had spent the hours in conversation with mermaids and devils and djinns.

The second thing she noticed was that she wasn't angry so much. Whatever it was that she was doing in Mrs. Zaccaroth's house eased the vexing tickle, and she didn't need to shout.

Many of the tales contained magic—what they called magic: potions, wands, charms, spells—and as Mira read, curled on the sofa in the sunny aerie, she longed to try out a spell. Now that she knew they were real in some fashion. Lifting her head from a page, she'd cast her hand forward with a twist, muttering.

One morning Mrs. Zaccaroth, coming up the stairs with a tea tray, caught her in the midst of one of these phantom spellcasts and said sharply, "No!" She entered the aerie and set the tray on a stack of books. "Not even in jest," she said. "Not even in pantomime."

"But when will you *teach* me?" Mira cried. "It's been nearly a month and all I've done is make chocolates and pull weeds and read fairytales."

"I know. I know, dearest child. The waiting is hard. But the waiting is also part of your education. You are learning patience, which is the key to control."

Mrs. Zaccaroth sat on the edge of the sofa. Between them Mr. Mugwort stood, stretched, and yawned. "What you possess is power," she said. "Raw power. It is enormous, and it is unharnessed. Your emotion releases it, which makes it dangerous if you are not able to control it. So dangerous, Mira. Watch." She raised her right hand, fingertips bunched, then let her fingers spring apart. There was a soft explosion and a pale flame quivered in her palm. Mrs. Zaccaroth lifted her hand slightly, lips moving, and the flame swelled, the slender turquoise tips licking close to the ceiling. Abruptly she closed her hand, catching up the fire as if it were a scrap of silk.

Mira let out her breath. "Lovely!" she said.

"The power can be used for beauty, and often is," Mrs. Zaccaroth said. "But I want you to imagine for a moment what would have happened if I had not been able to control the fire. If I had not been able to quench it." Again she made the catching motion. "In a minute the ceiling would have caught, then the books. In an hour the house would have been cinders."

"But you caught it."

"I caught it. You would not have had that ability. Now drink your tea."

* * *

So for a while Mira was chastened. Still, though, she longed to create—to coax a flame from thin air, to change a pebble to a shell, a shell to a flower, a flower to a butterfly, and *mean* to do it.

A week after the conversation in the aerie, she was kneeling in the garden. Mrs. Zaccaroth had gone shopping. Mira was training a bean vine along a crosshatched lattice, tucking the tendrils into place. It was midmorning, the sun scalding her neck, her hair making walls of ruddy gold on either side of her toiling hands. As she worked, she recalled a fairytale she'd read the day before, in which a jealous godmother had placed a charm on the rosebushes surrounding a castle, and they'd knotted and woven themselves into a hedge too dense to penetrate.

Scarcely aware of what she was doing, Mira murmured the words of the godmother's spell, then chanted them, a little work song to accompany the dance of her hands:

"Over, under, inside out,
Twist and turn and roundabout.
Knot a net of stem and leaf.
Catch a sparrow, catch a thief."

As she chanted, her fingers took up the rhythm of the rhyme and a strange gladness came over her, almost as if she'd become a vine herself, toes rooting in the damp loam, rich as the chocolate she tempered in the kitchen; green fire coursing through her veins; sunlight nourishing the roots of her hair.

Something brushed her left ankle. Thinking it was Mr. Mugwort, she ignored it. But then it tightened and she looked down. A tendril of the bean vine was wrapped around her leg. Giggling, still in the pleasure of the chant, she tried to tug her leg free, but it slithered tighter, surprisingly tough. She started to reach down to untie it, but her right wrist seemed to be caught. And now she realized with horror that the vine had loosed itself from the trellis and was wrapping thin green fingers around her thighs, elbows, waist, drawing her closer, drawing the nooses tight. Struggling, she screamed, and screamed again.

With a clang, the door in the garden wall opened and Mrs. Zaccaroth was beside her, in her ridiculous wide-brimmed black hat topped with a crow's feather. She said a word, and the vines lost their grip. She said another, and they swarmed back onto the trellis like thin green flames.

Mira forced herself to look at her, flinching, but there was no anger in the old woman's eyes, though they were not comforting either.

"Go wash your hands," she said, and Mira felt suddenly weary—as weary as if she'd just run a race. She went in and washed her hands. Her wrists were marked with pink where the vines had clung. Her eyes were suddenly so dull and heavy she could hardly keep them open. Stumbling to the sofa, she laid her head on a doily and slept.

*　*　*

That afternoon, after they'd sipped their soup and drunk their tea and eaten a truffle each, Mrs. Zaccaroth cleared the little table in the sitting room and placed in the center of the glass a petal from one of the small scarlet roses that grew beside the front door.

Perhaps by chance, a cloud passed across the sun and the shadows thickened in the room, all sparkle doused.

"Spellcraft is a profoundly serious and dangerous business," Mrs. Zaccaroth said. "Spells should be used sparingly, and never lightly, never in jest."

"But you," Mira said, "when the boys threw the stones, you hexed them. Wasn't that … ?"

"A woman's dignity is not a trivial matter," Mrs. Zaccaroth said. "What—did you think I placed those curses with no thought for the consequences? No, they were hours in the contemplation, hours in the execution. And you will note that those spells, among others, have provided us with the space and peace we now enjoy."

Mira nodded slowly.

"Watch," said Mrs. Zaccaroth. Extending one hand toward the petal, palm up, fingers slightly cupped, she whispered something and raised her hand slightly, and the petal lifted a hand's breadth into the air and hovered there, subtly trembling. She lowered her hand, and the petal sank slowly to the glass once more.

"Now you," she said.

"But what did you say?" Mira asked. Her heart was pounding.

"There is … well, I can't say that the words are not important—they are—but the words I use will not be the ones you use. You must discover what works for you."

"How will I know?"

"You will know when you succeed. Now, lift the petal."

So Mira did as Mrs. Zaccaroth had done, if a little more hesitantly: she extended her hand toward the petal and whispered, "Lift up!" and slowly raised her hand … and nothing happened. She took a breath and tried again, straining at the petal, willing it to rise. Nothing. A third time she tried, and then sat back, tears prickling the corners of her eyes.

"I don't have it," she said.

"Try again," Mrs. Zaccaroth said.

So she tried again and again, using different words, speaking now louder, now softer, raising her hand slowly, then quickly, and all the while feeling a knot tighten between her shoulder blades.

"I guess I'm not so dangerous after all," Mira said ruefully at last. "You needn't have worried."

"Take a break," Mrs. Zaccaroth told her. "If something is not coming, I often find it helps to look at the river for a time. I'll do the washing up."

Mira knelt on the window seat, forehead pressed to the glass, watching the long, flexing muscles of the river and endlessly shifting filaments of sun, rubbing her wrists where the bean vines had bitten. She was caught between the fear of her power and the fear that she didn't have it or couldn't control it. In the kitchen, Mrs. Zaccaroth was whistling and clattering the pans.

Mind still filled with currents and the blinking moments of sun, she went back to the table and extended her hand to the petal, but it would not lift. Then she wept, looking down at her grubby, gnawed fingernails. When she looked up, Mrs. Zaccaroth was standing across from her, tugging a dishtowel between her fists. She wore a look of scorn and derision that Mira had not seen on her face before: a look she recognized from the faces of her mother and her aunts. Disapproval.

"Well," said Mrs. Zaccaroth. "It seems your mother may be right. I had hope for you, Mira, but you're too lazy to—"

Mira gripped the cotton of her dress, knuckles blanching. "No I'm *not!*" she snarled, and let out a wordless shriek of fury, and suddenly the table was heaped with rose petals—dozens of them, piled high and spilling onto the carpet like a tender crimson rain. She sat back, horrified.

"Now," said Mrs. Zaccaroth. She brought thumb and forefinger together, and the heap of petals coalesced until a single petal lay on the glass once more. "Now," she said again, urgently. "Use that, Mira."

So, with the rage still within her like lemon on her tongue, Mira extended her hand, and knew before she spoke that the petal would move. It was easy as breathing: lifting the petal, holding it in the air a moment, letting it fall.

"Again," said Mrs. Zaccaroth.

So she did it again. And again and again and again.

III

MRS. ZACCAROTH'S COOKBOOK

Every afternoon the storms arrived, spilling across the river with their bursting parcels of wind and rain, their burdens of havoc, but the mornings were mostly clear. After breakfast, Mira walked down to the river, eyes on the clouds piling up like whipped cream on the horizon. Sometimes Tolly the fisherboy would be at the shore, mending his nets or patching his sail. The cats adored him, leaning against his thighs, knocking their skulls on his wrists as he sewed. Mira usually ignored him, but occasionally, if she was brimming with the stories in the aerie, she'd sit on an upturned crate and toss stones into the waves and tell him one of the fairytales, feeling it squirm free, shifting and spiraling. He listened with head tilted and mouth open, eyes on his toiling fingers.

The day after she'd told Tolly the story about the brother and sister and the dry land, she asked him how far downriver he had sailed.

"Only to the cataracts," he said. "There is no passage after that."

"How do you know when to turn back?"

"The Sentinel marks the edge. In the long-ago times, they used to light a fire in the hollow as a warning. That's what one of the older fishermen told me."

Mira looked to the north, past the sharp church steeple and the chimney of the brick kiln. The Sentinel was a great sullen shape of black stone, which some said was an ancient sculpture, chafed and mauled by weather into an anonymous form, though others said it was a natural formation. It had a nook near the top, which in certain lights could resemble a hooded face watching over the town. Many, including Mira's mother, made the sign of the cross when the Sentinel was mentioned, and refused to speak of it, but some of the older women used it as a threat: "I'll send you to the Sentinel," they'd say to a recalcitrant child. Or "Take care, the Sentinel is watching." The other children claimed the Sentinel was haunted and stayed away. Mira, even from a distance, sensed its somber strength, similar to that of the church, though there was a thick, opaque quality to it. She'd never walked to it.

This morning the hooded face of the Sentinel was stern, as if it harbored grim tidings. She shivered and returned her gaze to the water, which was always a good place to rest her spirit.

Later, as she tempered the chocolate, she told Mrs. Zaccaroth what Tolly had told her—that the Sentinel had been used as a lighthouse. The old witch frowned and shook her head slightly; almost a shiver. Then she said, "Well, yes and no." "What do you mean?" Mira asked, and she said, "It was indeed used for fire, and for warning." But, though Mira pressed, she would say no more, and spent the rest of that morning in a brooding silence.

* * *

That afternoon a storm arrived, the thunder rattling the boards of Mrs. Zaccaroth's clinker-built house, the raindrops like gravel flung against the windows. Mr. Mugwort hated the thunder. He whined and patted Mrs. Zaccaroth's skirts, hissing at shadows. Mira laughed at him. She liked the flash, which she felt in her mind, and the aching pause while her heart beat, and then the clap and diminishing concatenations.

While Mira set out their customary cups of tea and a saucer of truffles, Mrs. Zaccaroth went into the kitchen and returned with the enormous cookbook from the highest shelf. Mira had never looked into the book—Mrs. Zaccaroth had forbidden it, saying she must learn to trust her instincts before relying on recipes.

"It is time," Mrs. Zaccaroth said, sitting with the book on her lap and running a thumb along its craggy spine.

Mira looked at her expectantly. "Time to start using recipes?"

"Recipes, yes. But I'm afraid I've misled you slightly. This is a cookbook, but it is also my witch's book—a book of our craft."

And Mira's heart gave a great leap.

After a pause that might have been hesitation or ceremonial gravitas, Mrs. Zaccaroth passed the book into Mira's lap. It was massive as a flagstone, heavy as a block of mahogany.

Mira, nourished on fairytales, expected illuminated capitals glittering with gold leaf, pages dense with mystical symbols, arcane diagrams, illustrations of robed, bearded men posed in flaming pentangles. But when she lifted the warped, stained cover, she was disappointed to see a brown scrawl across the first page, and a slightly awkward sketch of a latticed pie, showing how to lay down the strips of pastry. Mira bent to the first line. "A recipe for apricot tart," she read. There was a list of ingredients: flour, salt, lard, apricots, sugar, cinnamon. They seemed perfectly ordinary. She looked up, trying to keep the disappointment out of her eyes. "But I thought …" she said. "I mean, it *is* just a cookbook."

Mrs. Zaccaroth gave a nod. "This apricot tart is superb," she said. "Though the lattice takes a bit of practice. At first I kept breaking the strips and had to press on patches to hold them together. Then I got the trick of folding them over my wrist." She drew a line across the back of her hand with one finger. "We'll try it later. But for now, let's move on."

Mira turned the page. This was in the same handwriting, though it was not a recipe from any earthly cuisine. She read something about moonlight, the dispelling of shadows, but the language was heavy—heavy as the language in the Bible—and several of the words were opaque. Nevertheless, she felt something rumble through her brain, even as the thunder rumbled through the sky. She looked up at Mrs. Zaccaroth. "It's too hard," she said with a little shiver.

"I remember having the same thought when I first opened the book, how many years ago," Mrs. Zaccaroth said. "Yes, it is hard. But within this book lies great beauty, great power. Read slowly, take your time, and the meanings will surface."

"Is it a book of spells?" Mira asked.

"Let's call it a cookbook," Mrs. Zaccaroth said. "A witch's cookbook. The book contains recipes, but many of these recipes are not like those in other cookbooks. A woman without power, though she followed the instructions to the letter, would achieve nothing at all. And a recipe that worked consistently for the witch who wrote it might not work for you or, more dangerously, might go awry. Many a witch has come to an ugly end because she attempted a spell she did not fully understand and that wrestled free of her control."

"Is that what happened to …"

"To who?"

"To the other … your other pupil."

"Her? No. No, she was a very fine student of magic."

"Better than me?"

"That remains to be seen."

"What happened to her?" Mira asked.

Mrs. Zaccaroth compressed her lips, and Mira wondered if she'd angered her. But then Mrs. Zaccaroth swallowed and blinked, and Mira saw she was trying to keep her tears bottled. "She was forced to leave the town," she said.

"Why?"

Mrs. Zaccaroth sighed. "They took her child from her."

"Oh, how awful! Do you know why?"

"They took her child from her because she was a witch. Now." Mrs. Zaccaroth rapped the page. "What I'm trying to tell you, Mira, is that you must approach this book much as you approach the fairytales in the aerie: with skepticism and wonder and appreciation for the bones, the flow. But refrain from attempting a spell at this time. For now, just read."

So, as the storms surged across the river, Mira made her way through the magical cookbook. Every morning Mrs. Zaccaroth took it down from the high shelf and carried it to her. Mira laid it on the coffee table and leaned over it, and the shadows of the purple parlor and glimmer of the mineral spheres and blue roil of the thunderstorms seemed to enter the pages. And what pages they were: each a world, as tall as her torso and twice as wide. Like those of her mother's cookbook at home, the pages were stained, but some of these stains were verdigris and violet, and in places had eaten entirely through the paper—if paper it was: the pages weren't delicate rippling things but were warped and crackly, the color and texture of a fingernail. Between some pages were pressed flowers and sprigs of herbs. Once a flattened salamander. Once a black feather. There were even a few fairytales and lullabies sprinkled among the recipes like glades in a forest: nooks of respite within the branching thicket of spells.

Reading the magical cookbook was unlike any other reading experience she'd had. It was like sitting by the river shore, watching the immense pour of the current, entranced by the surface glitter, but recognizing the river's power, and recognizing as well that its origins were hidden, that it held mysteries in its depths.

She read slowly, sometimes just a page a day. That was partly because the words were difficult and the pen work could be hard to unravel, but also because between every line and across the margins, in spidery ink, other voices joined, echoing certain elements or recommending a different technique or offering alternative phrasing. Between some pages other papers were stashed, or were actually sewn onto the bound pages, extending the conversations. Mira read these as well, and learned to recognize the various hands. The gently questioning tone of the witch who made her periods into little circles. The imperious witch with the jagged strokes. The witch who offered little drawings that seemed unconnected to the recipes, including, once, a tiny sketch of her face in a handmirror, and Mira gazed a long time at her shadowed eyes and stern mouth and frothy hair. There was even, here and there, Mrs. Zaccaroth's severe copperplate, which Mira recognized from the labels in the kitchen.

She read recipes for dove in wine with capers and bay laurel, for lamb simmered with dates and olives and orange rind, for a yellow cake speckled with poppyseeds and flavored with cardamom. She read a spell to cloak herself in darkness, a spell to summon rain from a cloud, a spell to uncover a lie. Some spells were delightful: a spell to make a child laugh, a spell to create an easeful dream that might be breathed into a sleeper's ear. But many had a grimmer intent: a spell to slip invisible needles beneath an enemy's kneecaps. A spell to cause temporary blindness. Spells to inflict an alarming variety of diseases and ailments: gout, croup, lupus, along with many others Mira had never heard of. Some of these involved adding potions to a drink or wafting carefully prepared powders into a room at evening, but others could be created in the solitude of one's house and cast from a distance. And there were, as well, spells to cure those diseases, though these often resembled regular recipes: a tisane of ginger and cherry juice against gout, for example, or fennel and peppermint against croup.

Occasionally as she read she sensed stirrings in her mind, in the shadows of the room, in the world at large—she couldn't have said where precisely, but she could almost taste the power. It was enormously tempting to try out a spell, but, remembering the swarming vines in the garden, she forced herself to refrain; to read on.

* * *

The book ended abruptly in the middle of a strange spell, something to do with changing what is inside to what is outside, though many blank pages followed. One of the readers had tried to complete the truncated spell, though she noted that the attempt was a failure. "The spellcraft of witches is always in ferment," Mrs. Zaccaroth said mysteriously, but shook her head when Mira pressed her, and stared out at the river. The current below the window was a heaving mass of bright fragments. Still looking out at the horizon, which was bruised with storm, Mrs. Zaccaroth said, "Let's try one, shall we?"

"Yes please," Mira said.

"Something benign. Relatively benign." Mrs. Zaccaroth pulled the book over to her side of the table and hauled at the pages with both hands till she reached a recipe near the middle. "Casting the Gaze" was written at the top, and in the center of the page was an eye with wavy lines radiating from it.

"I didn't really understand that one," Mira said.

"Farsight, some call it," Mrs. Zaccaroth told her, "though it is often misunderstood and is not entirely foolproof. If cast correctly, it will allow you to peer from the eyes of another. However, it will only work if you are familiar with the person, and the closer the connection the clearer the vision. Physical distance is also a factor. I recommend Hecabah's variation here, placing the palms over the eyes as you recite. The other notes I have found less helpful, but they might work for you."

Mira murmured the recipe a couple of times, getting the cadences. "Where's north?" she asked. She knelt on the carpet, facing the direction Mrs. Zaccaroth had pointed. Touching her tongue to the tips of her little fingers, she dabbed spittle at the corners of her eyes. Then she recited the spell, summoning the power with gestures that reminded her as she made them of the priest's invocation to prayer. As she spoke the closing lines, she pressed the heels of her hands into her eye sockets and cried aloud her mother's name.

Geometric spangles broke and reformed like a twisted kaleidoscope, cleared ... and, as though she were dreaming, Mira saw the kitchen sink at home, her mother's chapped hands, a blue milk jug rising from the foam. The vision was edged with shadow and silvered with a light gauze, as if she peered through a misted window. She tried to raise her eyes, but her gaze was chained to her mother's. Faintly she heard the chink of the crockery, though she also heard the crashing waves below Mrs. Zaccaroth's house. Suddenly the gaze lifted, darted right, left, and glanced behind. Her mother muttered something, and a sudsy hand came up and crossed her breast.

Mira pulled her palms from her eyes, blinked, and shook her head slightly. She looked across at Mrs. Zaccaroth. "She knew," she said.

Mrs. Zaccaroth nodded. "Some do, especially if they have a kernel of power."

"My mother does? Is she a witch as well?"

"No. But your power derives from that side of the family, and she carries a thread of it. Undeveloped, of course, and deliberately suppressed, but, as you saw, enough to sense someone is shadowing her."

Now began days of wonder, days of thrill, scored by thunder and raked by lightning. Every morning they worked their way through a fresh page. They'd read the recipe together first, bent over the book, and Mrs. Zaccaroth would walk her through it, demonstrating a gesture, pointing out the moment when the spell shifted, when the words became reality.

Mira learned to cast binding spells, to banish evil thoughts, to press someone into telling the truth. She learned the arts of duplication and vanishing. One day she learned to craft a light. "There is a way to do it," Mrs. Zaccaroth said, "in which the light remains a part of yourself, attached to your finger, as if you're a candle. Watch." She said the spell, weaving it with spare, elegant gestures, then snapped her fingers, and a soft greenish globe rested on the tip of her index finger. After several attempts, Mira too was able to craft a light, though hers was a pale purple. And as soon as the purple globule rested on her fingertip, she understood what Mrs. Zaccaroth had said: the light was part of her, like the coursing of her blood or the sparkles of her brain. To detach it would have required an effort, but allowing it to bloom from her finger was no strain at all.

"Why is mine a different color?" she asked.

"Each witch produces her own light," Mrs. Zaccaroth said. "Note as well that mine is brighter, with cleaner edges. That will come with practice."

In the subsequent weeks, Mira learned spells to find things that were lost and to hide things in plain daylight. She learned to open locked doors and mend a cracked pot. She learned to shape fire, to sing a snail from its shell, to harness the wind. And she learned as well elaborate recipes for dishes as sumptuous and satisfying as any magic. Recipes for soups and ragouts, for tarts and soufflés, for sauces incorporating butter and cream and wine.

* * *

In the middle of every afternoon they paused for tea and truffles, and Mira learned that Mrs. Zaccaroth would sometimes grow expansive during these interludes.

"So, can we do anything if we have the power?" Mira asked one afternoon. "I mean, if the most powerful witch knew all the spells, could she do whatever she wanted?"

"Not necessarily," Mrs. Zaccaroth said. A storm had just blown through and the river bore bright flotsam as clouds tattered in the sky. The old woman's face passed through light and shadow as she spoke. "Magic is malleable," she said. "The results depend on the person, on the circumstances. Think of breath. You can blow through a trumpet or a fife or your own pursed lips"—she whistled a little three-note melody—"and each tone is distinct. It depends, you see, on the shape of the instrument. Furthermore, an incantation that works on one day may go astray the next, or may be dependent on the weather or your mood.

"The cookbook contains suggestions. Gestures. You must try on the recipes even as you try on dresses, tailoring them to fit your frame, and once you know the ingredients and the essential movements, you can begin to create your own recipes.

"In this way we are at odds with the church—with the priest and what he stands for. Though the processes are similar. Though he deals as well, whether he recognizes it or not, with the arts of sorcery. But where we are hoping to set the world free of its fetters, he hopes to confine it. To use the laws, the codes, the single immutable text chained to its stand in order to harness the powers, subdue them, contain them."

"And does it work?"

"Of course it does. But in the process, if he is not careful, he can create imbalance. If all the passengers in a boat sit on one gunwale, the boat will founder. If you keep your eyes on the sky, you will trip on a stone. If you paint only the light and ignore the shadows, your painting will be depthless, lifeless."

She sipped her tea. "Many novice witches have grown frustrated and abandoned their art because they did not understand the fickle nature of the witch's craft. They imagine magic to be a religion, a set of laws, a set of instructions they can recite that will produce the same results every time. But magic is merely recognizing that reality is not solid; that we are creating it in tandem with others, with the wind and the rain and the soil, with our fairytales and lullabies. 'Tricks,' they call it. 'Smoke and mirrors.' And this is, of course, precisely correct. What they do not realize is that the entire universe is tricks, is sleight of hand, is smoke and mirrors."

"But we can make light. And fire."

"Certainly. However, the fire is not something I am summoning. It emerges from within. We are, after all, creatures of fire, and of mud and air, iron and ink. A witch, in essence, is someone whose mind is untethered, who recognizes the power of dreams and imagination, who is aware of the unruliness of the world. But she cannot make something entirely new. Only the gods and the djinns have the power to create something from nothing."

"What about the demons? Can they do magic?"

"Demons." Mrs. Zaccaroth turned to look out the parlor window. "No. The demons are animated by magic and can be contained by magic, but they are not capable of wielding it."

"What do they want?" Mira asked.

"You know what they want," she said. "They want the children to come out and play."

"The other children say the demons are my fault. That they came after I was born."

"Well," said Mrs. Zaccaroth. Her gaze was locked on the tattering clouds.

"Is it true?" Mira wailed.

Mrs. Zaccaroth dragged her eyes from the window, and there was something in her face that Mira had not seen before. A sorrow that flavored her voice when she spoke. "Is it true that they came after you were born? Yes. That it was your fault? No, child. No, of course not."

* * *

Occasionally in the afternoons, women from the town arrived at the witch's house. Mira sometimes passed them as she walked home, and they either avoided her eyes or gave her a stiff, nervous nod. If they came while she was still there, Mrs. Zaccaroth would send her home or up to the aerie or south along the river to gather the thick-stemmed marshmallows that grew there. But one day, when the brass bell beside the front door jangled as Mira was heading out, Mrs. Zaccaroth called her back.

"Go put the kettle on," she said.

From the kitchen, Mira could hear voices, and she peeked around the jamb. Mrs. Zaccaroth was settling the miller's wife onto the sofa. The woman seemed out of breath, and she startled when Mr. Mugwort jumped up beside her.

Mrs. Zaccaroth turned. "Mira," she called, and Mira stepped out of the kitchen. "You know Mira, don't you?" Mrs. Zaccaroth said.

The miller's wife twisted her hands in her lap. "Yes. Yes, of course. Your father's at the kilns, isn't he?"

She nodded.

"Mira helps me from time to time," Mrs. Zaccaroth said.

"So she … is she … ?"

"She has the gift, yes."

The kettle sang, and Mira made the tea. On Mrs. Zaccaroth's lacquered tray she placed a lace doily, and then the porcelain cups with their patterns of thistles and bumblebees, and the cut-glass sugar bowl and the silver pot of cream and a plate with half a dozen chocolates from the batch she'd made that morning: blackcurrant and vanilla.

She carried the tray in and set it on the coffee table and was about to head out the door once more when Mrs. Zaccaroth said, "Why don't you sit with us, Mira? Fetch a cup for yourself."

So Mira perched on the end of the sofa, sipping, while Mrs. Zaccaroth and the miller's wife talked about the weather and the price of sugar and how hard it was to find good-quality butter these days. Mira had decided she wasn't going to have a chocolate—she'd eaten three that morning—but then she saw the miller's wife eyeing them with mingled longing and wariness. So she took one and leaned back with her eyes closed, savoring the silky chocolate with its tart heart.

"Mira made those this morning," Mrs. Zaccaroth said.

"I suppose it couldn't hurt to try just one." The miller's wife popped a chocolate into her mouth and her painted eyebrows arced. "Oh," she said. "Oh my goodness!" Reaching across Mr. Mugwort, she patted Mira's knee and nodded.

"Now," said Mrs. Zaccaroth.

"Yes." The miller's wife glanced at Mira and took a sip of her tea. Then: "It's my mother. She's been sick for a week. She lies in bed. It's her legs, see. Her feet. They're too swollen to walk."

"Pain?" Mrs. Zaccaroth asked.

"A little."

"Appetite?"

"Oh, she eats. Yes. She adores my pastries and pies."

"And what treatment has she received?"

"The apothecary gave us a bottle of something, some brown syrup, but it hasn't helped. He said she was drinking too much tea and it was settling in her ankles. So I've been trying to keep her to a cup a day."

Mrs. Zaccaroth frowned. "She must drink," she said. "Tea, water … whatever she likes, but she must have liquids. No more pastries, though. No sugar. No salt."

"No salt? At all? But … well, for how long?"

"For one month. After that, only a teaspoon a day. And that goes for you as well, unless you want to end up like her." Mrs. Zaccaroth extended a slender finger.

The miller's wife swallowed and her hands floundered in her lap before they found each other and locked.

"Now, you have another cup of tea, and I'll prepare a potion. Mira."

Setting down her teacup, Mira followed Mrs. Zaccaroth into the kitchen.

"Dropsy," Mrs. Zaccaroth said. "Not the first time in that family. Fetch my mortar and pestle from under the sink and wipe them down."

While Mira did so, Mrs. Zaccaroth took two bottles from the shelves and placed them on the marble island. "The goldenrod is what does the trick," she said. "The licorice root helps it go down smoothly."

She tipped a portion from each bottle into the mortar and had Mira grind them into a fine yellow powder. This Mrs. Zaccaroth poured into a lavender envelope, which she sealed with a drop of scarlet wax. On the envelope, in her compact, barbed hand, she wrote: "One teaspoon in a cup of mint tea twice daily."

When they returned to the parlor, the platter of chocolates was empty. The miller's wife gestured at it helplessly, and Mrs. Zaccaroth smiled. "Here," she said, handing her the envelope.

The miller's wife took it gingerly by a corner and held it slightly away from her body, as if it were dripping.

"Give it five days," Mrs. Zaccaroth said. "As soon as she is able, she should start to walk, even if it's painful."

"And what do I owe?" the miller's wife asked, tugging a pouch from between her breasts.

"Two sacks of your finest flour," Mrs. Zaccaroth said briskly, "delivered to my doorstep."

After that, Mira attended the afternoon healing sessions, and sometimes accompanied Mrs. Zaccaroth to a patient's house, observing her calm, unfussy manner. Most of the healing involved herbs or potions, but occasionally Mrs. Zaccaroth would craft a small spell to help a patient breathe or sleep. The patient usually didn't even notice: the spells were concealed within rhymes and songs, but Mira could feel the changes like a shift in the weather.

Once she began participating in the healing sessions, the women of the town began to look at her differently. She still received glances of derision or fear, but now also a grudging nod from time to time.

* * *

Her mother sensed that something in her had changed, was changing. However, as there were no more incidents, and Mira did the dishes and scaled fish and peeled potatoes without complaint, there was nothing she could latch on to. Mira kept her eyes lowered at the dinner table. She spoke softly, and only in reply. But spells teemed in her mind like a thicket of roses, thorny and gorgeous as the book itself. The cookbook whose pages she turned as she lay in bed with her eyes closed, whose words she mouthed when she sat beside the river in the mornings, whose tendrils wound through her veins. When she was with her parents, though, she bit her lower lip and sat on her hands, keeping the words locked away.

Then one evening as she sipped her soup, something shifted in the window across from her. A storm cloud was coming in over the rooftops, its belly succulent as a plum. The cloud's slow roil snagged her gaze and her thoughts strayed back to the morning with Mrs. Zaccaroth. They had been working on a spell to shape smoke, the blue-gray fronds writhing about the coffee table. It was like drawing—like the drawings in charcoal Mira and Paulus had made on the cobblestones long ago. A girl and a boy, red hair and black hair bent together, kneeling on the stones ...

There was a sudden clatter and a gasp, and Mira looked down to see her mother staring at her. Her father had dropped his spoon into his soup.

"Mira!" her mother screeched, flapping her hands in front of her breast as if to chase off a bee.

And now Mira saw what she had done. The candle in the center of the table had gone out. Above the wick, carved in smoke, was a slender face—a face she almost recognized. As she watched, the features slurred sideways, and then some minute breeze wafted it toward the open window.

"Into your room!" her mother shouted. "Evil child!"

Mira set down her spoon and went to her room and lay looking up at the ceiling. She wasn't frightened or angry, just annoyed she'd let her guard down. She summoned the candle-smoke carving in her mind's eye. A slender face, beautiful and severe. Where had she seen it before?

* * *

The priest came again that night. This time he didn't pull the censer from his bag or open the Bible. He just sat with his head bowed, looking into his hat. His hair, in the past year, had lost its dark grain and turned quartz white. The hat had pressed a dent into it all the way around. When he looked up, Mira was surprised to see a crust of tears against his lower lashes. He shook his head and a tear fell onto his cassock, leaving a tiny round stain.

"You have been granted power," he said. "I do not know why. Who can say why these powers are bestowed—these gifts or curses." He turned the hat in his hands. "What I know is this: the power may be used for good or for evil. We are waging a battle here. The demons are growing stronger. Two more children were taken yesterday evening—a brother and sister. Their footsteps were seen along the shore north of town.

"The rumors have reached me, young Mira, that you are visiting … that woman—the woman on the cliffs. She is an agent of darkness, as you have no doubt discovered. You are opening yourself to the darkness. Come back, my daughter. Return to purity. Return to the light."

Mira watched him. His words made sense, or seemed to. But when she tried to label Mrs. Zaccaroth an agent of darkness a giggle erupted and she had to grip her mouth. She hoped he thought it was a sob.

"Who are the demons?" she asked quickly to cover her indiscretion. "Where do they come from?"

"It is best not to talk of them," the priest said. "To talk of them is to bring them to mind, to summon them. And you must keep your mind turned always, always to the light."

"But how can we fight them if we don't know who they are?"

"The demons come from the wrong side of the world," he said. "We fight them with the truth, with the light, with the word." He laid a hand on the Bible.

"How do they get through?"

"The boundary is worn thin. The seams are fraying. I do not know why."

Seeing the befuddlement and panic in his eyes, her fear of him fell abruptly away. He wasn't cruel. He was, like her, just trying to understand.

IV

STORM

For three days, Mira was forbidden to leave the house. If her mother went to market, she summoned an aunt to watch over her; at night they locked her in the bedroom. The storm winds battered the shutters and the demons howled until Mira could not disentangle them. Crouching on her bed, which was still at an angle in the room, she clutched her pillow over her ears, but the ranting was impossible to shut out, and she wondered if it came from within her: she had read in one of Mrs. Zaccaroth's fairytale books of a girl who was a storm bringer.

After supper every evening, her mother set candles thick as leeks on the windowsills around the living room and kitchen, and Mira and her parents knelt on the carpet with their hands at their breasts while her mother prayed and her father coughed softly. Through the fiery fronds of her hair, Mira watched the candle flames and their echoes in the glass, pulsing in tandem. Though her mother kept the lamps and candles burning all night long, gilding the window panes, Mira could still see the writhing of the demons' limbs, sometimes a glint of tooth or nail, sometimes an eye. And their chanting wove over and under her mother's voice, occasionally seeming to deliberately harmonize with her—dark harmonies that sent beetles scuttling through her brain.

From the market, along with cucumbers and cabbages, her mother brought tales of stolen children, snatched from doorways, from open windows, from their mothers' breasts even—the demons had grown that bold.

The third evening, as they knelt in the living room with the rain and the demons' fingers clawing at the panes, Mira sensed a sudden rise in energy, in tempo. Her mother must have felt it too, because her prayer became a scream, and she pulled her hands from her breast and beat at the coffee table with her palms. Even as she did so, the brass clasp of the window swelled, then snapped open, and the double panes burst inward. A curtain of rain soaked them. Through the cacophony, Mira heard her mother shrieking, "Do something!"

The torrent had sent Mira sprawling backward, but now she rose, though it seemed she pressed against a tremendous weight to do so. She rose and stood straddle-legged on the soaked carpet, nightdress clinging, and spread her arms. And abruptly, in the midst of the raw storm, the charm came to her, easy as a nursery rhyme—a closing charm from the middle of Mrs. Zaccaroth's cookbook. It was on the left-hand page, and there was a drawing of a door with a circular tea stain on it. Even as the scrawny arms scrabbled over the sill, she was able to close the windows by bringing her palms together, and the demons' shrieks abated. But as the shutters closed, she glimpsed through the swarming rain a white-clad figure darting, and heard a voice she knew.

She went up to the quivering windows and latched them. Turning, she saw her parents on the carpet, drenched, staring at her with mouths agape. And then weariness overcame her and she fell.

* * *

The next morning, tiles and glass and branches lay on the cobbles, and when Tolly came to the door Mira heard him tell her mother that windows had smashed in several houses and a dozen children were missing. Two boats had foundered; a third had been swept downriver and was lost in the cataracts. Tolly's boat had survived, but the sail was in shreds. He waved a hand at the horizon. "More clouds are rising," he said. "Tonight will be worse."

Mira didn't even have her shoes on and was still in her nightdress, but she ducked under her mother's arm, brushed past Tolly, and, ignoring her mother's cries, scampered down the cobblestones. There might be a storm percolating on the edge of the world, but the morning air was polished and tangy, and it was delicious after the days of confinement to be out of the house and running, toes finding the washed cobbles among the branches and broken tiles, dress cavorting about her knees.

On the cliff top the destruction was more general. Several of the twisted trees were down and lay humped on the bracken, their roots filthy talons brandished at the river. The silhouette of Mrs. Zaccaroth's house seemed misshapen, and at first Mira thought a tree had landed on it; then she realized the aerie was gone—what she had taken for branches were snapped boards and rafters. Hurrying to the door, she tugged the bellpull. After a minute she tugged again, harder. After another minute she climbed the wall and jumped down into a patch of mint, releasing a pocket of bright scent, muddying her hands and knees.

The door was open and she went in, calling. There was no answer. The parlor was empty; so were the kitchen and bedroom.

Without much hope, she ran up the stairs. Sodden books lay on the top step. She stepped over an illustration of a magpie in a nest, surrounded by cut gemstones. It must have been hand-tinted—the colors of the gems had bled into the margins.

Mrs. Zaccaroth lay arched beneath the sky on a heap of tumbled books, arms spread, sopping nightdress tamped over her sparse frame. Her eyes were shut and her hands were empty and open, and Mira thought she was dead. Kneeling on a volume of nursery rhymes, she wept and bent her head to Mrs. Zaccaroth's ribcage. Pillow of bones. But as her initial hectic sobs subsided to moans, she felt the ribs shift slightly, and swallowing her tears she heard a heartbeat.

Mira tried to lift the old woman, arms under her knees and back, but she was too heavy, so she gripped her by the armpits and tugged her to the top of the stairs. As she started down, she saw what she had missed on the way up: stiffened hindquarters poked from beneath a fallen tome, the silver fur pewter now, matted and spiked. One glance told her it was too late, and she looked quickly away.

She dragged Mrs. Zaccaroth down the stairs—wincing as her heels bumped on the wet wood—and into the bedroom. When she had dried Mrs. Zaccaroth's hair and gotten her into a fresh nightgown and under the counterpane, she went to the kitchen and brewed a pot of tea. Though the carpet beneath the stairs was squelchy and scattered with wet paper, the rest of the house seemed untouched. The doilies lay on the backs of the armchairs, and the kitchen was in its usual impeccable order. The cookbook still lay on the top shelf. A batch of truffles stood on the marble counter—Mrs. Zaccaroth must have made them the day before.

When the tea was ready, she carried the cups into the bedroom. Mrs. Zaccaroth was awake, watching Mira with her green eyes that seemed to carry the light.

"I made you some—" Mira began, but her voice stuck in her throat. She sat shakily on the edge of the bed. The teacups rattled in their saucers.

"Set the cups down, child," Mrs. Zaccaroth said, her voice like a dry leaf blown across a flagstone. "You'll spill the tea."

Mira gave a sob-chafed chuckle and put the cups on the bedside table. Tentatively she touched Mrs. Zaccaroth's hand where it lay beneath the covers.

"You're all right then?" she asked.

Mrs. Zaccaroth blinked. "I may have a touch of fever," she said. "Lift me. Tea will help."

So Mira arranged the pillows behind her and eased her into a half-sitting position and handed her the tea.

Mrs. Zaccaroth raised the cup carefully to her lips and took a tiny sip. "Delicious. Thank you."

"I saw you in the night," Mira said.

Mrs. Zaccaroth watched her. Her eyes, now that Mira was in their full beam, seemed too bright, too glittery.

"What happened?" Mira asked.

Mrs. Zaccaroth took another sip of tea, and another, before she answered. "The breach has grown wide," she said. "They are strong, child. Very strong. Only with your aid could I hold them, and that barely." She looked down into the diminished circle rocking against the porcelain. "Once you had closed the window, I was able to lay a charm about the house to keep you safe, at least through the night. But I had neglected to do so for my own house." She breathed, looked up. "They were waiting for me. Waiting in the wings of the storm. As soon as I entered the house they plunged. All night we struggled, Mr. Mugwort and I, against the demons. At last, with dawn, their power broke and they retreated, howling."

"I heard them," Mira said.

"Yes. They retreated, but I had spent my power. If you had not come this morning ..."

"I came," Mira said, and patted the blade of Mrs. Zaccaroth's shin beneath the counterpane.

"You came. Yes, you came, my Mira. But what happened? You were absent for some days."

Mira told her about the candle—the smoke crafted in the shape of a face—and the priest's visit.

To her surprise, Mrs. Zaccaroth summoned a narrow smile. "You are lucky," she said. "It was precisely such a mistake that sent me to the asylum. I was told to sweep the floor and my mother caught me manipulating the broom, making it dance. I had thought she was out shopping." She closed her eyes and held out the teacup. "I must sleep," she said. "Give Mr. Mugwort his breakfast if you will."

Biting her lip, Mira helped her slide back down and tucked her in. Then she fetched a clean sheet from the linen closet and went up to the aerie. Lifting the book off the cat's body, she wrapped him in the sheet and carried him outside. With a garden trowel, she dug a grave beside the stone wall—the soaked earth came up easily—and laid the stiff swaddled shape inside and covered it. Over the grave she planted a sprig of catmint.

All that morning, Mira labored in the aerie. The books too

damaged to salvage she tossed down to the garden. The worms and beetles would work on them; they would become earth. She imagined the passage of the letters through the worms' bodies and then up a stem, into a leaf. Would she be able to taste a name in a sprig of rosemary? she wondered. A rhyme in a twig of thyme? Using butcher's string, she laced a lattice across the parlor, attaching it to pegs in the cornice molding. On the lines she hung the rest of the books, pages-down, like bulky laundry, and laid folded towels beneath the rows to catch the drops.

The fainting couch she tipped overboard, and watched it careen end over end, ripping open, stuffing bursting abruptly free like gouts of white smoke, until it vanished beneath the spray. She did the same with the shards of roof and the shattered bookshelves, saving only a few planks. With these she battened down the well hole.

It was nearly noon by the time she was done, and she stood on what had been the aerie floor and was now the roof, looking out at the horizon. The clouds were rising, a bank of thunderheads frothing merrily into the blue. But their bellies were ripe purple, and beneath them lay vaults of cobalt. She could feel the approach of thunder like a grimace in her brain.

She moved to the eaves and lowered herself over the edge. Gripping the gutter with her fingertips, she pressed off from the clapboard siding and landed in a patch of verbena, arms wheeling, toppling onto her rump.

In the kitchen she made soup and another pot of tea and cut a slice of the light, golden-crusted bread Mrs. Zaccaroth made every three days, and carried a tray into the bedroom. Mrs. Zaccaroth was awake.

"That was Mr. Mugwort in the garden, wasn't it?" she asked as Mira set the tray down.

Mira nodded. "I'm sorry."

Mrs. Zaccaroth closed her eyes, pressing out two chains of teardrops. She brushed them aside with her palms and looked at Mira. Gaze of green ice once more. "Thank you," she said.

"I made some soup," Mira told her. "And there's tea." She set the tray on the bedside table and took a bowl and perched on the counterpane. The morning's labor had given her an appetite. "I cleared off the aerie," she said between sips. "I was able to save a lot of the books. Not all. They're hung up to dry in the parlor. I'll come over tomorrow to see if they're ready to take down."

Mrs. Zaccaroth watched her over the rim of her teacup. "You will not come tomorrow," she said.

"Of course I will." Mira put down her spoon. "This is the last of the bread, and I—"

"Child," Mrs. Zaccaroth said, her voice low, but so firm Mira ceased prattling and stared. "Have you not understood? Their power has grown too strong. Last night they nearly broke through. If the dawn had come but a few moments later it would have been over. Oh Mira, I wish ..." Her gaze strayed from Mira's eyes to her hair, and then over to the window, where a snapdragon blossom nodded.

"What do you wish?" Mira asked, alarmed. It wasn't like Mrs. Zaccaroth to leave a sentence unfinished. Her conversations were always so tidy.

Mrs. Zaccaroth shook her head. "No matter," she said. "I have done what I could in the time we were given. But tonight ..." Suddenly Mrs. Zaccaroth's gaze was full upon hers, and Mira felt the green chill in her belly, as if she'd quaffed an icy drink. "It is time, Mira," Mrs. Zaccaroth said. "You must leave before sundown."

For a long time Mira was silent. The snapdragon had ceased its nodding and the leaves of the pomegranate lay painted on the spotless sky, as if the world were holding its breath.

"How do I go?" she asked at last.

"I have spent many days pondering this," Mrs. Zaccaroth said. "The river brought you the key, so I believe you must follow the river. There are therefore two ways you can go: north or south. Bring me my crystal from the mantel."

Mira didn't have to ask which one. Going into the parlor, she lifted down the heavy sphere of smoky quartz and carried it back to the bedroom. It was cool and smooth in her hands, like a congealed shadow.

"Look into it," Mrs. Zaccaroth said.

Sitting on the edge of the bed, Mira held the crystal ball in her lap, and this time she could gaze unflinching into its depths, where facets and crevices lay like a distant city seen through mist. The daylight seemed to dim as though drapes had been drawn, and the forms within the stone churned like storm clouds and parted. Mira drew in her breath and looked up.

"What did you see?" Mrs. Zaccaroth asked.

"The Sentinel," Mira said. "The Sentinel, but its face was on fire." She shivered.

"It is as I suspected," Mrs. Zaccaroth said. "You will go north."

Mira walked back slowly along the shore. From time to time she picked up a river-polished stone and cast it into the waves, which were jade now, and surging. Spume blew from their soft tips like flicked cream. Behind them thornbushes of lightning quivered in the grottoes of the clouds and she thought she could discern the shrieking of the demons above the crashing waves.

She entered the house through the back door, which was now the front door, and heard the slosh of sudsy water in the laundry room. Leaving the door ajar, Mira went to the kitchen and quickly dropped into a sailcloth shopping bag a loaf of bread, a wedge of cheese, several tangerines, and a stoppered bottle of water.

Going to her bedroom, she changed—she was still barefoot and in her nightdress—and stuffed some clothes into the bag, and added her toothbrush and hairbrush. On her way out, she peeked into the laundry room, taking care to keep the bag behind the jamb. Her mother was on her knees with her back to Mira, plunging her arms into the suds, shoulders churning. Mira watched her for a moment. Then she turned and walked out into the breathless afternoon.

The bag was heavier than she'd anticipated, and awkward. She slung it from one shoulder, then the other, and finally put her arms through the straps and wore it like a knapsack, jouncing on her spine.

She walked down the main street, past the boats on their sides in the sand where the fishermen had pulled them high, past the market, past the apothecary and the bakery and the church, past the brick kiln with its tall smokestack, past Tolly's shack on the northern fringes of the town. Tolly was sitting outside on the grass, patching his sail. He raised a hand, and she was in such a state of excitement that she grinned at him. This gave him the courage to pipe up. "Where are you headed?" he asked, but she retorted, "Mind your own business!" and he bent to the net with carmine cheeks.

Then she was beyond the houses, trudging through the unkempt riverside brush, releasing the sharp scents of wild sage and river bracken. The storm was coming in fast, and now the first keel of wind cracked the air, casting leaves about, tousling the bracken, brushing the kiln smoke over the rooftops. Waves smashed along the shore like abruptly blossoming chrysanthemums.

The Sentinel was larger than it had seemed from the town,

though its form grew no clearer as she approached: a hulking shape, creviced and craggy, the hollow a hooded face watching her approach. She hadn't known what she would do when she got to it, but when she reached its base she realized a series of shallow notches curved up the structure, and was certain they had been carved by human hands. She set a foot on the stone, reached for a handhold. Then another.

In a minute, fingers chafed, she reached the nook: a snug chamber as tall as she was. Crumbs of char lay in the recesses, and the walls and ceiling were scorched. To either side, at waist height, rusted iron rings were socketed in the stone. She wondered what purpose they had served.

She sat on the edge of the hollow with her feet dangling and looked out. Set beneath the extravagant cliffs of the storm, with its colors of peacock and plum, its lobes and crevices, the town seemed puny—just a smattering of houses. The grim cube of the church, its spire a wedge in the sky. The masts of the fishing boats like a stand of leaning cane. The tawny speckling of the terracotta rooftops. Among them her backward house stood out, like a flaw in a tapestry, like a misplaced tile in a mosaic. And beyond the town, on a rise, the off-kilter patch that was Mrs. Zaccaroth's house and garden.

The clouds bent over the river, and from this perch she saw what she could not have seen from her home: the storm was confined to the town. Like a great disheveled bird of prey, it lowered rumpled gray wings across the houses, but beyond those wings the air was clear. However, she scarcely had time to notice this before her attention was dragged back to the river by a sound she had previously heard only from within the shelter of her house. Here it was raw and chaotic and incredibly loud—the choral shrieking of demons, hurtling across the river on the wings of the storm and rushing northward along the riverbank with outstretched fingers. She watched their approach with a terror the flavor of poison: it nearly stopped her heart.

They were smaller than she'd imagined. Their eyes were wan. They wore necklaces and gnarled bracelets that might have been fashioned of broken stones or broken bones. Skinny hands raised or beating chests and flanks. Some were entirely naked, their pelvis bones sharp, their ribs like spoon handles. Others wore tattered remnants. Sliding away from the entrance, Mira pressed herself against the back of the hollow, drawing her knees to her chest.

The demons seemed to drag the storm with them, tugging it

northward like a vast cape of thunder, and now the first of the rain arrived—a handful of pellets dashed against her ankles. Then it descended in solid sheets, making a wavering curtain before her small shelter. The demons chanted as they massed at the base of the Sentinel, and she could hear the scratching of their fingernails on the stone.

Hastily Mira kindled a nubbin of light on the tip of her forefinger. Then she screamed. A hand had ripped through the curtain of raindrops—thin, pale, the gnawed nails violet. As if through warped glass, she glimpsed a narrow face, great lidless eyes. In a spasm of panic, she flung out her palms and a panel of fire shattered against the wall of rain. A howl of rage tumbled away, as if her parry had sent the demon end over end. The voices shrieked in fury.

She did not possess the strength to keep the curtain of flame permanently erected, but it served to stave off the demons temporarily. When she raised the fire they retreated, howling. Then they would regroup and surge forward, swarming up the stone.

The spontaneous spell wrought from panic and the small light she'd crafted had given her an idea. Deep within the magical cookbook was a mending charm that could be used to shore up a crumbling wall or patch a ripped blouse. It would not suffice for long-term repair, but was intended, Mrs. Zaccaroth had told her, for emergencies. Now, with terror feeding invention, Mira realized she could tailor the spell to suit her need. There was no time to wonder if it would work. Swiftly she recited the altered incantation, hands at her breast, then raised. She indicated with lifted palms the edges of the scorched stone ceiling and brought her hands down in a sweeping, curling motion, embracing the space as the spell was cast. At once the shrieks of the demons and the clamor of the storm diminished, the cold prickling of raindrops against her ankles ceased, and she sat within a shimmering room created by her words and her strength and the stone and the rain.

Mira had known long nights cowering under her counterpane while the demons ranted and beat at the glass, but nothing had prepared her for this toil. Hour after hour she sat squeezed into the nook, spine against stone, mind and hands straining to keep the spellcast wall sound. Though she was starving and desperately weary, though she could feel her strength ebbing, leaching into the spell, she could not pause for even a second to snatch a bite or close her eyes: the demons scrabbled at her makeshift shelter. She could see their small teeth grinding in their ruined lips, could see their curdled eyes. She could not block her ears from their cries.

Toward dawn she began to hallucinate. She had visions of a hand creeping up her leg, of a slavering mouth against her nape, and she would twist and shriek and firm up the fiery walls, muttering the incantation. But inevitably the moments of involuntary slumber grew longer, and at last she jerked awake, knocking her skull on the stone, horrified to find she'd drifted off. Swiftly she raised her hands to shore up the spell, then paused. The world was quiet. The rain had ceased, and the watercolor edges of dawn stained the damp arc of sky. Gray clouds still coiled across the town, but among them were scraps of blue. To her left, the swollen torrent bore drowned cats, capsized boats, uprooted bushes.

She ate a tangerine and made a sandwich, but only ate half before sleep overcame her. The sailcloth bag her pillow, she curled up and slept, a small, filthy redheaded troll high above the careening river.

She woke, flailing, from a dream that a demon sat upon her chest. It had been lighter than she'd anticipated, blue shadows in the hollows between its ribs, and it grinned at her with teeth like smashed pebbles. Its thin fingers with their bitten nails had been reaching for her throat. Her heart was clattering as though she'd swallowed a rattle, and her head throbbed.

Climbing down the Sentinel, she walked a few paces along the riverbank and stood for a while, mesmerized by the slashed, raucous tumult. The river was narrower here, filled with tremendous canines and molars of black rock. The swollen torrent gnashed among them, tearing and spitting, flinging into the air shards of rainbow that clung a moment like iridescent butterflies.

She had an almost uncontrollable urge to walk back into town once more. She wanted to see her mother again, even if she would be smacked and scolded. She wanted a cup of tea with honey and a bowl of fish soup and a quilt around her knees. But as her gaze lighted on the cliffside house, something crackled in her mind and, vivid as day, she saw Mrs. Zaccaroth, propped on her bed, watching her with those stone-green eyes, and she turned and looked out to the north.

The river tumbled across the rocks, and on either side the land fell away in long, uneven shelves, the cloak of greenery diminishing. As the landscape leveled out far below, the river eased into curves, silver shavings thinning till they were subsumed under volumes of dust-laden oxygen. To east and west the desert sprawled, its palette similar to the jars on Mrs. Zaccaroth's shelves: cinnamon, nutmeg, turmeric, with vortices of shadow and patches of stipple and expanses smooth as a child's skin. The whole glinted and seemed to subtly tilt. The landscape was too big. Too big for a girl to walk through. What secrets did the desert conceal? And she realized for the first time the immensity of this decision. Though many of the fairytales in Mrs. Zaccaroth's aerie described journeys, she could always stop reading or flip to the end to see how they turned out. But she had not recognized until this moment that a journey creates its path.

She took a step northward. Then another.

V

MOTHER GOTHA

As Mira descended across the shelves of the land, the air grew warmer. At first her surroundings seemed little different from those she was accustomed to: the same tough bracken and pungent herbs by the water's edge. The same sunbirds in the acacias. The same emerald and sapphire dragonflies skittering like shattering prisms across the water.

By the evening of that day she had not yet reached the base of the slope. She made a nest beneath a tree and ate bread and cheese and a tangerine, watching her surroundings dissolve into shadow, listening to the antiphonal chanting of crickets and frogs in the reeds by the river's edge, not daring to light a fire lest it summon beings from the night.

At the top of the long slope to the south, the Sentinel was a finger snared in the erratic cat's cradle of lightning. But she was beyond earshot of the thunder, and knew she was beyond the clutches of the demons: they were creatures of the storm, tethered to the storm. Making a pillow of her sailcloth shopping bag, she told herself fairytales to lull herself to sleep.

* * *

It took her another day to reach the base of the long escarpment. As she walked, her spirit expanded into the space, and she felt something lifting from her mind. Some burden she hadn't realized she was carrying. In the town, it had been present even though she had tried to extricate herself from the leaden nets of the church and the disapproving glances of the market women. Her thoughts had remained trapped. Now, in this expanse, she could breathe. But with that freedom came a strange new terror: the terror of the release, of the plummet.

The third morning, after a breakfast of dry cheese and stale bread, Mira sat watching the river, which had ceased its headlong careen and was now wider, gentler, a sequence of interlocking planes pocked with copper dents. It was already hot. She stood and walked on, the sailcloth bag so light now she scarcely noticed it. The acacias grew smaller and more twisted. The dragonflies vanished, replaced by clinging, biting flies she slapped at to no avail. And instead of bracken, there was a narrow, tough grass that sliced her ankles. To escape the flies and the grass, she moved away from the river, into the sands.

She peered forward into the parched land, but could discern little save the heat-addled globules, warping even as she watched. For hours she waded through the heat as though through syrup. Once she found herself on her knees and couldn't remember having fallen. Once she thought she saw a bend of the river before her, but as she approached it lifted into the air, diminished to a bead of mercury, and was gone. There was not a speck of shade.

She mounted a low hillock and sat on its peak, gazing through the warping heat. And for a moment, as she looked northward, she saw the black angles of a wall. A house, she thought. A house of black rock. But when she looked again it was gone, like the phantom curl of river.

She struggled on, and once more saw the black walls, but this time upside down, dangling queerly in a drop of molten sky.

Terribly thirsty, she made her way down to the riverbank, where a single stunted acacia cast a lacework shade. She filled her bottle with the brown river water and drank and filled it again. Draped in the skimpy shade, she laid her head against the trunk and closed her eyes.

When she woke, the sun was in her face and the flies had found her, clustering on her crusted lips. She drank and filled her bottle and headed back into the desert. The landscape was less tormented now, only the horizon rippling softly. She'd entirely forgotten about the black walls she'd glimpsed, but as she crested a dune she halted and peered forward with scraped eyes. Something lay out there—she was certain of it now—in a hollow between two low hills: a dark clot of walls and shadows.

An hour later she realized it was not a single building, but a walled compound containing a number of buildings, one a chapel. And she saw as well that some of the interior structures were cratered. A ruin. Strange that she had never heard of this place—a walled compound three days' walk from the town.

Mira approached cautiously. The place appeared deserted, and no footprints marked the sand around it. The walls loomed, windowless. There was no doorway on this side, but part of the eastern wall had collapsed and boulders thronged the gap. Only when she started climbing did she realize how weary her limbs were. Her fingers were pliable as old celery; her kneecaps hiccupped. At the top of the heap, she stood looking into the compound.

Sand clogged the doorway of the chapel and had all but submerged the flagstones in the courtyard. Picking her way down the pile of rocks, she dislodged one, and it banged three times and shattered. From the caved dome of the chapel a dozen crows burst forth, like the stones come to life. The clap of their wings echoed from the walls. As they wheeled over Mira's head, their shadows a vortex, she felt an unaccountable terror. Cowering on a boulder, she shielded her head with her arms until the crows subsided and the compound was silent once more.

The place sent shivers up her spine, as though the walls harbored creatures more malevolent than birds, but she shook off the dread, telling herself she was beyond the darkness and the demons; she was simply overtired. Nevertheless, as she picked her way down to the courtyard, she felt something settle over her like an ancient, clotted spiderweb, and she brushed at the air with her fingers. Nothing was there.

Turning on the sand-strewn flagstones, she called out: "Hello?" Her voice caromed. "Hello!" she called again, but only echoes answered. She walked over to the chapel and peered in. Decaying pews, an altar all but obscured under sand and cobwebs, and in the center the cairn of the fallen ceiling, chalky with crow droppings.

The entire northern wall of the compound was a bank of chambers. Scraps of wood clung to rusted hinges. Mira peered into several. There was a slumped cot in one, a dusty candle stub on a ledge in another. A third held a painting in a simple frame, but the image had long ago faded to gauze and scabs, illegible.

Walking around the chapel, she stopped short. Someone lived here, or had until very recently. Beside the far wall was a wide rectangle of tilled ground in which grew potatoes and carrots, peppers and beans, marjoram and basil and other herbs. A pomegranate tree stood beside the garden, the fruit glowing among the leaves like lanterns with thin leather shades. Sharp-edged footprints marked the soil. Someone in sandals had trodden this earth within the past day or two.

And when she peered into the last chamber, the one tucked into the corner of the compound, she saw that it was swept and the ceiling was free of cobwebs. A mattress rested on a cot, with a blanket folded at its foot, and several garments lay on a shelf.

How strange. Why had no one answered her greeting? Standing

in the doorway of the room, she called again, but this time not even the crows replied.

She plucked a pomegranate. Sitting on the threshold of the tidy room, she took from her bag the last hunk of bread and the last nubbin of cheese and had her breakfast. When she was finished and had spat the last seed into the garden and licked the sour juice from her stained fingers, she was suddenly impossibly weary, head wilting on its stalk. Hardly aware of what she was doing, she slipped off her shoes and collapsed on the mattress.

* * *

From a dream that she was ensnared by black vines, she woke into darkness. She tried to stretch her legs, but encountered resistance. Panicking, she lifted her arms above her head. They too pressed against something: something hard, something cold. Sitting up, heart thrashing, she realized she was no longer on the cot. She was in an iron cage just tall enough for her to sit upright. Prodding blindly at the bars, she found a padlock and banged it against the metal. She tried to mutter a spell of opening, and with a jolt realized she was bound by more than iron; invisible coils lay across her lips so nothing emerged from her mouth but sighs. And this theft of her voice was even more terrifying than the physical cage.

She made a little light—the purplish glowworm on the end of her finger, fuzzier and dimmer than usual. The cage lay in the center of a windowless room. There were shelves on three walls—perhaps this had been a storeroom at one time—and a door in the wall to her right. The light dimmed and went out: whatever spells had been laid upon her siphoned and stifled her strength.

It was the first time she had been in the thrall of another's power, though she had tasted Mrs. Zaccaroth's from time to time, and she tried to discern who or what was oppressing her. She had only the sense of something ancient. Ancient and clotted and solitary.

She lay on the slats of the cage so long in the darkness that she became certain she'd die there, and she was furious with herself. She should have known a place like this would harbor magic, and now that she thought back she realized she had scented the danger. She had felt this presence as soon as she climbed the fallen wall, but in her weariness and her desire for shelter had failed to recognize it.

When finally something tapped, echoing, accompanied by a swelling seam of light beneath the door, her tears had long since dried and she'd succumbed to dull despair. Metal scraped on metal and the door rasped open.

By the light of a candle she saw her captor for the first time: an ancient woman—older (in appearance at any rate) than Mrs. Zaccaroth. She was hunched, and the hand that gripped the candle was knobbly as a cluster of olives, the knuckles swollen. Discolored fleshy growths marred her face, and from certain of these long white hairs curled. She wore enormous black-framed spectacles, though the left lens was smashed and that eye peered through fangs of filthy glass.

"So you're awake at last, intruder," she said. Her voice was soft and dark. Mira could taste the power in it, sour and potent as communion wine.

Mira opened her mouth, expecting to still be silenced, but the invisible muzzle had fallen away. She cleared her throat. "Who are you?" she asked. Her tongue felt thick, as if she'd been sucking on ice.

"Not so fast. Not so fast," the woman said. In the corner by the door was a wooden stool, and she sat, hunched like a great lumpish spider, and aimed her cloudy, half-shattered spectacles at the cage. The candle fumed at her breast.

"You came down from the cataracts," she said. "I was watching you, moving toward the abbey like a flame in the sand. Why? What are you seeking in this place?"

"You're a witch," Mira said, and at that the woman jerked and crossed herself. Mira nodded slowly. "You're a witch, aren't you?"

The woman shook her head violently, and her voice sharpened. "Answer my questions!" she ordered. "Who are you? Where did you come from?"

Mira passed a hand across her face. She shrugged. There seemed no reason for secrecy. "My name is Mira," she said. "I come from the town to the south, from beyond the cataracts."

"And why did you leave your home?"

"Demons. They come in the night, and they are growing stronger. They took my brother; every night they take the children. A storm came. A tempest. The demons rode the storm in, and they broke the windows of my house. They nearly killed my teacher."

"What are you seeking?"

"I was given a key." Mira patted her pocket. "Where is it?" she cried.

Without taking her eyes off Mira's face, the old woman reached inside the neckline of her garment and brought forth the gold key on a thin chain. She ran a thumb across its gleam. "Who gave it to you?" she asked.

"The river. It was my birthday present. Give it back."

"A gift from the river. I have heard of such things." She turned the key and it glinted in the candlelight, almost as bright as a flame itself. She looked up. "But you haven't told me. What are you seeking?"

"A door. A door somewhere, that the key will open. I don't know where it is. Do you know?"

"A door?" the woman said in her voice of black wool. "A door to what?"

"To the other side. That's what my teacher told me."

The woman sucked in her breath. Abruptly she stood and stepped out of the room. There was a clang and Mira was in darkness once more. "Come back!" she cried feebly. "What did I say?" But the woman did not return, and when Mira tried to call again she found that the muzzle had fallen over her tongue once more.

Much later—though there was no time in that chamber, and Mira sometimes did not know if she slept or woke—the door opened again, just for a moment, and something clattered through the bars of the cage. She fumbled at it with her fingertips. It was a mug, containing a stew of turnips and carrots and some tough stringy flesh. There was no spoon, so she slurped, scooping with her fingers. It was delicious.

With the sustenance in her belly, she began to turn her mind to escape, though the invisible bonds reached even into her thoughts, slowing and scattering them. A more accomplished witch, she was sure, would have been able to release herself from this cage, but try as she might she could not summon a spell that would avail her. Though she had turned her entire house somehow in her sleep, she could not open the padlock or bend these iron bars by her willpower. She leafed through her memories of the magical cookbook, recipe by recipe, examining each to see if it could be tailored to her need, but her thoughts were frayed and she could not bring the recipes entirely to mind.

She woke from troubled dreams to blushing eyelids and opened them to see the old woman again sitting on the stool in the corner. How long had she been there?

Mira cleared her throat and found that her tongue was once again loosened. "Thank you for the stew," she said dully. She rubbed her eyes. "It tasted so good. But I still don't know who you are. What's your name?"

The old woman was silent for a long time, watching her through the corroded lenses, smashed and whole. The candle wax dropped to the floor with a pock that seemed to grow louder each time. Finally she said, "You have the power."

Mira nodded. "Yes."

The woman fell silent again, but her breathing quickened and a single tear emerged from under the black frames of her spectacles and traced a jagged track down her cheek.

"You have it too," Mira said softly. "You have the power. I can feel it."

Angrily, the woman smacked away the tear, but another took its place.

"Did they try to press it down?" Mira asked. "Did they make you pray and recite the verses and do the oil?"

The woman stared at her.

"That's why you're in this place, isn't it? That's why you're alone in this falling-down place—because they called you a witch; because they were frightened of your powers." She could feel the sinews forming as she spoke, could feel her words traveling along them to the old woman's ribcage.

"How do …" the woman said, then shook her head. "Your powers won't work on me," she muttered.

"It's true, though, isn't it?" Mira said. "It's true. Tell me …"

The candle jerked, and Mira thought she was going to scurry out once more and bang the door shut, but the woman pressed her head back against the stones. She took off her ravaged spectacles and laid them in her lap and pressed the globes of her knuckles into her eyes. Then she put on her spectacles once more and looked at Mira.

"All my life I have been struggling against you," the woman said. "Against you and what you stand for and the powers you carry. When I saw you coming through the sands like a little flame, I knew … I knew you were danger. Dangerous as any spark. And then you stole a pomegranate and slept in my bed, and I should have done away with you then and there. I should have seized a stone and smashed your freckled forehead in. But you were so peaceful. Your lips slightly parted, your eyelids twitching—you were watching some dream. It was like … well, it was like looking into a mirror of the past. And I couldn't do it." She fingered one of her wens, which clung like an engorged lilac tick to her chin, and stroked the three hairs sprouting from it. "I couldn't do it," she said again. "So I told myself I'd torment you—stick you in a cage and watch you wither."

"I didn't mean any harm," Mira said. "I was just so hungry and tired, and the pomegranates were ripe and your bed looked so soft."

"You are a thief. An intruder and a thief." Once again, the old woman stood and patted down her skirts and bolted the door behind her, but Mira had a strange sensation that her presence lingered, as if the room were filled with suffocating black wool. Mira pressed against it with hand and mind, and this time, to her surprise, she felt the wool yield, melting like spun sugar under her prodding, and she was able to reach out, to soothe, to call.

And before long she heard the tapping, saw the swelling seam of light.

"What did you do?" the old woman asked, standing in the doorway.

"Nothing," Mira said.

"I was outside under the pomegranate tree, and I heard your voice." The candle flame cast black hoops of shadow across her eyes.

Mira shifted in her cage, leaning forward. "You made the bridge," she said. "If you hadn't, I don't think I could have called to you. But you made the connection." She could feel the old woman's mind waver, and she pressed, reaching along the black tendrils.

"If I let you go, what will you do?" the woman asked gruffly.

"I'll leave, I promise. I won't look back."

The old woman nodded. "Of course you will," she whispered, and the hoops of shadow trembled on her eyes. "Of course you'll leave. And ... and that's ... that's what ..."

"Oh," Mira said. "Oh, I see. Well ..." She hugged her knees and stared at the woman. "I don't think I can stay," she said finally. "I wish I could, but ... the key, you know. It's what I have to do. I'm on a journey."

The old woman gathered her skirts and made as if to stand, then sat back with a sigh. She picked up the candle. A bead of amber clung to the last morsel of wick. "I suppose I'd better let you out," she said, and her voice was suddenly as fissured as her skin.

* * *

After the days in cramped darkness, Mira emerged into the sunshine with a forearm raised as if to fend off a blow. Knees crackling, she shuffled over the sand-strewn cobbles, squinting and grimacing.

Beneath the pomegranate tree was a wooden stool. The woman

led Mira to it and fetched another from her room. Then she entered one of the doors on the eastern side of the compound and clattered and rustled within. Mira sat back with her legs outstretched and head pressed against the bark, eyes closed, relishing the melting coins of sun swaying on her skin and the odor of loam and the chanting of the bees.

"Here you go, dearie."

Mira opened her eyes. The woman was holding out her hands. From one dangled a chain with the key strung on it; the other proffered a glass of tea. Mira slipped the chain over her neck and tucked the key into her dress. Then she took the glass in her fingertips and sighed the steam into her face—fragrance of mint and honey. And for a moment she was back in Mrs. Zaccaroth's house, getting ready for a lesson in magic, Mr. Mugwort beside her on the sofa. She looked up, and the old woman blinked at her.

"Tell me your story," Mira said. "How did you come to this place?"

The woman sighed, and sighed again. "Well," she said. "Well. Where to start? It has been many years since I told a tale."

"Start from the beginning," Mira said. "Start with your name."

"Yes," the woman said. "My name is Gotha. Mother Gotha, they called me here. I was for many years the abbess of this place. I still am, I suppose, though you are the first underling to arrive for many years.

"I was born in the city to the north, the youngest of three sisters. And it was clear from the first that I was different. I had the red hair, of course, while my sisters were black-haired, but there was something else: my sisters were calm and obedient and charming—when my mother asked them to sweep the floor and wash the dishes they did so without complaint, and they sang as they worked, for both had lovely voices. My voice was that of a crow, and I detested housework. So I'd skip out of the house in the mornings and wander down to the riverbank, and there I'd play with stones and bottles and snail shells and tell myself stories—yes, I used to be a storyteller. And in all the stories I was the heroine and my sisters were spurned.

"I can't remember when I first realized I possessed the power—when you're young the world is full of wonder, and it's only in comparison that you recognize what is strange. I do remember the time it got me into trouble. My mother had sent me to hang out the laundry—we had washing lines strung off the balcony. It was a breezy day, and the wind snatched a handkerchief from my hands. I remember thinking it looked like a white dove as it went tumbling away, and somehow, before it touched the cobbles, I was able to snatch it up and turn its hemmed corners to wings and send it flapping up into the sky, a bird of my own devising. Oh, it was such fun to see it up there against the smoky blue, and I could turn it this way and that. So I released another handkerchief, and then one of my father's shirts, and then a cotton dress belonging to one of my sisters, and soon the whole batch of laundry was flapping and circling like a flock of doves, and I was clapping and jumping up and down.

"My mother heard my cries and opened the balcony doors, and she seized my elbows from behind. Then, of course, I lost my grip on the flying laundry and it blew off who knows where. The only article we recovered was a single black stocking, draped over a lamppost."

Mother Gotha sighed and pinched a swollen knuckle. "Well," she went on, "it was clear that evening, when my mother let me out of my room and brought me into the parlor and my uncle the priest was there, as well as my father and my sisters, that I'd done something wrong and that it was not the first time. They'd known, you see—known that I had the power—and they told my uncle about the time I'd turned my bath over and flooded the hall and the time I'd made all the eggs hatch and the time I'd ripped my oldest sister's best dress to shreds just by staring at it. And all of these I recalled as they said them, though they had seemed at the time just more strange, wonderful things in the world, like thunder or the taste of cinnamon or the blue rim of a candle flame.

"I had never before been told it was wrong. And this was utterly terrifying—to be told that this thing inside you, which feels so gorgeous, is wrong. The priest told me I had to press it down—to find out what it was, where it came from, and stamp it down or pluck it out, as though it were a weed in a patch of thyme.

"I was young, and you believe them when you're young. So I wept and said I was sorry and that I didn't know, and I promised I wouldn't do it again, though I scarcely knew what the 'it' was that I referred to. 'I'll stop it,' I told them. 'I won't do it again.' You know how it is when you're young."

Mother Gotha peered at her with naked, moist eyes. Mira nodded, her mouth too full of emotion to speak.

"That evening, my uncle the priest came again," she went on. "He offered my mother a solution. There was a place, he said, where girls like me could be sent. A place where they could get the evil out. They never asked me if I wanted to go, and I was too young, too naive, to understand the glances that passed between them.

"The next morning, I woke to find three gray-robed women in headscarves standing over my bed. They bound my hands and gagged me with a cotton cloth. I thought I was being kidnapped, but as they pulled me through the living room I saw my mother watching from the bedroom. Though she was weeping, she made no move to stop them."

Mother Gotha drained her cup. "Would you like more tea?" she inquired, peering at the pattern of leaves at the base of the porcelain.

Mira shook her head and wrapped her hands around her elbows. The sun had passed beyond the western wall, gathering the coins of light into a shawl of shadow. "Where did they take you?" she asked.

Mother Gotha looked up from her tea leaves. "In the southwestern quarter of the city," she went on, "there is a great structure of gray stone, surmounted by dozens of towers. This is the Convent of the Sisters of the Light. Viewed from the street it must seem to passersby a delightful sanctuary, an abode of peace, for there are fortifying aphorisms carved into the walls, and in the reception area are lilies in vases and cross-stitched verses. But look closer and you will notice that the lower windows are narrow and heavily barred. The girls do not enter through the main doors, but are dragged in through a small door of solid iron in a side alley. For the convent is a prison. A prison and an asylum.

"The initial weeks in that place were utter horror. I was caged in a dark cell with a single high window, my hands bound so I could not work a spell. The sisters beat me with knotted ropes and forced me to memorize long passages and repeat them endlessly, withholding food if I missed a word. I thought I would go mad. And many of the inmates did go mad, though the sisters said they were mad already—that, of course, was why they had been brought to the convent in the first place, do you see? But somehow, even bound in a dark room, even beaten without reason and tormented with verses, I was able to cling to my senses.

"At last I was released to the dormitory—a great room on the third floor, lined with bunk beds. And this space, though a relief after the days of confinement, contained its own horrors, because if the young are caged together, their spirits curdle. There were not enough sisters to adequately oversee all the girls, and so certain girls had been chosen as prefects. These were the cruelest of the older girls, and they carried whips of their own with which they were permitted to beat us. The beatings were not the worst punishments, though. At least they'd be over in a minute or two—whenever the prefect's arm grew tired. But they would sometimes make the girls kneel for hours on the stone floor, or perform meaningless tasks such as counting grains of rice or braiding an endless cord, or they'd make the younger girls walk around their beds in circles, hour after hour, until they collapsed from exhaustion.

"I remember the day I broke, during an evening chapel. I'd been without food for three days. The Mother Superior was giving the homily. She framed it as a choice; as a choice between darkness and light, between the locked door and the open window. And suddenly I saw how easy it was to choose the light. The darkness, after all, was where nightmares came from. And so, when she called us forward, I stumbled up the aisle, dazzled by tears. I knelt and she touched my forehead, anointed me, and raised me with a kiss on each cheek. 'Welcome to the light,' she whispered. 'You are reborn.' And so it was.

"I became a watcher. I was given the task of sweeping the hallways, and this allowed me to slip into the shadows, away from the prefects; it also allowed me to explore the crannies of that vast structure—if you're holding a broom, no one questions your presence. So I learned that certain of the mistresses crept into each other's rooms in the evenings; and that the cook was selling the finer cuts of meat to a pomaded scallywag who came to the scullery door, and could herself be bribed to make sweetmeats; and that two of the prefects had blackmailed one of the mistresses and were granted special favors, including being permitted to go out from time to time, dressed in ordinary clothes. And I discovered something else. I discovered that six girls gathered in the library in the evenings—for a Bible study, they said.

"The library was in the tallest turret of the convent, high bookshelves between narrow windows. The librarian was a slender mistress named Agate, with a mouth like a papercut and eyes tucked beneath brows like moss. She had a reputation for being the harshest of the sisters, and was stingy with library privileges. The most intractable cases were sent to her for correction. The six girls who gathered in the tower were of all ages, all shapes, but they had something in common; something I recognized but could not have named. I don't think I could name it now. What I was certain of was that they were not praying behind that door. I eavesdropped on them several evenings, and though I could not discern words, I heard exclamations and laughter and once a small explosion that rattled the hinges and caused purple smoke to seep beneath the door.

"The next day after morning prayers, I went to Sister Agate and told her I wanted to be admitted to the library. She shook her head, but I insisted. Then I saw something in her eyes, which I thought at the time was anger, but now I recognize was fear.

"Frustrated and furious, I stomped directly over to the Mother Superior and told her what I had heard behind the library door. Well, that was the end of the gathering of witches. The library was shuttered and locked. Sister Agate was never seen again, and the six girls were broken. I won't tell you what they did, but it shattered their minds. Three died; the others, when I left, were little more than babbling idiots.

"Because of my perceived good deed, I received privileges and favors, and after several years I became a prefect, and then a sister myself. I was known as one of the strictest, and could often bring wayward girls to heel by applying the force of my mind. Thus, subtly, I worked my way up the ladder of power and eventually was sent to be mistress of this place—this refuge, where the most recalcitrant girls wound up, the ones the city could not contain. But I could break them. Because I understood them, I could break them; could warp and subdue their power, turn it back on itself, and place my chains on their minds. I was lauded, and this abbey was considered a model of success.

"After a number of years, though, the river of girls thinned to a stream, a trickle, and then dried up altogether. The other sisters grew old and died. For seven years I have lived alone here, with only the crows for companions."

"Why did they stop sending the girls?" Mira asked.

Mother Gotha shook her head. "They never told me, and the girls of course did not know. Perhaps they have successfully contained magic in the city. Or perhaps they found another solution."

Mira gave an involuntary shiver, and Mother Gotha reached out and patted her knee. "Come," she said. "I'll heat some stew."

From the soot-stained rafters of the scullery hung herbs and onions and bunches of garlic and net bags of potatoes. Against the wall lay piles of acacia wood. Mother Gotha blew the ash off the embers in the stove and fed it with twigs and then sticks, and soon the fire was clicking and lisping and the concoction in the cauldron started to ripple and then bubble sloppily.

Beside the woodpile was a heap of black feathers. Mira picked one up and smoothed the wispy tendrils at its base. She looked at Mother Gotha, who nodded.

"The crows and I have an agreement," she said. "They can plunder my garden and eat my pomegranates if I can snare one of their number every so often." She stirred and tasted the mixture, and added a couple of diced potatoes and an onion.

"My seven-year stew," she said. "I just keep it going."

"Don't you get tired of it?" Mira asked.

"Well, it's always changing, see? Every day a little different. Sometimes I add pomegranate seeds, sometimes dill weed, sometimes a crow's egg. Sometimes if the rains come mushrooms crop up in the decaying mattresses, like the delicious ghosts of the girls who slept there."

After they had eaten, Mother Gotha made up a cot for Mira and for the first time in a week she had a decent sleep, free of storms and demons, cages and binding spells.

* * *

Mira stayed another two days in the abbey, eating the good stew and drinking the herbal teas. Mother Gotha, now that she'd released her story, was keen to gather Mira's. She was especially curious about Mrs. Zaccaroth, and questioned Mira intensely about her house and habits, about the lessons in magic. She sighed often as Mira told her of Mrs. Zaccaroth's tidy kitchen filled with labeled bottles and the row of mineral spheres on her mantel and the gigantic cookbook of spellcraft and the library of fairytales in the aerie.

They were sitting beneath the pomegranate tree in the afternoon, drinking peppermint tea, watched by a crow bobbing on a low branch.

"That could have been me," Mother Gotha said. "In a mirror world, that could have been my life—crafting potions, curing the sick, assisting the lovelorn, cursing miscreants, and nourishing those with the gift. But instead I have done the opposite. My work has been to quench the spark, to stifle magic in all its forms. And I thought I was in the right—I was so certain I was doing the right thing all this time."

The cup rattled in her saucer and she set it down.

Mira reached over and touched her knee. "You helped me," she said.

Mother Gotha pressed the heels of her hands into her cheeks. "Move forward, that's what I used to tell those in my charge," she muttered. "Don't squat with your face to the past. Move forward. As you are moving forward, my dear."

"But I still don't know where I'm going," Mira said.

Mother Gotha lowered her hands and looked up. "You have a key," she said. "You have a key, and you are seeking a door it will open. The city in the north has ten thousand locked doors. Surely that is where you must go."

* * *

The next morning Mother Gotha led Mira to a small gap in the western wall. Mira took her arm, and together they made their way up the hill flanking the abbey to the north. It was capped with black rocks, and Mother Gotha, panting, plumped herself down on the flattest of these. Mira took the next rock over. Before them, the desert deliquesced into a sky of pearl.

Mother Gotha raised her right arm and aimed it northward, at the diminishing silver slivers in the glittering expanse. "The safest route is to follow the river. You would be certain of water, you could gather dates and pomegranates, and you might fish or shoot waterbirds."

"I don't know how to fish or hunt," Mira said, her mind returning to Tolly with a smidgen of remorse. Perhaps she should have been friendlier.

"I could teach you," Mother Gotha told her. "There are rods in one of the storerooms here. Several of the girls would go to fish from time to time. When I was younger, I used to join them."

"You said that's the safest route. Is there another?"

"The other way is shorter," Mother Gotha said. "Much shorter, much riskier." Taking up a fallen crow feather, she used the quill to sketch in the sand a shape like a sideways S. "The river loops around, see. North of here it curves back to the south, and then curves to the north once more." And she drew a line linking the starting point of the S to the lower curve. She stretched her hand to the left. "If you walked that way, toward the setting of the sun, you would cut ten days from your journey."

"How long would it take?" Mira asked.

"Three days," Mother Gotha told her. "Three days if all went well. There is an oasis midway, where you can find water and shade. So I have heard. But if you missed the oasis, or if you strayed too far to the south and missed the river, you would have little chance of survival."

Mira looked out at the expanse before her. She saw in her mind's eye a frail figure trudging through the sands, and she quivered. But ten days was a long time. And with the sun to guide her … surely she wouldn't wander off course.

"I will take the shorter way," she said.

"It is not the safe choice," Mother Gotha said, "and not the one I recommend."

"I'll be fine."

"Well, if your mind is made up, I will prepare a parcel for the journey." And she placed her palms on the rock to heave herself to her feet.

"Wait," Mira told her.

Mother Gotha turned her head.

"Give me your spectacles," Mira said.

"But why, child? They are too strong for your young eyes. And they are broken."

"Give them to me."

So Mother Gotha took the spectacles from her nose and, blinking, held them out. Within her bewenned and age-clawed face her eyes were shockingly gorgeous: long-lashed, the color of woodsmoke at twilight.

Laying the spectacles in her lap, Mira closed her eyes, summoning the pages she required from Mrs. Zaccaroth's cookbook. If both lenses had been broken, it would have been difficult to mend them. But she had realized she could use a mirroring spell in tandem with a mending spell and make the broken lens whole.

She muttered, crafting the mirroring spell with her left hand while weaving the mending spell with her right—a tricky task, and one that made her breath come short and sweat spring out on her forehead, tickly. Resisting the urge to wipe her face and catch her breath, she bent over the spectacles and felt the tiniest tremor on her thighs. Gasping, she opened her eyes and looked down. Then she grinned. They were whole: a second lens glinted beside the first.

She polished them on the hem of her dress and set them gently back on Mother Gotha's nose, tucking the earpieces in. Mother Gotha blinked and looked around.

"Bless you," she whispered. "Bless you, my child."

* * *

Mira left in late afternoon, under a coil of calling crows. Mother Gotha had prepared for her a package containing seven hard-boiled eggs and five pomegranates. Her sailcloth bag was heavy, but, as Mother Gotha reminded her, it would get lighter as she journeyed.

As they stood on the knoll once more, looking west, where the descending sun drew a line behind every stone, Mira put a hand on Mother Gotha's shoulder.

"What will you do?" she asked. "All alone here."

"Oh, don't you see, child?" Mother Gotha exclaimed. "You've released me! I thought I was releasing you, but no—you released me from my chains. I know what I am now. I'm a witch. I'm a witch, and I'm going to spend the rest of my days making magic."

And for many steps, as Mira set off westward into the desert, she could hear Mother Gotha's gleeful cackle behind her.

VI

THE LAST DJINN

At first it was delightful to be on her way again, to feel the sand give under her soles and the lumpy sailcloth bag jounce on her spine, to taste the clean air of the desert and squint out at the unscrolling expanse. She kept herself from turning until the sun was a handspan above the horizon. Then, on the crest of a dune, she looked back along the way she'd come. Her footprints, like rips in rucked silk, made a narrow swaying chain back to the rock-capped hill, behind which the abbey lay; behind which, perhaps, Mother Gotha was at this moment crafting a spell with gnarled hands. At that thought, Mira smiled.

She stood with her fists on her hips. She could still see, on the edge of the world, the green fringe of the river, and for a moment she ached for that certainty: for water close by and a sure path, however tortuous, to her destination. It was not too late—she could reach the river by nightfall if she walked briskly. She even took a step back down the slope of the dune. But then she stopped, toes releasing a scoop of sand that crumbled down the dune's face. With a bitten lip and a shake of the head, she turned westward once more.

As night fell, she chose a little hollow, out of the wind. She peeled a crow's egg and ate it with salt dipped from a paper spill, and then ate one of the five pomegranates, teasing each faceted garnet from its nest and releasing its tartness against her palate. There was not a morsel of sound in this space unless she moved, unless she breathed. Her heartbeat loud as a clock. The first star nudged through the indigo, sending a quavering beam to crumple on her gaze, and all at once solitude was in her throat like a fishbone, and she beat her hands softly on the sand and squeezed her eyes closed to keep the panic at bay.

Later the stars were so plentiful the sky could not contain them. They plummeted in great numbers, trailing stuttered tails of fire, and she tried to spot the gaps they'd left behind.

She woke chilled, an hour before dawn, and sat with her arms wrapped around her knees and jaw clenched. Her legs were sore and her shoulders ached from the tug of the bag. She craved a cup of tea. When the first cotton dab shimmered on the eastern horizon, she set off, simply to keep herself warm, looking over her shoulder every so often to ensure the sun was at her back. As it rose, laying warmth and glitter across the world, her shadow swelled to a vast compass needle aiming along her way.

By the time she halted midmorning to eat another egg, her shadow was precisely her height and the glare smote from the sand as if from an opened oven. She drank again, sparingly, and set off into the tussling heat.

Mother Gotha had told her the oasis lay halfway, and she scanned the horizon as she walked. The heat mauled the land so violently she wondered at one point if it was under a vast spell, but her muttered words of revelation had no effect. She walked on, constantly uncertain, tipping her head this way and that, shielding her eyes. She tried to imagine a charm that would indicate the way she should go, but could find nothing in Mrs. Zaccaroth's cookbook. Nor could she summon a charm to keep the sun off her head. So she trudged on, hour after hour, taking scant sips of water when she could bear the thirst no longer.

In midafternoon she thought she spotted the oasis: a clot teased by the heat into forms she read as tree or lodge or lake. But, stumbling forward eagerly, she arrived after an hour at a heap of rocks, as if sprinkled by the hand of a sky giant. She was so disappointed she moaned and nearly walked past it. Then she turned and clambered up the pile, scalding her palms, chafing her knees. From the small peak she looked out upon the landscape. To the west the desert was vacant: flimsy tissue of sand and light.

Only as she turned to climb down did something catch her eye. Not west, but due north. A dark sliver, thin as an eyelash, as if the horizon were flaking and a splinter had sprung free.

She came to it in late afternoon, and when she realized what it was she sank to her knees in dismay. It was a single leaning palm trunk, denuded. In the sand around it lay other trunks, toppled and half submerged. The dead palms were ranged about a depression in the sand, rimmed with a pastel mineral crust, but perfectly dry. At the edge of the depression lay an arc of polished white stones, which she prodded at with a toe before realizing they were the bones of some beast.

Dropping her bag, she knelt in the center of the depression and used her hands to dig. Under the surface the sand was cooler. After a while, she went to the row of vertebrae and scrabbled till she found a shoulder blade. With that rudimentary trowel the work was easier, but though she dug nearly half her height, the sand remained dry.

By the time she climbed out of the pit, dusk had fallen. She went over to where she'd cast her bag at the base of the leaning palm. Taking out the water bottle, she held it to her ear, shook it, and replaced it in the bag. With her back to the trunk, she ate a pomegranate and the last crow's egg.

That night she woke every hour from dreams that scorpions scuttled in her hair; that she held up a hand to ward off the sun and was looking through a fence of bones; that she was still digging in the dry depression, deeper, deeper, till she could no longer climb out and knew she'd have to dig through to the other side.

Long before sunrise, she was once again sitting with her back to the trunk, arms around her knees. As she counted the hours till dawn, she cursed the gift that had brought her to this place. What use was magic if it turned your house backward, chased you from your home, and couldn't even provide you with a glass of water? For a moment she longed to be a different sort of child; a child like Paulus; a child who would put on pinching church shoes without complaint and set the table without being asked, who never shouted, never grew angry, and prayed for her enemies rather than taunting them and yanking the heads off their dolls. But she knew even as the thoughts rose that an instant of magic was worth all the tribulations, and she kindled a purple flamelet on her shivering forefinger and watched it awhile.

As dawn bloomed, sending the shadow of the leaning palm to the edge of the world, she started digging again. For an hour or more, while it was still cool, she clawed into the desert with the shoulder blade, heaving the sand over her head, until when she stood upright she could no longer see the surface: she was in a shady grave of her own making. But still the sand at her toes remained dry. The walls were beginning to crumble inward and, fearful of being buried, she clambered out.

She sat cross-legged in the sand and took the bottle from her sack. A single swallow remained. Shrugging, she held the bottle over her mouth till the last drop fell. She had eaten all the eggs. All she had left was one pomegranate. With some ceremony, she peeled and ate it slowly, savoring each brilliant morsel. She ate even the seeds, but when she'd sucked the juice from the last she plucked the pearl droplet from her tongue and stuck it in her pocket—sole keepsake from her days with Mother Gotha.

Now she was faced with a choice. The oasis was halfway between the abbey and the lower curve of the river. She had no water and no food, so it was unlikely she'd survive a trek in either direction.

With a little rueful shrug, she stood and shouldered her bag: she'd go on. Better to perish pursuing one's goal than retracing one's steps.

****

Before she set off, though, she walked once more to the hole she'd dug, to see if by some miracle water had started to seep into it. It was dry as ashes. However, as she turned, something caught her eye—not at the base of the hole, but halfway down, in the sloped side of the pit. A smooth green curve, embedded like a fossil in the strata. A stone? A shell? Lying on her belly, she reached in and pried it free.

It was a lamp, one of the old kind, with a narrow spout and a handle that curled up at the base. Rubbing the tarnished green surface with the hem of her dress, she got down to a patch of some gold-glinting metal: brass or bronze, she didn't know which. Etched arabesques swirled around its flanks. Clearly it had once been gorgeous.

The spout was tightly plugged with something—oiled cotton, perhaps. Using her fingernails, she worked it free … and then cast the lamp to the sand and sprawled back on her elbows.

From the spout of the lamp, smoke was pouring forth: dense smoke of deepest blue. It did not dissipate into the sky like the smoke of a fire, however, but seemed to congeal, gaining edges. And a minute later a vast figure fashioned of indigo smoke was hovering in the air before her, arms folded. The smoke still trickled from the spout, wavering, as if feeding the form.

"Who—what—who are you?" she gasped as she gazed up at the immense form, partly just to hear her voice and reassure herself she wasn't hallucinating.

"My name is Baliel, mistress." The voice was a distant rockslide, a thunderstorm on the horizon.

"Baliel. And you're a …"

"I am a djinn, mistress. I am yours to command."

"A djinn," she whispered. She still couldn't believe it, though Mrs. Zaccaroth had mentioned djinns more than once. She remembered the pictures in one of Mrs. Zaccaroth's books. That djinn had worn an orange turban and an embroidered vest, and had gold hoops in his ears. This real-life djinn was flimsier—she could see the horizon faintly through his inky torso—but much more terrifying. He seemed to have no mouth, though when he spoke something glimmered in the hollows where his eyes should have been.

"And how long have you been here, Mr. Baliel?" she asked.

"For many centuries I have lain dreaming beneath the sands," he said.

"Dreaming. What do djinns dream of?"

"I dreamed of my masters and mistresses in many lands."

"Oh, I'd love to hear about them," Mira said, apprehension abating, though her heart still throbbed. "But first, I'm … well, I'm afraid I'm in a bit of trouble. I'm on a journey and I ran out of water, you see, and I was hoping to fill my bottle at the oasis. But it's dry, and now I'm so thirsty. You said you're mine to command. What does that mean, actually? Can you … would you … ?"

"Would you like me to fill your flask, mistress?" the djinn asked.

"Oh, yes please!"

"It is done."

He had made no motion, and she hadn't felt the tremor, the little buckle in reality she usually sensed when a spell took hold, so she wasn't quite sure what to think. But when she pulled the bottle from the sailcloth bag it was sloshing full and cold droplets were already beading on its surface. She uncorked it and, gasping, drank and drank. The water was exquisitely cold, keen as a steel blade: utterly refreshing.

"Oh," she said, wiping her mouth with the back of her wrist. "Oh, that was good!"

"I am pleased to be of service," the djinn said.

"So, Mr. Baliel … You're the first djinn I've met. I've read about djinns, but I don't think I really believed in you. Until now, of course. You have the power. The power to do magic, right?" Though it was odd, and slightly alarming, to be talking to a being who hadn't been there a moment before, the gift of water had given her confidence that his intentions were benign.

"I have the power," the djinn said, inclining his head ever so slightly.

"I have it too," Mira said, "but my power isn't like yours. I have to have something to work on, see? I couldn't just summon something out of nothing, like you did. How did you do it? How did you make the water appear from nowhere?"

"This is the power bestowed upon the djinns," Baliel said. "Though we are by nature immaterial, we have the ability to create material things. However, we are not gifted in the arts of instruction. We execute commands."

"So you don't know how you did it? How you put water in my bottle?"

The djinn seemed to ponder this. Then he said, "Does the wind know why it blows? Does the sun know why it shines? These powers are bestowed upon us, but are not ours to explain."

Mira held the cool flank of the bottle against her neck. "Yes, I see," she said. "Or, I think I do. And part of my magic—the best part—is the part I don't have to think about. In fact, I guess I could say that a lot of magic is trying to get my mind out of the way so the magic can bubble up from wherever it comes from."

"Others of my masters and mistresses have uttered similar sentiments," the djinn said. "But though the race of djinns lives adjacent to the race of humans, we are in many ways very different."

"The race of djinns," Mira breathed. "So, what are you, really? What are djinns? It's so odd to be sitting here in the middle of a desert, talking with someone made of smoke."

"Is our story no longer told in the dwellings of the humans?"

"Well, it is, but they're fairytales, you know? Not real. At least, not real the way you're real and standing here talking to me. Anyway, I'd love to hear it. Can you tell me your story?"

"Certainly, mistress." And the djinn seemed to settle in the air—you couldn't really have called it sitting. "Listen: In the early years of our existence, humans and djinns lived side by side, in almost equal numbers. Humans dwelt in the houses, djinns in the drains and wells, nooks and eaves. In the nights, while the humans slept, we ventured out to frolic, dancing across the rooftops, flinging bolts of lightning across the cities as boys fling balls, and all the while speaking our poetry into the wind. Our poetry, which is not like the poetry of humans, locked in boxes and pinned to paper and chained to shelves. Our poetry is like breath released, like the clouds and shadows from which we were created: evanescent, ever changing, ever new …

"For a time we were free, the djinns, and we existed alongside the race of humans, in companionship, and each race delighted in the other's company. Eventually, however, certain of the humans realized they could contain us and use our power to their own ends. Soon many of the powerful had in their possession bottles or lamps, within each a djinn. And they would call us forth to wreak havoc: to turn the blood of their enemies to molten lead or create vast palaces filled with gold and gemstones. Some realized we had the gifts of manipulating language, and ordered us to create poetry or tales they passed off as their own.

"As the djinns wreaked terror and created imbalance in the service of their masters, the less-mighty humans developed incantations that could be uttered to thwart our power, to keep us penned. They muttered as they poured tea down the drains, as they opened doors, as they settled in bed at night. And the incantations were, of course, efficacious—even the lowliest human can control a djinn with a word. Eventually, as the cities burgeoned and the masses uttered the incantations daily, the djinns were forced into the crannies, into the cracks in foundations and the forgotten spaces behind walls. They emerged only stealthily, for they relished their freedom. When human masters died, the djinns who were free released the djinns who were caged. And in time they fled the habitations of humans."

Mira thought she sensed sadness in the djinn's tone. "Where did they go?" she asked. "The other djinns—the ones who got away."

"In the midst of the desert, far to the west, in a landscape of sun and stone, sand and shadows, the djinns dance," Baliel told her. "They pirouette on stones and swirl across the crests of dunes and create their poetry, which is dispersed by the winds and strewn among the stars. During the day the djinns dream, crouching under rocks, so a traveler entering their land might see only blue shadows. At night they dance, but even then a traveler might blame the visions of frolicking djinns on faulty eyesight or thirst or sandstorm, and might imagine the poems came from within her own head."

"Oh, I'd love to see them!" Mira said. "I'd love to watch the djinns dance and listen to their poems."

"So would I, young mistress. So would I."

"Why didn't you go with them?" she asked.

"I was left behind. My master was returning from a trek to the eastern salt pans when he was waylaid by bandits in this place, which at that time was verdant and hospitable to human travelers. In the skirmish, the lamp tumbled into the waters of the oasis and was forgotten. For centuries I remained here, within the stoppered lamp, until you found me and released me. I am the last djinn remaining in the lands of the humans."

"The last djinn," Mira said. "Then I must be the only person alive who has had a conversation with a djinn."

"I believe that is true, mistress."

It was midmorning already, and the sun was hot on Mira's head. She looked around. "I wish there was shelter here," she said. "The dead palms cast no shade."

"Would you like shelter from the sun, mistress?"

"Oh." She giggled. "I forgot. Yes, of course. If it's not too much trouble. And …"

"Yes, mistress?"

"And … breakfast?" she said timidly. She wasn't used to giving commands.

Again Baliel didn't move or make a gesture, and Mira thought that perhaps his powers had failed him this time. But then she heard behind her a little flap, as of laundry in the wind, and she turned.

A pavilion lay in the sands: a striped awning of tasseled silk, with a sumptuous carpet beneath it, scattered with embroidered cushions. And on the carpet lay covered silver dishes and a bottle in a bucket of ice, perspiration beading on the brown glass. Mira walked hesitantly over to the awning, expecting it to vanish at any moment, and extended a foot as though testing the temperature of a bath. The carpet was soft and cool as river sludge beneath her toes. Entering the blessed shade, she knelt and lifted the lids of the silver dishes, releasing gouts of fragrant steam. Saffron rice studded with raisins and hazelnuts. Tiny sausages spiced with cloves and cinnamon. Halved lobsters, the delicate flesh dripping with clarified butter. Roast quail stuffed with quinces. Oranges and green grapes and apricots, all perfectly ripe, unblemished. The bottle in the bucket of ice contained tamarind juice.

"Is the breakfast to your liking, mistress?" Baliel asked.

"Oh my," she said. "Mr. Baliel, I've never … I mean, it's simply amazing. Like something out of a storybook."

"It is identical to a breakfast I saw served to the empress of a distant land in the early weeks of spring, seven and one half centuries ago."

She nibbled at the charred end of a sausage. "Did you ever … in any of the places you've been, did you see the land of the demons? The land the demons come from?"

"No, mistress."

"So you, the djinns, you're not like the demons. I mean, you don't come from the same place."

"We do not."

"Who are the demons, then? Do you know?"

"What I know is this: demons are severed shadows, tarrying on the other side. They can cross over if there is a breach; if the boundary is worn thin."

"Severed shadows? I don't understand."

The djinn was silent for a moment. Then he said, "I will tell you a story that was told by one of my mistresses, who had the red hair like yourself."

The Boy and His Shadow

There was once a boy who grew weary of his shadow. If only I could be rid of this troublesome stain that follows me everywhere, I would be free, he thought. Then I could run as fast as the wind, which casts no shadow, and leap as high as thought, which casts no shadow. He tried shouting at his shadow, but it would not leave; he tried striking it with a stick, but it would not leave. Then he asked everyone he met how he could get rid of his loathsome shadow. He asked the priests and the merchants and the learned men, but all told him it was impossible—his shadow was tethered to his soles, they said, and it could not be removed. Still he asked everyone he met how he could get rid of his shadow: the fishermen and the delivery boys and the lamplighters, and they laughed at him and said it was impossible—his shadow was tethered to his soles and it could not be removed.

One day, as the boy was sitting in his room, fretting because he could not get rid of his shadow, he heard a tap-tap-tapping in the street. The sound came closer, and soon it stopped at his door. Tap-tap-tap he heard on the door itself. He felt an unaccountable chill, but nevertheless he got up and opened the door. And there stood an old, hunched woman, almost too ugly to look at. She had greasy knotted hair with bits of twig and beetle wing tangled in it. She had a bristly mustache and her teeth were as gray and angled as gravestones and she wore a patchwork dress pieced together from a hundred filthy rags. He couldn't see her eyes, as they were concealed behind opaque black spectacles, but he was sure they were just as hideous as the rest of her.

In one hand the old woman held a stick (it was the stick he'd heard tap-tap-tapping); in the other she held an ancient handbag of cracked black leather. She stank of smoke and sloe gin and unwashed undergarments.

The boy tried to close the door on her, but she stuck her stick in so he couldn't get it shut. Then he was angry. Holding his nose, he said through the crack in the door, "What do you want, stinky old woman?"

"Are you the boy who wishes to remove his shadow?" she asked in a voice every bit as cracked as her ancient handbag.

"Oh. Yes." And his tone changed. "Do you know how I can do it?"

"I do indeed," she said. "I do indeed."

Though he could hardly bear to allow such a creature into his room, the boy stepped aside and the woman tap-tap-tapped her way over to his bed. Before the boy could stop her, she sat down.

Oh well, the boy thought. I can launder the sheets later. It will be worth it if she can give me what I desire. "So," he said. "Tell me, old woman. How do I get rid of this troublesome shadow?"

"I will tell you," she said, setting the stick to one side. "But I must warn you, first, that it will be painful. And second, that there is a price."

"I don't care about the pain," the boy said. "The pain of carrying this shadow around all day is surely greater than the pain of removing it. As for the price—so long as it is within my means, I will pay."

The old woman nodded briskly. "The price is within your means," she said. "Now sit." She patted the bed, leaving a greasy handprint.

So the boy sat, keeping as far from her as he could.

The old woman opened the clasp of her handbag, rummaged inside, and pulled out a knife. It was as long as a finger and its handle was of bone and its blade was of glass or quartz or ice. And as soon as he saw that colorless knife the boy knew it was what he'd been searching for. A pure knife for a pure deed.

The old woman held the bone handle between finger and thumb. "Here," she said. "Take this knife. Its blade is the only thing sharp enough to cut away your shadow."

The boy seized the knife and without further ado he bent and ran the blade along his soles. Oh, it was painful—the worst pain he'd ever felt—and he bit his lower lip to keep from crying out. But there was also the pleasure of feeling his vexatious shadow peeling away from him. At last the deed was done, and his shadow, released from his soles, leaped on skinny legs out the window and ran down the street. The boy paid it no heed. He stood in the square of sunlight by the window, and though his feet still smarted, he did a little dance. "I'm free!" he said. "Free of my shadow at last! Thank you, old woman. Thank you, thank you."

"You're welcome," said she, returning the knife to her handbag and snapping it closed. "But now I require my payment."

"Yes. Take it," he said. Opening his arms, he twirled, shadowless, in the sunlight. "Take it, old woman. Take whatever you wish."

"Come," said the woman. Again she patted the bed. So he came and sat beside her. Fumbling forward, she found his face and patted his cheeks with her filthy fingers. And then, before the boy understood what was happening, she'd plucked out his eyes.

For a moment the boy sat there in total darkness, too shocked and horrified to speak. Then he reached out to where the old woman had been sitting, seeking to get his eyes back. But she was gone, and all he clutched was her stick, which she no longer needed. He thought he heard a cackle in the street, but it might have been a passing crow.

The boy stumbled out of the door on his still-painful soles, and with his arms before his face he blundered this way and that down the street, until he came to the river. And some say he foundered in the water. And some say he is chasing his shadow still, in sunlight and in moonlight, a boy without eyes stumbling across the waves, and the fisherfolk hear his melancholy calling.

* * *

The story seemed to be over and Mira looked up from the lobster carapace she'd been ransacking. "Is the story true?" she asked.

"I do not know, mistress."

"And ... what does the story have to do with demons?" she asked.

"I do not know. I know only that this is the story my mistress told when her apprentice asked about the demons."

Mira sucked her fingers and wiped them on her dress. She tugged the key from her neckline and held it out on her palm, heavy and warm and beautiful. "I'm here in the desert because I'm running from the demons," she said. "I was given this key. Can you tell me what door it opens?"

"Naturally, mistress."

"Oh!" Mira gripped the key in her fist, hope flapping like a fish in her belly. "Where is the door?"

"I cannot tell you that. What I know is that this is the key that will open the door to the other side."

Suddenly weary, Mira tucked the key back into her dress. "I know *that*," she said. "I was hoping you could tell me where the door was."

"No."

"But how will I *find* it then?" She was suddenly close to tears, and she beat her fist on the carpet to keep them in.

"You must make the journey."

She nodded with a sodden sigh. "It's so hard," she whispered. "I tried to throw it away once, you know. I threw it into the river because I'd decided I was done. Done with magic, done with everything. But it came back in the belly of a fish." She paused and looked up. "Could I give it to you?" she asked plaintively.

"No. The key is bound to you even as your heart is bound to your mind, as your breath is bound to your tongue. Though I were to cast it into the whirlwind, it would return to your hands."

"Yes, I see." A tear escaped and fell onto the carpet. She pressed a fingertip over it.

"Why do you weep, mistress? What is your desire?"

"My desire? Oh, you know—for everything to be the way it was. For Paulus to come back and my house to be turned the right way and Mr. Mugwort to still be alive and Mrs. Zaccaroth's aerie to still be standing. But everything's wrong, and here I am in the middle of a desert and you can't even tell me where the *door* is." Now she was weeping in earnest, and the tears dripped off the end of her nose, making dark circles in the crimson nap.

"I could perform certain of those deeds for you, mistress, but know that it would not release you from your task. You would merely have to begin again. You would still have the key."

"Yes, I know. I see. I do, really."

"I am sorry, my mistress," the djinn said in a softer voice—a rockslide of gypsum rather than granite.

At last Mira took two heaving breaths and chafed away the tears with the heels of her hands.

"What about you, Mr. Baliel?" she asked. She looked up at the djinn.

"I do not understand."

"What about you? What is your desire? I mean, if *your* wish was *my* command, what would you wish for?"

The djinn was silent for a moment, and something seemed to sparkle in his eyes; in the hollows where his eyes should have been.

At last he said, "In all the centuries of my existence, no one has asked me this question."

"Well?" she said, looking up at the djinn and squeezing her hands between her knees. "Do you know? What do you want, Mr. Baliel? What's your desire?"

"If I were truly given a wish of my own," the djinn said, "it would, of course, be to leave the habitations of humankind and dance on the winds of the western desert with my fellows."

She nodded. "So why don't you?"

"Do you not know?"

Mira shook her head.

The djinn crouched or compressed his smoky body slightly, so his head was beneath the silk awning. "I am under your command," he told her. "As long as you desire it, little mistress, I am in your thrall."

Mira thought for a minute, running her finger along the cold flank of the bottle of tamarind juice. She took a sip and corked it again. "So if," she said finally, "if I let you go, you'd be free? You could go where you wanted? Out into the desert to be with the other djinns."

"That is correct," the djinn said, his voice a distant sandstorm. He turned his head slightly.

Mira followed his gaze, staring out at the western horizon. In the hazy furrow where sand met sky, she thought she caught a shimmer. At last, almost in a whisper, she said, "I've been caged too, you know. I've been caged, and my tongue was tied down. And the woman who caged me had herself been caged, as had the women who caged her. But she set me free. Mother Gotha set me free to continue my journey, and when she did so she set herself free as well. Free to do magic." She looked up at the djinn. "I'm not saying it isn't tempting, you know." She offered half a grin. "Having a personal servant who could ... well ... all this." She wafted a hand over the dishes and upturned lids, the spilled rice, the orange peels. "But also, I can't keep you. I know that. I can't keep you caged, now that I know what you want. So, Mr. Baliel, you're free." She cleared a little grit from her throat. "I release you. You're free to go now, to join your companions in the western desert."

The djinn seemed to take a breath; at any rate, his smoky torso swelled slightly. "Oh my mistress," he said, "this is generosity beyond compare. You have given me my desire, which is my freedom, and in my poetry your name will be forever exalted. But before I take my leave, allow me to perform one last deed for you—a deed freely given, in gratitude for your gesture."

"What is that?" Mira asked.

"Allow me to transport you to anyplace you desire."

"You could do that?"

"Yes, mistress."

"Well," Mira said. She raised her arms. "Take me to the city then. The city in the north. The city of ten thousand doors."

Reaching into the shade of the pavilion, Baliel plucked her forth, lifting her effortlessly in his hands of smoke, and it was like being lifted by the wind. Though she sensed his strength, there was no pressure against her skin. Then, trailing a spun cord of sand, she was high above the desert, rising with a rush of wind in her ears, hair flailing like a flame when a window's flung open. She felt no fear—only exhilaration as, cradled in the djinn's indigo arms, she arced like a spark across the sky.

Far below, the serpent river curled—just as Mother Gotha had said—to the south, and then northward once more. From this height she could see that the desert was patterned like the veins of leaves or as if colored inks had been spilled on linen. Looking back, she saw stamped into the sand the glyph of the abbey where Mother Gotha was surely practicing her magic, and the meager speckling of the town. In that little corner of the world, so small she could erase it with a thumb, her mother was folding laundry and her father was walking home from the brick kiln, coughing softly into the back of his hand, and the priest was having a cup of tea as he went over his sermon and Tolly was mending his nets and Mrs. Zaccaroth was whistling as she tempered chocolate in her kitchen … From this height, the tensions of the town seemed puny, ridiculous.

Reclining in her evanescent indigo hammock, Mira cast her gaze wide once more. Far to the east, beyond the river, a soft rind of darkness lay across the world.

"What's that?" she asked, flinging out an arm.

"Night is approaching," he told her, and she realized with a shock that she was watching the creeping edge of dusk. She looked up into a sky graded to a darker blue and sprinkled with stars, though it was plain day. The moon so close she could almost touch it, carious as a wasp's nest.

"Oh, it's so pretty," she sighed, and the djinn laughed—a preposterous cacophony that rumbled like thunder for ages in their wake.

All too soon they were descending, and she saw that what she had taken for a blemish in the sand was the city, the streets intricate as veins in jasper, etched on either side of the river. Three bridges stitched the banks together, and between them lay a slender island. Thick walls girdled the city, creating an irregular octagon with nodes at the corners: watchtowers.

As they dropped, the city grew spiky and angular, black rock hacked with spines, diced into skewed cubes. Cross section of a dark crystal, the river a seam of chalcedony. Though the city was enormous, it gave her a sensation of claustrophobia. Even the river was tamed here, trammeled by stone walls, laced by bridges.

The djinn slid down the scalloped breezes, and suddenly the odors of the city were in her nostrils: charcoal smoke and rotting limes, toasted almonds, river slime, urine, jasmine, frankincense. And a moment later she heard the first sounds: cries of children, clink of coffee cups, clatter of horse hooves on cobbles, combined in a choral murmur not unlike the wave-jostled pebbles at the river shore.

All she had known was the little town in the south, where she could name every inhabitant, where she knew every birth, every marriage, every stolen child. The profusion below struck a sudden panic in her breast—she hadn't been aware the world was so full— but then she realized that with profusion came anonymity: a fresh face would rouse few questions here.

The djinn alighted softly as a mist on the tallest tower of the island in the center of the city, and set Mira on her feet. She looked up at him, blinking, the journey across the sky an ember in her belly. "That was marvelous. Thank you," she whispered.

His eyes glimmered faintly like the first stars at twilight, like the last stars at dawn. "It was my pleasure to serve you, mistress," he said—far too loudly, she thought. What if someone heard his rumble and came to investigate?

"And now you're free," she told him. "Go, my friend." She spread her arms.

Baliel bent down, indigo rainbow, and bestowed a djinn's kiss on her forehead, of which she felt nothing save perhaps the vaguest breeze. With a thunderclap "Farewell!" he rose like an inky whirlwind, arced to the west, and was gone.

For a minute after his departure, Mira watched the sky, heart aching slightly. And then she turned to see where she'd landed.

VII

CITY OF LOCKS AND TOWERS

The tower was at the northern tip of the island. Kneeling with her hands on the parapet, she could gaze almost straight down at the green strands of river braiding, releasing whorls that skittered off like bobbins and tapered into the pour. As she bent out, as if she'd triggered an alarm, a sudden whirring and clanking seemed to emerge from the very floor she knelt on, and she swung round, hands outspread. Then she was almost knocked off her perch by booming tones. Only when they had pulsed into silence did she realize what had happened: the djinn had set her down on a clocktower. She counted backward: five chimes.

The top of the tower was just a few paces across. Moving to the other side, she peered down into a thin alley, vacant save for a preening rat. Then she stood and looked across the rooftops of the island, strewn with bird bones and broken kites and fragments of fallen stars. Beyond the last roofs was a weightier shape, almost as tall as the clocktower, a triangle torn out of the sky. And on all sides lesser spires rose—a city of a hundred churches.

In the center of the roof was a trapdoor with a handle. She lifted this a finger's width and peered into darkness. Spaced metallic knocks and whispers surfaced, but as her eyes grew accustomed to the shadows she saw no human form or movement. She lifted the door higher. A ladder descended vertically. Climbing down, she pulled the trapdoor into place once more and kindled a lavender light on her fingertip. She was in a room almost entirely filled with shifting cogs and springs and spools, reeking of oil. From this room a staircase whorled through the belly of the tower, where a few slit windows cast garbled shadows across the walls. Trying to tread softly, though the staircase groaned and swayed alarmingly, she moved down through the tower, heart throbbing.

At its base was a locked door: no barrier to a witch. With narrowed eyes, hand on the knob, she muttered an opening spell and felt the latch slip aside. She peered left, right, then stepped out and closed the door behind her. Straightening her shoulders, with a huff to give herself courage, the young witch set out into the strange city.

Cobbles underfoot, similar to those of her town, though these were of darker stone, polished to an almost obsidian gloss by centuries of soles. In her town, the only structures taller than a fig tree were the church and the smokestack of the brick kiln. But here the buildings rose story upon story, seeming to angle inward, so she walked beneath jagged creeks of sky. The lower windows lay behind iron latticework and latched shutters. She caught no glimpse of the interiors. The doors were not the plain wood of those in her town, but were armored with iron grates, with knobs and hobnails and spikes, and the keyholes were surrounded by chased brass plates. A city of ten thousand doors, as Mother Gotha had said. Ten thousand doors and ten thousand locks. Was she meant to walk through every street of this vast city trying every lock, hoping her key would fit? Suddenly her task seemed all but futile.

At the end of the alley, she angled right and then left, onto a more generous street she guessed ran down the center of the island. And now she came among people. For a few minutes she leaned in a doorway watching them, the inhabitants of this city. They seemed all in a great hurry, the men in dark hats and dark suits, black shoes clacking like shiny beaks on the cobblestones. The women likewise clad in muted colors, hair concealed under veils similar to the one Mira's mother wore to church. They walked with short steps to keep their hips from swaying, their eyes lowered. The girls wore pale dresses, though some had a little froth of lace at cuff or hem, and a few clutched dolls to their chests. Only the youngest children's heads were uncovered, the boys' hair closely trimmed, the girls' bound by ribbons and clips and ties.

As Mira stepped out into the street, her tangle of tangerine hair and embroidered aubergine dress and open, inquisitive gaze drew horrified looks and muttered imprecations. She heard sharp inhalations, saw fingers go to lips, and one mother even turned her daughter's head away, gripping it by the curly crown and forcing it ahead. A priest passed, older than the priest of her town, though with a less luxuriant beard. With a hiss, he plucked the iron cross from where it dangled on his cassock and brandished it against her.

Rounding a corner, Mira caught a glimpse of herself in a shop window and stopped and gaped, shocked as any of the citizens she passed. In this landscape of dark stone and subdued attire, her hair was a wildfire, a wildflower, wayward and thrilling. As she swiveled, the yellow cats she'd embroidered onto her dress seemed to writhe and stretch and arch their backs. She grinned, then sighed and wished she hadn't sent Baliel away quite so soon. She couldn't walk through the streets of the city dressed like this, not if she wanted to remain anonymous.

She passed clothing stores, fruit sellers, cafés where men smoked thin black cigarettes and sipped coffee from small cups, hats on the tables beside their saucers. A carpenter, a candlemaker, a shop selling copperware. There were moments of fancy—a curlicue in wrought iron, a twisted serif in a shop sign—but they were overwhelmed in the surfaces of dark stone. So, when she found a pale blossom sprouting from a crack in the wall, she cupped her hands around it for a moment and breathed a protective charm.

From the top of the clocktower, the rock had seemed immaculate, polished and trimmed. However, as she moved through the streets she began to notice remnants of an earlier time. On some of the stones were etched rain-worn, sand-scoured glyphs, too shallow to make out with certainty. These were sometimes sideways or upside down. Once she saw a curve of carven wing, once a black lily, once in a pillar the twisted torso of a woman, her face chiseled away—by time or human hands, she could not tell. What stories simmered under these layers? What quarrels fermented behind the shutters? What bones lay beneath the sole-scoured cobblestones? And she wondered as she walked whether some of these walls had harbored magicians who kept djinns in boxes or bottles or lamps, all released now, reveling in the winds of the western desert, where Baliel, the last captive djinn, had now joined them.

Despite its size, the city was tidier than her town in the south. In her town, rags and fishbones and mango seeds and broken crockery littered the cobblestones. But these streets were clean, the sidewalks swept. The shops she passed were similarly chaste—no peppers scattered on burlap or gaudy hillocks of spices, as there had been in the market in her town. The wares here were confined to labeled bins, most of them lidded, some of them locked. She went into a fruit seller's, hoping to find a bruised apple she might have for free, but the fruit was unblemished and neatly stacked, and the shopkeeper watched her from behind the counter, lips compressed beneath a bottlebrush mustache.

Exiting the shop, she felt a sudden pang of homesickness for her little town with its saffron tiles and colorful laundry flapping and painted fishing boats and the gorgeous marketplace thronged with amiably squabbling housewives. Here all seemed constrained, concealed, even the giggles of the children silenced.

The only laughter came from a bakery. She had followed the warm brown scent around corner after corner, until she finally entered a back alley and heard a guffaw. A young man with two days' stubble on his chin was dipping an enormous wooden paddle into a tawny half-moon maw, pulling out round loaves and tipping them into a basket by his side, and all the while chattering to someone in the interior.

Mira watched him for a full minute before he spotted her and gave a little twitch of his eyebrows. With a grin, he flicked the loaf on his paddle twenty feet into her hands. She gasped and juggled the loaf—it was scalding—and then fled, ignoring his shouted "What about a kiss then?"

Before the loaf was cool enough to hold comfortably, she came out from an alley and found herself at the river shore. Fifty paces to her right a bridge spanned the water on arches of stone, hemmed with stone balustrades. The bases of the arches, where the river slurped and belched, were hairy with weed. Beside the closest a fisherman swayed in a dory, holding a rod and smoking a long-stemmed pipe.

Mira walked out to the middle of the bridge and stood with her elbows on the pitted stone, looking down at the water. As if it had gained substance on its journey, the river seemed thicker here than it had in her town, more sluggish—a gray-green soup, softly etched with spirals and scribbled lines. To her right, the buildings were more loosely grouped, with here and there scraps of green: gardens, perhaps, or tiny parks. To her left, the facades of the island shore leaned together as if closing ranks, their shuttered windows lidded eyes. Lights were winking on in windows across the city, reflected like stars in the water ambling below. There were no stars in the sky, though. The city, it seemed, had banished them. From this vantage, she could see that the island was bookended by the two tallest towers in the city: one the clocktower where the djinn had deposited her, the other the spire of an enormous cathedral.

Setting the loaf on the parapet, Mira hauled herself up and swung round so her legs dangled over the river. Elbows on thighs, heels bumping the stone, she broke the bread, releasing a blossom of fragrant steam, and crammed a hunk into her mouth. Oh, it was good. She closed her eyes, immersed in the bliss of hot, crusty bread.

And now, above the river, she at last allowed herself to gather what she'd begun to think of as the city's murmur or heartbeat: the massed voices of power, active or quelled. There was certainly power here—she could feel it in her fingertips, in her bellybutton.

And she sensed that much of it was a rotten, repressed power similar to Mother Gotha's, as if dozens, maybe hundreds of women squatted behind shuttered windows, muttering prayers and burning incense in an effort to tamp down their magic. But she also sensed moments of sparkle and knew native witches labored here, perhaps hidden, perhaps unconscious of what they meddled in.

All this, however, lay beneath a tremendous leaden lid, fitted precisely over the city walls, which she recognized instantly as the presence of the church. It terrified her—there was none of the fumbling kindness of her town's priest here, or even the soft woolen malevolence she'd experienced in Mother Gotha's abbey. This was a grim architecture, calculated, stifling, and she sensed within it a deep structure of magic. An unaccountable terror gripped her; she felt too exposed, as if the windows were eyes, and all peering in her direction.

Finishing the bread, she brushed the crumbs from her dress, swiveled, and hopped off the balustrade. There were fewer people in the streets now and the shops were closing, iron grates hauled down over the windows and padlocked to rings socketed in the thresholds. In the failing light, she made her way back through the alleys to the clocktower. Glancing left and right to ensure no one was around, she slipped into the recessed doorway and with a whispered charm slid the bolt aside. The stairwell was a great echoing chamber of shadows, the clock room grim and clicking, and she was relieved when she emerged onto the roof. For a while she sat with her back to the low parapet, watching the bats take flight like splintering shadows. What a long, strange day: begun in despair in the middle of a desert, finding the djinn, eating the extraordinary feast under a summoned pavilion, hurtling northward across the sky, and landing in this strange, enclosed city; a city like a fist, like a pocketful of secrets, like a cluster of dark crystals. She curled on her side in the dust and told herself fairytales to carry her to sleep.

* * *

All that night, Mira was woken every hour by the bells below her, tremendously loud, and after the five o'clock chimes was unable to get to sleep again. She sat up, wishing she had a cup of tea. As dawn dabbed pink across shutters and spires, Mira made plans. She needed clothes so she could blend in. She needed a scarf to conceal her hair. But first she needed breakfast.

The shops were just opening. She passed cafés where men with bruised pouches beneath their eyes sat smoking and sipping coffee. She passed pastry shops from which housewives emerged with plump brown-paper bags marked with archipelagos of grease. She passed a restaurant where a waiter set a platter before a diner: charred sausages, a green-flecked omelet, white beans in tomato sauce. Finally, by chance, she found the alley behind the bakery where the boy had tossed her a loaf the evening before, but this morning a middle-aged man wielded the paddle, and he just scowled when she took a step toward him. She walked on, stomach festering.

At the far end of the island, the streets converged on a wide courtyard whose flagstones undulated like a rucked carpet. Convoluted fig trees ruptured the paving on three sides. The fourth side was the facade of the cathedral.

Mira stood beneath a tree and looked up at the immense structure, formed of the same black rock as the rest of the city. Beneath a peaked portico, the tall doors were shut, though the round stained-glass window above them glimmered dimly: wine, ivy, moonlight on dark water. Someone was within. And as she stood there, she knew with a dreadful certainty that this was the center of the leaden power she had sensed. From this architecture emerged a stiff, stifling magic; not the blind, benevolent gestures of the priest in her town, but a carefully crafted span of spells that held the city in its grip. She could feel it settling on her like a terrible crown. Slowly she backed away, and then, once she was in an alley, turned and ran.

Panting, she came out alongside the river. She walked along the bank until she found a stone bench, and sat watching the water, gray as smoke at this early hour. Once there was a fillip of silver: a fish, followed by soft sky-tipped furrows, easing as they spread. After a while, she moved on.

Half the morning she wandered, till the chimes of the clock beat ten, and finally she grew so hungry she loitered by a café until a diner paid and stood, leaving a corner of croissant unfinished on his plate. This she snatched, and dashed off, ignoring the shouted curses of the waiter.

She couldn't simply snatch clothes, though—the shops were scrupulously watched over by humorless attendants. As she nibbled her morsel of croissant, wishing she had a slice of cheese or a pear or a cup of milky tea to go with it, a gust of wind blew a napkin along the cobbles, and its ungainly tumble gave her an idea. She'd remembered Mother Gotha's story of sending the laundry flying through the air—the escapade that had led to her incarceration. So she retraced her steps to a street where some of the sellers displayed their wares on frames along the sidewalks.

She waited until a breeze tousled her curls, and with a subtle gesture and a whispered chant pressed it on its way, gathering air into it until it hurtled among the dangling skirts and dresses, sudden gale, plucking them free of their hangers and hooks and sending them skyward, along with men's hats and children's dolls and a parasol or two. Some of the garments snagged on café umbrellas, some sailed over rooftops, some scurried along the street ... but a few clustered like crows in a stormy sky, waltzing a moment, then toppling together into an alley.

The street was suddenly filled with screams and laughter, children dancing to seize the stray clothes, entirely consumed by the havoc. None noticed the redhaired girl leaning in a shadowed doorway, hands clenched, gaze intent.

As the shopkeepers ran snarling after their wares and the men pursued their tumbling hats, Mira turned into the alley where clothes the colors of ash and smoke lay heaped in a doorway. Hastily she tugged on a gray dress—a little long for her, but no matter—and tied a dark scarf about her hair, tucking in the curlicues of flame.

Checking her reflection in a window, she gave a smile tinged with chagrin. She'd successfully doused her hair, successfully erased herself, though she couldn't help feeling she'd managed to douse something inside her at the same time. She stuck out her tongue at her reflection and, clutching the rest of the clothes in a bundle at her breast, walked back to the clocktower.

* * *

The next morning, after breakfasting on a stolen peach, she wandered, this time allowing herself to be swayed by the submerged voices of power. She found herself drawn toward the southeastern corner of the city—drawn by fine filaments, by a scent of brewing magic. It was nearly noon when she emerged from an alleyway to see a wide building, bands of stone fraying above into a myriad towers and thin windows. In an empty courtyard before it stood a tapered tower of chafed stone, which Mira took at first for a sculpture, though one so eroded its form was lost. It reminded her of something ... something she couldn't quite bring to mind.

Around the lower flanks of the tower, honeysuckle swarmed like flames.

Mira took a step back, into the shadow of the alley, and gazed up at the building beyond the tower. No movement in the tiny windows. Along a gray band were incised aphorisms: "For we have forsaken the darkness and stepped into the light." "Day has broken and banished the fears of the night."

Despite the pretty words, Mira felt a prickle across her scalp as she cast her eyes along the ranked windows. This was the convent where Mrs. Zaccaroth and Mother Gotha had been incarcerated. Within these walls, she knew with a strange certainty, young witches lay in chains. Chains of iron, chains of will. Within these walls, witches were broken. Some lived, maimed in the mind. Some died.

She lingered for longer than she should have, perhaps, watching the door, but it never opened. No maid arrived, no gray-robed sister emerged. Only once during that hour did something happen—in the window of the tallest tower there was a flash of silver, a bright tattoo that remained printed on her vision as she walked away.

VIII

ROSA'S CHOCOLATERIE

Within the tyranny of trapped time, within the walls of cut rock, through the chained alleyways, among the sidelong glances of shrouded women, flame concealed beneath an ash-colored dress and a smoke-colored scarf, Mira eased her way into the city. For three days she lived on snatched scraps, using magic on a couple of occasions to secrete an apple into her pocket, though she sensed magic must be wielded sparingly here: there were watchers. She entered restaurant after restaurant, asking if she could sweep the floor or wash the dishes in exchange for a meal, but received only chilly stares and clicked tongues. And she soon realized there were no women in these establishments, no girls—all the work was done by men and boys. The only women she saw tended clothing stores or hair salons, but these places appeared to need no assistance.

On the afternoon of the third day, she was wandering in the northeastern quarter of the city, where the houses were more loosely spaced, where she encountered from time to time nooks of green: a bench set beneath a dusty palm or a trellis of threadbare jasmine. The only thing she'd eaten that day was a stolen plum, and she was so hungry that when a tendril of chocolate entered her nostrils, summoning a vision of Mrs. Zaccaroth's purple parlor with its high-backed chairs and crocheted doilies and window overlooking the river, she guessed she was hallucinating—the hunger was tampering with her mind. Nevertheless, she tugged on that thread, reeling it in turn after turn, and after a minute arrived at the prettiest storefront she'd seen. "Rosa's Chocolaterie" arced across the glass in crimson-shadowed gold, and beyond the letters, arranged in the rooms of dollhouses and spilling out of miniature treasure chests, were chocolate truffles. Mira studied them with an educated eye. They weren't as exquisite as Mrs. Zaccaroth's, but they were uniform, well-crafted, sturdy.

As she entered, a bell tinkled somewhere. The fragrant interior was empty, but she heard a clatter from beyond a door with a round, mist-clouded pane. Mira had her elbows on the glass of the case and was peering down at the wares in their chambered boxes, each truffle nestled in gold foil, when the door swung open, releasing a billow of scented steam. She straightened.

The woman who bustled into the room had comfortably round limbs and a bosom like risen dough, concealed under a red apron daubed in umber.

"Now then," she said, a smile printing dimples in her cheeks. "What looks appealing today?"

"Oh, they're all very pretty," Mira said politely, "but I'm afraid I don't have any money."

"Well, longing gazes are free," said the woman. "And since you're new, here's a morsel to whet your appetite when your mama gives you a coin." With a dainty silver tongs, she plucked from the case a truffle topped with a gold-dipped cashew and dropped it into Mira's palm.

Mira nibbled. Cherry at the heart. She closed her eyes and blissfully allowed the chocolate to melt across her tongue, then crunched up the scrumptious cashew.

"Oh, delicious," she said; then, automatically: "But perhaps a smidgen too much ..." She smacked a hand to her lips. "Sorry!" she exclaimed. "I didn't mean—"

The woman's eyebrows went up. Amusement pricked the corners of her lips and deepened her dimples.

"Too much what?" she asked.

Mira sighed. "I can make them," she said. "I can make truffles. I had a teacher, and—"

"A smidgen too much *what*?" the woman insisted.

"Almond extract," Mira said softly. "It doesn't let the cashew flavor get free."

Eyebrows descending, the woman took a truffle for herself and ate it, watching Mira the whole time. She swallowed and ran her tongue around her lips. "You're right," she said after a moment. She nodded once, twice. "You're right, much as I hate to admit it."

Fortified by the praise and the chocolate, Mira clutched the corner of the case, bitten fingernails on the glass. "Let me work here!" she blurted. "Let me help you. I can temper chocolate. I can chop nuts. I'm good at decorating."

The woman laughed. "I'm hardly making it as it is," she said. "I certainly can't afford an employee."

"I'll work for food," Mira said. "For bread and cheese and fruit. One meal a day. Please. I have a place to sleep but I'm starving."

She felt the woman's mind waver, and knew in that instant what she had to do to sway it. Barely moving her lips, as though uttering a little prayer, she spoke a spell of turning, and the woman suddenly opened her eyes wide and breathed in sharply.

"Why yes, child," she said. "If you're starving, of course. When can you start?"

"Right now," Mira said with a grin, and she stepped around the counter. "My name is Mira."

"And I," said the woman, "am Rosa." She took Mira's slender hand in her plump one, and for a moment indecision or confusion flickered on her features. Then she gave a little shake of her head as though to dislodge a gnat, and said, "Well, let's see what you can do."

The kitchen wasn't much larger than Mrs. Zaccaroth's, though the mixing bowls were colossal. There was a rectangular island in the center, topped with cream-colored marble. On shelves along one wall stood corked bottles of all colors, labeled in a handwriting more generous than Mrs. Zaccaroth's. Mira ran an eye over the bottles, greeting the labels like old friends: rose petal, gold leaf, hazelnut, vanilla pod …

For her first creation in this city she chose a combination that had been a favorite of Mrs. Zaccaroth's, plucking the bottles down: dried mango, smoked salt, pink peppercorn.

"Are you sure you want to try something so … so unusual for your trial run?" Rosa asked, one finger pressing into her cheek.

Mira shrugged. "Let's see how they turn out," she said mildly.

She tipped chunks of chocolate into a double boiler, then sugar, and melted them together slowly, till she was turning a luscious, glistening mass in the pan. She dipped a spoon, tasted, and added a pinch of cayenne. Tipping two-thirds of the mixture onto the marble, she used a pair of spatulas to temper, lifting, turning, watching for the subtle shifts in color and texture, sensing the seed crystals form. At the moment of change, she scraped the mass back into the pan, mixed it all up, and then dipped a spatula and set it aside to cool.

When she looked up, Rosa was watching her sidelong, head canted. "Where did you say you learned to make chocolates?" she asked.

"At the house of a friend. A teacher. Her name was Mrs. Zaccaroth."

Rosa shook her head. "I don't know her."

"How long have you had this place?" Mira asked to avert her prying.

"A year … almost a year and a half now. It's been an adventure. People aren't accustomed to new things, and truffles are … well, they're pretty and frivolous and a bit too delicious. A bit too addictive. One of the priests even gave a sermon denouncing chocolates and there was talk of shutting me down, until it was discovered that he sent his housekeeper to buy them in secret." A giggle rippled across her voluminous bosom.

Mira set about making a mango ganache. When that was ready, and the shells were prepared, she filled them, dabbing the mango at the heart like liquid flame. Now she took up the bottle of salt and poured an amber hillock into her palm. Before the truffles were entirely firm, she swept the salt across their surfaces, the grains scattering evenly, like blown sand. Finally, at the corner of each, she laid two pink peppercorns.

Going to the sink, she washed her hands beneath the great brass spigot and turned.

"There," she said.

"Well, I'm intrigued!" Rosa said. She reached for the truffles, but Mira held up a hand.

"Give them a moment to rest," she said.

Rosa sat on a tall stool, and Mira did likewise, elbows on the marble.

"What does your mother think, then?" Rosa asked. "Or is she the one who sent you looking for work?"

"My mother … my parents aren't here," Mira said. "They don't know." She didn't want to lie to this pleasant woman, but couldn't tell her the truth.

"You're an orphan?"

"No. Not an orphan. I have a place to stay, like I said. I just need food. And something to do; something to keep my hands busy. But tell me about yourself. Do you have children?"

Rosa shook her head. Looking at Mira, she opened her mouth; her chin quivered, and suddenly a tear spilled down each cheek. Using a corner of her soiled apron, she wiped them away, leaving small streaks of chocolate. "Well, that's not true," she said. "I had a child—a little girl, younger than you—but she was taken."

Mira's heart lurched. "By the demons?"

Rosa gave her an indecipherable look. "Demons? No, dear, by the priests. When I was your age, I always said I'd have a huge family—five, six, seven … I'd make their clothes and feed them cookies and we'd take picnics to the river shore. On Sundays I'd dress them all alike—blue scarves for the girls, blue caps for the boys—and we'd walk to church in a tidy row. But … well, it wasn't to be. It wasn't to be. And so." She gave a sodden sigh. "And so I have chocolates." She spread her plump hands and sighed again, offering Mira a broken smile.

"I think the truffles might be ready now," Mira said gently. "Shall we see how they turned out?"

They nibbled, and Mira watched the flavors detonate on Rosa's face even as they did on her tongue; supple, unctuous chocolate, slightly bitter, laced with salt and smoke and cayenne, then the gold pop of the mango, and finally the twin prickles of the pink peppercorns. The flavors lingered, melded, melted away, leaving a little ache.

"Oh my," Rosa said. She nodded slowly, eyes closed. "Yes. Yes. Perfection." She opened her eyes. A fresh set of tears trembled on the lower lids: it was clear that tears were always close to the surface with her. "All right, Mira. You're hired. For one meal a day and all the tea you can drink."

Mira hopped off her stool. "When do I start?"

"Tomorrow's Sunday. I'll see you at eight o'clock on Monday morning. Does that sound all right?"

In answer, Mira scurried around the corner of the marble table and gave Rosa an embrace that nearly knocked her off her perch.

* * *

So Mira crafted a little existence in the city. She salvaged an orange crate from a fruit seller's in which to keep her clothes. She found a mat so she could sleep out of the dust. She got used to the hourly chimes, and sometimes even slept through them, though they then entered her dreams in disconcerting ways. She borrowed a kettle from Rosa and fashioned a charcoal stove from a tin that had held olives, and after the six o'clock chimes she'd light the charcoal and brew a cup of tea, pouring filched sugar from a white paper sack and stirring with a stolen spoon. Then she'd sit with her back to the parapet and sip, cup propped in her fingertips, watching the diminishing smoke of her fire trickle into the dawn. Occasionally, though she knew she shouldn't, she'd scrawl a word or carve a little design in the smoke, loving the way the edges frayed, dispersed. From below rose the clatter of opened shutters, the cajoling of mothers, the voices of children, the clink of spoons on porcelain. This was thinking time, yawning time—a time to finger fragments of dreams before they floated free, a time to imagine the possibilities of the day.

Before the chimes beat seven, she descended the tower, listening at the door, then cracking it and peering out. Only when she was sure she was alone did she slip into the alley.

She walked down to the river and along it to the bridge. At the top of the stone curve she always paused a minute, forearms on the balustrade, looking down at the shredded reflections, the shadows slipping ripple to ripple, blessedly tender, blessedly changeful. She sometimes felt the river was a long cord of braided colors, reaching back to the town in the south, to her house and to Mrs. Zaccaroth, and then beyond, raveling into fable, into mist and mystery, and somehow tying her story together, binding it, making a single bundle of the disparate, chaotic threads.

Beyond the bridge she entered wider streets, which by this time had started to fill with pedestrians and carriages and carts of lemons and strawberries. Now that she was concealed in her drab garments, savage hair doused by a headscarf, the grownups paid her little heed. But occasionally a child would stop and watch her pass. Something in her face, her bearing was still a little too loose, and she strove to rein in her steps, to keep her head bowed, eyes lowered.

The now-distant chimes would ring seven as she arrived at the chocolaterie, its iron grate tugged down and padlocked over the glass. Rosa generally arrived a few minutes later, out of breath, unruly curls bouncing free of her headscarf.

"Sorry, sorry!" she chirruped, fumbling for her keys. "Late again! And how did you sleep, Mira my dear?"

"Very well, thank you," Mira replied. She helped Rosa raise the grate, using a forked stick to prod it the last few inches, and then Rosa unlocked the door and they went in.

Entering the chocolaterie was a relief after the black angles of the city: the shop was all curves and sparkles and the cozy scents of cinnamon and burnt sugar. The first thing Rosa did, after she yanked off her headscarf and checked the traps—she was in a constant battle with rats—was put the kettle on, and Mira had her second cup of tea with a croissant or rusk or triangle of shortbread, sitting on one of the stools at the marble-topped island. Rosa would tell her about the latest escapades of her wayward nephews or about her mother's moodiness, and Mira listened politely. Then Rosa would catch sight of the clock above the door and give a little shriek. Placing the cups in the sink, they'd tie on their aprons and get to work.

The initial task was to make the chocolate itself. Rosa did the stirring, as the wooden paddle was too large for Mira to wield comfortably. But Mira could do the tempering on her own, a process she adored. It was so similar to magic, to making a spell: the careful manipulation, watching for transformation; she could almost feel the minute crystals forming in her mind.

As Mira worked the mass on the marble slab, Rosa chattered away, and Mira gathered some of the tensions in the city, which was not as orderly and straitlaced as it appeared. Rosa told her about scandals: rebellious boys who scribbled blasphemous poems in dead-end alleyways, girls refusing to wear their headscarves, pregnant sisters in the convent, housewives who dressed as men and ventured out after dark.

When the chocolate was tempered to a glossy sheen and spaded into a voluptuous mudpie in the center of the marble, it was time to decide on the flavors of the day. This was an enormously pleasurable interlude. Rosa would prod idly at the chocolate with a spatula. "Well, we almost sold out of those peanut-brittle truffles yesterday," she might say, and she'd quirk an eyebrow at Mira. This was her opener.

Mira pulled up a stool. "What if, instead of peanuts, we used hazelnuts this time?" she said eagerly. "And maybe stick in some of those gin-soaked currants as well, for a bit of chewy texture."

"Well, I do like the hazelnut idea. Yes. The currants ... could those go on top?"

"Oh, of course. But they'll blend into the chocolate. Color-wise, you know. We need something else, for contrast."

Rosa scanned the shelves. "Orange peel?" she asked dubiously.

"Yes! Some of that candied orange peel. And it will add a lovely texture."

"Mmm. Yes. This is shaping up." Rosa slid a scrap of paper over and extracted a pencil from her hair. "So ... hazelnut brittle and currant. I love that!" She jotted a few items in her round hand. "Now, did you have anything special in mind?"

Rosa always gave Mira an opportunity to get her zaniest ideas out. Sometimes she even took them on, though she was often skeptical. And in truth, they didn't always work. Or, if they did, they might not sell.

Mira leaned forward. "So, here's what I've been thinking," she said. "You know that smoked sausage we had yesterday in our sandwiches?"

"Mira—"

Mira held up a hand. "Wait. Just listen."

"Mira, no! I am not serving my customers sausage chocolate."

"But just *listen*."

Rosa crossed her arms, trying to erase her dimples. "All right. I'm listening."

"Here's what I was thinking: that sausage went so well with

those green apples. If we could get that excellent sharp apple flavor—somehow concentrate it—that would balance the smoke and the salt. We could candy tiny crumbles of the sausage, maybe wrap them in apple. And then on top, two crispy strips, one of dried apple, one of bacon. And we just call it apple and bacon—crunchy on top, with the salty, spicy, smoky sausage hidden away."

"Apple and bacon. Apple and bacon ..." Rosa's eyes grew filmy and she swallowed. "All right, Mira. All right. Let's try it."

By nine, Rosa had to be out front, making sure the glass was spotless and the boxes of truffles were impeccably arrayed. She came back in to remove her apron and tie on her scarf in front of the pier glass, then hurried out again. And by nine thirty, from within the kitchen, Mira heard the first tinkle of the bell as a customer entered, and Rosa's ecstatic burble of a greeting.

* * *

Midmorning, Mira would head to the market and the specialty shops with an eccentric list of items: cinnamon, arugula, almonds, kumquats, olives, peppers, honeycomb. Or rosemary, radishes, nutmeg, blue cheese, raisins, pears, star anise. Or tangerines, sweet cream, dill, fish roe, orange water, salt, paprika. She loved these expeditions: they gave her a chance to explore the city, poking her head into shops and nosing through lidded bins.

After their initial suspicions—even shrouded, Mira was still too wide-eyed and openmouthed and loose-limbed for this city—the fruit sellers and spice vendors got to know her. They called her the chocolate girl. Curious about the odd assortment of items she'd purchase in outlandish quantities, they'd found out where she worked. And sometimes, if a vendor had slipped her an extra apple or had wondered how she was going to use, say, smoked chilies or pickled portobellos, she'd smuggle them a foil-wrapped truffle the next day. "Don't tell!" she'd murmur with a wink as she dropped it into his palm along with the coins. The vendor would wink back. And, likely as not, he'd come by that very afternoon to buy a dozen for his family.

Rosa normally brought most of the lunch fixings from home, enhanced with items from Mira's excursions. But one day, after Mira had been working in the shop for a month, Rosa came in even later than usual, chestnut locks tumbling from her scarf.

"Sorry, Mira!" she exclaimed. "So sorry to keep you waiting. My mother had one of her attacks, and I had to make sure she took her medicine." Rosa's mother was prone to fits of weeping from time to time—Mira heard all about them—and Rosa would have to wait till she calmed down enough to sleep.

"Anyway," Rosa went on, "because of all the ruckus, I'm afraid I completely forgot to bring lunch things. So why don't I give you a little extra when you go shopping, and you can buy whatever you like. After all, yesterday was an especially good day. We're down to one box of the cashews, and that gooseberry batch is sold out."

Mira had been living on tea, sandwiches, and chocolates for a month, and she was delighted to buy ingredients for what she thought of as real food. At the market, she bought a thick leek, two carrots, garlic, ginger, small white beans, and a good meaty bone, the latter parceled up in white paper.

The first thing she did when she got back to the shop was set the bone to simmer, along with the beans, star anise, cloves, and cardamom. And all that morning, as she tempered chocolate and crafted truffles, she got whiffs of the rich, spicy broth bubbling lackadaisically on a back burner.

After the noon rush, she sliced the leek into thin green and white rounds. She cooked it slowly in butter and added garlic and ginger and finely diced carrots. As the mixture seethed, the sliced leek slipped into silky strands and the garlic turned tawny.

"Oh my!" Rosa exclaimed when she clattered through the kitchen door. "Something smells wonderful. What have we got cooking here?" But Mira only smiled secretively and turned back to stirring. After ten minutes or so, she tipped the vegetables into the broth and let it bubble awhile before fishing out the bone and whole spices. She turned off the heat and added pepper and cream and a squeeze of tangerine.

"Soup's ready," she called.

Mira ladled the broth into mugs and handed one to Rosa. Rosa leaned over her mug and inhaled the fragrant steam. She blew on a spoonful, sipped, and leaned back. When she opened her eyes, her expression had changed. She peered at Mira with an indecipherable emotion.

"Do you like it?" Mira asked.

"You're … what are you, Mira?" Rosa said. She took another sip and shook her head. "You're not a normal girl." She seemed almost angry.

Mira sipped her soup. It was rich and creamy, with deep layers of flavor. "I think it tastes all right," she said.

"Listen to the child," Rosa said. "All *right?* It's magic. Pure magic. You're a magician is what you are."

And Mira had to hold the mug to her lips to cover her smile.

* * *

After that, Rosa often had Mira make a soup or a stew for their lunch, and would carry the leftovers home in a lidded container to share with her husband and mother.

These were delectable days, brimming with chocolate and spices and cups of tea, with steam and flame, with the laughter of delighted customers from beyond the swinging door, with Rosa's praise and embraces. This could be a life, Mira sometimes thought, as she strolled out with her shopping bag on her midmorning excursions. And she flirted with the idea of making a home here, of building up the chocolaterie to the point where she could ask for a wage, of renting a spare room somewhere, and perhaps eventually becoming a partner: Rosa and Mira's Chocolaterie. It had a pretty ring.

But then the gold key on its chain would tap her breastbone and she'd remember that this time at Rosa's was respite, interlude. She was a witch on a journey, though the journey seemed to have foundered in the tangled alleys of this city of ten thousand doors. At night sometimes she woke from dreams that she was moving from door to door in a dimly lit street or a dimly lit hallway, trying her key in lock after lock, but the doors remained closed. Behind those dream doors, girls lamented, but she could never make out the words, and woke with the flavor of sorrow on her tongue.

As she got to know the layout of the streets on her shopping excursions, she began to roam wider, taking in a fresh slice of the city every morning. There was no rhythm to the streets. They angled this way and that, but she was always able to find her way back if she could spot the clocktower: it was like the anchoring pin of a compass needle, keeping her tethered.

During these rambles, she picked up lightning stones and snail shells and chipped marbles, as she always had, and stuck them in her pockets. Back at the clocktower, she arranged these objects on the parapet, a little gathering of prettiness to keep her company. And she also, with her practiced witch's eye, spotted herbs and medicinal plants growing on the verges, in the tiny communal gardens, along the riverbanks. Occasionally she came a upon of pocket of feverfew or cinquefoil tucked behind a bench or bush, and was certain a surreptitious witch had planted them.

Sometimes the streets shunted her wider than she'd anticipated and she'd return to the chocolaterie panting, headscarf tamped to her forehead, but Rosa never said a thing—punctuality was not high on her list of priorities. Thus the city etched itself on the inside of Mira's skull, and she woke from dreams of wandering its quarters.

In her wanderings, she avoided the cathedral. She was terrified by the power that emanated from it. A power she did not have the strength or the courage to confront.

* * *

She also tried to avoid the convent, but one morning, when she headed out to the market, there was a strange bright fizz in her head. She told herself she'd let the tea steep too long, but when she got to the marketplace it was nearly deserted. An old apple seller remained in one corner, and Mira went up to her.

"Where is everybody?" she asked.

The apple seller tipped her head to the right. "There's a burning." Her lips peeled back, revealing a single blackened tooth clinging to her upper gum.

Unwilling to betray her ignorance, Mira headed in the direction the old woman had indicated. A group of caterwauling children rushed past, and housewives emerged from doorways hastily tying on their scarves. As she crossed the southernmost bridge, she heard in the distance a chaotic susurration that reminded her of the sound of the cataracts, though this was spiked with shouts and laughter.

The space in front of the Convent of the Sisters of the Light was a seething mesh of compressed bodies, and from every balcony faces craned, mouths writhing in grins or grimaces. The thin windows of the convent were similarly crammed with faces, though there was no joy in them: beneath stricken eyes, tears glittered on cheeks like the seed pearls on Mrs. Zaccaroth's skirts. Mira squirmed through the mashed flesh, pinching thighs and poking ribs to ease her passage, until she could see what they were staring at.

A wooden dais had been erected before the stone tower in the center of the square. From where she stood, Mira could see what she had not seen on her first encounter with the convent: iron rungs ran up the tower to a black oval near the top. She could not see into the hollow, but had a brief black-framed vision of the thin windows and their contents of tear-spangled faces.

Now the doors of the convent opened and a priest emerged. He mounted the dais and scanned the crowd, and as soon as Mira saw his face she knew with a jolt of horror and fascination that he was a man of power. She could taste it: flavor of salt and iron. He wore the black robes and an elaborate hat, and he held a short rod of dark, polished stone with a cross at one end. Other than the hat and the rod, nothing set him apart: a man of ordinary height and medium build, trimmed beard grained with white.

He stood looking up, running his right hand slowly along the length of the rod. Black lightning seemed to gather about his head; twisted, jagged shapes like lacerations in the air, like altered letters that vanished if she focused on them, so she knew she was seeing them with her witch's eye.

The priest raised the rod in his right fist and said something, but the clamor of the crowd swallowed his words, and the answer, if there was one. He spoke again, while the crowd hushed. The third time she could hear his voice: "Do you repent?" And the reply from the hollow, shrill and tremulous and incredibly strong: "I do not."

The priest bowed his head, lips moving. His eye sockets were wells of darkness, and the dark lightning seemed to crouch in to his form. Then he stepped forward, leaned, and in sudden silence touched the tip of the rod to the base of the tower. A bright insect scurried up the stone, and with a sound like an abrupt exhalation flames burst from the hollow.

Mira felt the burst in her brain, felt rather than heard the scream, and a curtain of fire engulfed her eyes. Cheers erupted around the square.

Unable to catch her breath, she turned and clawed her way through the crowd and out of the square, and then she was running through the empty streets, only stopping when she reached the river. Every breath a blade between her ribs.

"No!" she said. "No, no, no!"—each word a little shriek. And she pressed her bitten fingernails into her temples as if she could rip out the flames that still flickered behind her eyes, as if she could rip out the scream that echoed in her skull.

Returning emptyhanded to the chocolaterie, she dropped the bag on the marble and sat on a stool and placed her head in her arms.

"What's wrong?" Rosa asked, alarmed. She came around the table and put a hand on Mira's back. "What's wrong, Mira? Why is the bag empty?"

Mira lifted her head and stared bleakly down at the marble. She traced a black vein with a fingernail. "There was a burning," she said.

Rosa sat as well, clutching the countertop. In a shattered voice, she said, "That explains why we haven't had the noon rush. You didn't ... you didn't happen to see who ... ?"

Mira shook her head.

* * *

The next afternoon, as Mira was finishing a fresh batch of hazelnut chocolates, the door swung open. Intent on decorating the truffles, she didn't look up till Rosa said, "Mira, I'd like you to meet someone."

Mira tapped a gilded hazelnut onto a truffle and raised her head. Standing beside Rosa in a dark-gray pinafore, nutmeg curls swarming exuberantly from beneath a blue headscarf, was a girl about Mira's age.

"This is my brother's daughter, Aster," Rosa said. "She was at the apartment yesterday afternoon and had one of our apple-and-bacon truffles, and when I told her you'd come up with the idea, well, she just had to meet you."

Aster took a step forward. Like Rosa, she was comfortably plump, and she had Rosa's star-flecked, thick-lashed eyes. However, unlike Rosa's symmetry, only her left cheek bore a dimple. "So you're the famous Mira," she said. "Auntie Rosa never stops talking about you. And what are you making here?"

Mira, ordinarily brash, was unaccountably abashed before this pretty, open-faced girl. She wiped her fingers on her apron. "Oh, these ... these are just our normal hazelnuts." She nudged a truffle toward the girl. "Would you like to try one?"

"Ooh, yes please! If it's all right, Auntie Rosa."

Her aunt gave her a double-dimpled grin. "Go on. I might have one too."

Mira had one as well to keep them company. They were still a bit squashy, but Aster closed her eyes and shook her head gently as she crunched up the hazelnut. Her tongue emerged to lick a chocolate beauty mark from her downy upper lip. She opened her rain-washed eyes, still shaking her head.

"I don't know how you keep the shop running," she said. "If I worked here I'd eat them all up, every day."

Mira laughed. "I sometimes snitch one," she confessed.

The doorbell rang, and Rosa bustled out to deal with the customer. Aster sat on the stool. She nodded at the mass of tempered chocolate on the marble. "So is it hard to learn?"

Mira shrugged. "It takes a while. My first ones were terrible. Really, you almost had to spit them out. But then you figure out the balance. You figure out what works."

"Could I learn? I mean, could you teach me to make one?" And there was no way to refuse that half-dimpled smile.

"Wash your hands," Mira said. "Then come over on this side."

When Rosa returned to the kitchen a few minutes later, she found the two girls bent over the table, giggling furiously. Aster, speechless with merriment, pointed to the dog turd of a truffle that was her first attempt.

Rosa stood with arms folded, shaking her head. "I leave you two alone for a minute," she said, but couldn't stanch her smile.

Aster stayed till they closed up shop that evening, helping to wash the marble slab and rinse out the huge pans and tidy away the boxes of chocolates and set the rattraps and sweep and mop the floor. As Rosa pulled down the grating, the streetlamps came on. Aster put her plump fingers, still damp from wringing out the mop, around Mira's elbow. "Can Mira come tomorrow afternoon, Auntie? Please?" she asked.

Rosa padlocked the grate and stood panting.

"What's tomorrow afternoon?" Mira asked.

"It's the birthday of Aster's twin brothers," Rosa said. "My rascal nephews. We're having a little party. Yes, I don't see why not. If you'd like that, Mira?" She cocked her head, tipping her headscarf askew.

"I'd love to," Mira said, though her heart gave a little gulp. "But I don't know where you live."

"Oh, you can just come with me after closing," Rosa said, and Aster gave Mira's elbow a squeeze.

* * *

Rosa's apartment was a few minutes south of the chocolaterie. They each carried a box of assorted truffles—one a gift, one to share. As Rosa unlocked the armored door at the base of the building, Mira felt a twinge of apprehension, coupled with thrill: this was the first time she'd stepped behind one of these formidable barriers. They wound up four flights of stairs that were smooth and bowed and gray as old soap, Rosa pausing to catch her breath on every landing. As they passed hallways, Mira caught whiffs of simmering stews and frying onions, the whimpering of babies, the shards of a quarrel.

Rosa's apartment was at the end of the hall on the fifth floor—a paneled door with a brass knob. The door opened onto a parlor crammed with furniture. On the walls were cross-stitched verses framed in gold, and in a corner cabinet stood painted porcelain angels and plates with patterns of vines and roses.

From the kitchen came clattering and a gorgeous aroma of roasting chicken. Rosa dipped her head into the doorway and said, in a voice verging on a shout, "Mother, come meet Mira, my helper at the shop."

Mira had expected an older version of Rosa, as Aster was a younger, but the woman who stepped out of the kitchen, still gripping a wooden spoon, was skinny and angular: pike chin, pointy elbows, tightly bound steel-wool hair, eyes sparking under tangled brows. Rosa must have taken after her father. The old woman leaned in the doorway, gaze flickering across Mira.

"So you're the little sorceress behind the chocolates," she said, her voice as sharp as her elbows.

Mira shrugged. "I just help Rosa."

"What's that?"

"You have to speak up a bit with her," Rosa said.

Mira leaned forward. "I just help out," she said, louder.

The woman gave a gap-toothed grin and beckoned with her spoon. "Come," she said. "Tell me what you think of my sauce."

Squeezing into the kitchen, Mira sipped at the proffered spoon: a silky, buttery lemon-tarragon sauce. She nodded, eyebrows raised.

"Not bad, eh, for an old woman?" the mother said. "That will go on the chicken, and I've got potatoes and green beans and a nice salad here as well. All right, out." She poked Mira's ribs with the spoon handle. "I'll finish up before the others arrive."

Mira had just taken a seat in one of the armchairs in the parlor when there was a great tramping in the hall and the door burst open without a knock. In came Aster, followed by what seemed like a dozen people, all shouting and laughing, but the throng turned out to be only four: Aster's mother and father and her two brothers. Aster plunged over to Mira, hauled her up, and gave her a kiss on each cheek. Then she turned and introduced her family, her brothers instantly shy, mumbling with eyes averted as they took Mira's hand, and then rambunctious, roughhousing on the sofa while their mother tried to calm them.

Aster grinned. "They're always like that," she said. "I don't even apologize anymore. Come. Have you been out on Auntie Rosa's balcony?"

The balcony was crammed with potted herbs and flowers. There were geraniums in a chipped tureen and mint in a teapot and a grapevine sprawling overhead, and to one side two wicker chairs and a little tin table. They leaned on the balustrade.

"Where do you live?" Mira asked.

"Just a few streets that way." Aster flung out an arm. "I'll have you over sometime."

"Why's your brothers' birthday party here? Why not at your house?"

Aster laughed. "My mother would say it's because this apartment's a bit bigger, but that's not the reason. The reason is that she's a terrible cook. Also because it's easier to bring people to Grandmother than shuffle her down all the stairs. And where do you live? Auntie Rosa says you're an orphan."

"No. Not an orphan."

"But Auntie Rosa—"

"I think Rosa wants me to be an orphan," Mira said. "Needs me to be an orphan, so she can mother me. But no, I have parents."

"Do you live with them?"

The grapevine had sent a tendril coiling around the balustrade. Mira gently tugged at its last loop, felt the strength and fragility of the thin green curl. She tucked it back into place.

"I don't live with them, no. Not here. But I can't tell you where I live. I wish I could, but I can't."

Aster looked at Mira, the single dimple appearing and vanishing as she tried to settle on an emotion. She shook her head. "Auntie Rosa said you were a strange one."

"Yes. Sorry." And suddenly Mira was on the verge of weeping. She desperately wanted to be able to tell Aster the truth, to tell somebody the truth—the whole story of her parents and her powers and the journey she'd made—but she knew it was too dangerous.

The balcony doors opened and Rosa stuck her head out. "Food's ready," she said.

They ate squeezed around an oval table in the dining room. There was a crocheted runner over a red tablecloth and a red rosebud in a little white vase in the center. Rosa lit candles. The china was chipped and the silverware mismatched, but it all seemed lovely and elegant to Mira.

"Serve Mira first," Rosa's mother called.

"It's *our* birthday," said one of the twins, and Rosa's mother rapped his elbow with a spoon. "Your time will come, young man," she said. She pointed the spoon at Mira. "We have a special guest tonight, and I want to see what she thinks of my cooking."

"Perhaps the birthday boys …" Mira said mildly, but Rosa had already forked a thigh onto her plate.

After the meal, they returned to the parlor for presents and chocolates and birthday cake. Mira was sitting by the corner cabinet filled with angels and painted plates, and as she scanned the glass shelves she realized one of the angels was perched on a slim book. She leaned. In gilt letters on dusty blue: *Tales from Under the Bed*. The first book she'd seen in this city. The first book she'd seen since she'd left Mrs. Zaccaroth's house.

"Oh!" she exclaimed. The whole room turned and she shoved a knuckle into her mouth. "Nothing," she said quickly. "I just saw your book here." She tapped the glass.

"That's Mother's old book," Rosa said. "She won't let me throw it away. You can take it out if you like."

Mira opened the case and carefully lifted the angel and slid the book out. The angel's base had left a shadow of darker blue on the cover. "This is the only storybook I've seen in this city," she said, turning the pages. A girl in the clutches of a great eagle. A fisherman with a net full of stars. A mermaid asleep on a stony shore.

"There are still a few old books around," Rosa said.

"Are there bookshops?" Mira asked.

"Bookshops?" Rosa looked blank.

"Where you can buy, you know, stories or … or books for reading. For pleasure."

Rosa shook her head. "Nothing like that, no."

"There used to be," said a voice from the corner by the kitchen.

They all turned. Rosa's mother raised a claw from the arm of her chair. "There used to be a lovely bookshop," she said. "I went there on Saturdays if I had a coin. It was down in the old quarter—don't remember the street. Tiny dead-end alley. And right at the very end was a bookshop. It was old even then. But you could still find books there. The old fairytales. Stories of dragons and giants and djinns."

Rosa crossed herself, which roused her mother's ire.

"Don't you go crossing and praying over me, now. It was a better time, I'll tell you that. A better time than all this button-up, button-down, obey-the-master nonsense."

"Oh, Mother."

"Oh, Mother nothing." The claw returned to scratching the arm of the chair and she subsided, muttering.

Mira leaned forward. "What happened to the bookshop?" she asked.

"Eh?" The mother ceased her scratching.

"I said, what happened to the bookshop?"

"It closed up."

"Went out of business," Rosa's bald little husband said smugly.

"No," snapped the mother, aiming the claw at him. "Shut down by the authorities. The same as they tried to do with my Rosa's chocolate shop. And they'll try again, dearie, you watch. But oh, I loved that bookshop. The smell of the books. The pictures. The owner was a lovely woman, knitting and reading all day long in her rocking chair, and a fat gray cat sleeping beside her. She didn't care if you just sat and read for a while. For a whole morning even. But that's all gone. All gone now." She sank back once more, breathing as though she'd just climbed the stairs.

The streetlights were coming on by the time Mira left, full of good food and good cheer. She was anxious to get back to the clocktower before the curfew, and had almost rounded the corner when there was a shout. She turned. Aster was running down the street with something in her hand. "Here," she said, panting, headscarf fallen back. "Grandmother wanted you to have this." It was the blue book of fairytales. Mira clutched it to her chest like a child with a new doll, too pleased to speak.

* * *

The next day, she sat in her clocktower and drank tea and read the book Rosa's mother had given her, and it was like a little holiday from the black stone walls and the watchtowers and the leaden lid of the church. She read it straight through, story after delicious story.

The Blue Girl

On another bend of the river, a boy sat on a rock in the rain, watching the fleeting diadems dance across the water. The rain came down harder, and he was just getting up to head home when a commotion caught his eye. Along the shore to the south, something was thrashing in the shallows. At first he thought it was a fish, but as he got closer he realized it was a girl with blue hair and translucent blue skin flailing in a tattered fishing net.

"Wait," the boy said, kneeling on the polished stones. "You're all tangled." Carefully he unpicked the knots, releasing her limbs one by one, until she was free.

The blue girl sat up in the shallows.

"What's your name?" the boy asked, but she only gave him a blue smile. Lifting off her necklace of blue driftglass, she held it out. The boy took it, letting the cool, smooth shapes slip through his fingers. He looked up to thank her, but she was gone.

When the boy got home, his mother scolded him. "You'll catch your death, sitting in the rain."

"I found a blue girl by the river," he said. "She was caught in a net, so I helped her get free. She gave me a present." He showed his mother the necklace of driftglass.

"Nonsense!" his mother said. "There are no blue girls. Now go change out of your wet clothes."

So the boy, a little disheartened, went to change into dry clothes. He put on the necklace, tucking it into his shirt. The smooth shapes of glass were cold at first, but his skin soon warmed them.

The next afternoon, he again went down to the river and sat on the rock. And before long, the water shivered and parted and the blue girl emerged.

"Do you have a name?" he asked. But again she only smiled her blue smile. She swam up to him and held out her hand, and this time he received a lightning stone: blue, with a white slash through the center. Then she turned and dove, and her blue toes slipped beneath the waves.

Back at the house, the boy went into the kitchen. "There *are* blue girls," he told his mother. "I saw her again, and she gave me another present."

"That's just a stone from the shore," his mother said. "Now go wash your hands and set the table. Supper's almost ready."

The boy put the stone in his pocket and went to wash his hands.

The next day the boy didn't come home for supper. In the twilight, his mother went calling for him along the river shore. By the rock where he liked to sit, she found his sandals and the lightning stone, and as she picked them up she thought she heard laughter. But looking out across the water, she saw only shadows and ripples like a thousand blue smiles.

After the birthday party, Aster sometimes came to the shop in the afternoons. Mira would set her to work shelling pistachios or dicing dates or filling foil shells with finished truffles. Occasionally, after days of pleading, Rosa would let Aster make a batch of chocolates from scratch, though these often had to be scrapped. Mira found herself channeling Mrs. Zaccaroth's teaching style, refusing to allow Aster to measure, exhorting her to taste at every step. But it was clear Aster didn't have whatever it was that made Mira a good cook—the ability to taste in the mind, the sense of balance, the intensity of focus.

One Friday, Aster asked if Mira could come to her house for lunch. Mira had finished making the truffles, so Rosa agreed. Aster took Mira's hand, and as they walked she chattered away—a scattered story about a boy in her Sunday school class who left her misspelled notes tucked into a hymnbook but blushed and ran off when she asked about his day. Mira grinned, remembering Tolly the fisherboy. She wondered idly what he was doing, and had a sudden vision of Tolly, who seemed taller and skinnier, standing in the shallows and scrubbing the side of his painted boat with a piece of pumice.

Aster's apartment was smaller than Rosa's, dingier, the low ceilings tarnished with candle smoke. She had her own room, though it was windowless and had clearly once been a linen closet. Her bed filled most of the space, dresses dangling from a dowel over it. On the smudged walls were icons and a filigree cross. A Bible spreadeagled on the pillow.

"It's tiny," Aster said shamefacedly, and Mira touched her arm. "It's more than I have," she told her.

Aster showed her the boys' room—bunk beds with rumpled bedclothes, and in the middle of the floor a reeking heap of soiled underwear, muddy socks, sticks, and balls. The boys were out playing in the street.

"Come onto the balcony," Aster said. "It's not as pretty as Grandmother's, I'm afraid."

The balcony was dusty, with a single dead plant in a flowerpot and a cracked wooden top in a corner. Mira leaned her elbows on the balustrade. They were close to the city walls here, and one of the eight watchtowers loomed above a rooftop. A uniformed man paced in a pillared cage there, black cap at an angle, face turned outward.

"What's he looking for?" Mira murmured.

"Who?" Aster was scouring the street below.

Mira pointed. "The man in the tower. What's he watching for?"

Aster straightened. "Oh, him. I've never thought about it. He's keeping us safe, I suppose."

"Safe. Safe from what?"

"Demons," said Aster.

"Have you seen them? The demons?"

"No. Of course not."

"Then how do you know?"

"How do I know what?"

"How do you know the demons are out there?"

"The priests, of course." Aster glanced at Mira. "They're always preaching about them."

"Do you know what they look like?"

Aster gave a beguiling frown, which incongruously summoned her single dimple. "What the demons look like?" she said. "Oh, you do ask the oddest questions." Then, seeing that Mira was serious, she said, "Well ... I guess, you know, they have horns. And red eyes. Tails, maybe. Just normal demons."

"Normal demons." Mira quenched a grin. "Do they ever get in? Into the city, I mean. Over the walls."

"Oh, no. Not for years and years. See, the walls keep them out. Our prayers keep them out. But why don't you know all this?"

Mira ignored that. "They used to come in, though? Before?"

Aster shrugged, nodded. "I've heard the stories. You must have heard them too."

"Tell me."

"Well, this is from my grandmother. And it's hard to know quite what to believe. She can be a bit outlandish, as you saw. So, she said once that in *her* grandmother's time, there were no walls. Or maybe the walls weren't as high. I don't know. Anyway, demons used to come in from outside. From the desert or somewhere." She gave a little shiver. "I don't even like to *talk* about it. It makes me all trembly inside, as if just by talking about them we might call them." And she put a hand on her breastbone.

"They came in from the desert," Mira said, squeezing slightly with her mind.

Aster breathed in sharply. "Yes. And then ... oh, it was awful. They used to take the children. Snatch them from the streets. From doorways, even, or open windows. So people started putting bars on the windows and spikes on the doors. And then they built the walls and the watchtowers."

"Where did the demons take the children?" Mira asked.

"Back into the desert, I guess. Or wherever they came from. I don't know."

"Did any return?"

"Not that I heard. But this was all long ago. Long ago. If it even happened. And isn't it nice to feel protected? Cozy. Like when you're in church, and the priest is giving his sermon. You feel so safe."

Mira was silent, and Aster turned to her. "Where do you go to church?"

Mira shook her head.

"What?" she exclaimed. "You don't go at all?"

"No."

"Why not?"

Mira gave a half shrug; just a twitch of her shoulder. "So, if there used to be demons in the city," she said—she wanted to know what ordinary girls believed, "was there also magic? Were all the fairytales true?"

"Magic? You mean like witches with cauldrons, making potions?"

Mira saw Mrs. Zaccaroth standing very straight before the stove in her tiled kitchen, the copper-bottomed pans like harvest moons above her head, the periwinkle strings of her apron in a neat bow at the small of her back. "Yes," she said. "Witches, cauldrons, all that."

"Well, no. I mean … no, of course not."

"Why not, though? If there are demons, you know, why aren't there witches as well?"

"Oh, Mira. Because …" Her plump lips pleated.

"Because?"

"Because if there were witches, we'd *see* them. I mean, we'd see the magic."

Mira nodded.

"What horrible things you like to talk about, though," Aster said. "Demons, witches. Do you want tea? I'll get some tea, and you think of something nice to talk about."

Mira hadn't spent much time with girls her age. She had always been too spiky, too volatile, too given to shouting. Dolls seemed to lose arms or heads when she was around, and she grew irritated with the girls' pretend parties—she wanted the real thing: real tea, real cakes. She always felt the other girls knew something was wrong with her—even after their mothers admonished them not to call names, she heard them whispering about her red hair, about her temper, half taunting. And, of course, they blamed her for the arrival of the demons, which made her furious. Mira wasn't one of the group. She would never be one of the group. So she'd head down to the river shore. The cats didn't care about her hair or her temper. And she preferred real stones to imaginary cakes. But Aster was so open, so blithe and serene that Mira didn't feel the need to snap, to lash out.

Mira had somehow assumed that under their polished surface—their shiny brushed hair and neatly buttoned blouses and gleaming shoes and unbitten fingernails—all girls had the same cravings, the same inclinations toward magic and fairytales, toward poison gardens and the secret arts of cookery. But Aster seemed to want nothing more than to conform: marriage, church, children … with the hidden heart of a truffle the most exciting part of her week.

Aster came back with two cups of sweet milky tea, a cinnamon stick in each as a stirrer. "So, have you thought of something nice?" she asked.

Mira breathed into her tea, eyes closed, immersed in a fragrant cloud. "What would you do if you could?" she asked. "If you could do whatever you wanted, have anything you wanted. Let's say you rubbed a lamp the right way and a huge friendly djinn made of blue smoke came out and gave you three wishes. What would you wish for?"

"Oh, I like *this*," Aster said. "Mm, let's see. Three wishes. So, first, I find a husband, like that boy I was telling you about the other day, the one from Sunday school, but with a mustache. A nice neat mustache, curled up at the ends." She twisted imaginary points at the corners of her lips. "And tall polished black-leather boots, with brass buckles. All right. That's one. So, two—we get an apartment like Auntie Rosa's, maybe even a bit bigger. Enough so that all our children can have their own rooms."

"How many children?" Mira asked.

"Three." Aster sighed. "Two girls, one boy. And their names would be, for the girls, Rosie after Auntie Rosa, of course, and Jasmine. The boy I haven't decided yet. Maybe Bramble."

"Wouldn't you feel tied down?"

"What do you mean?"

"I mean, husband, apartment, children … you'd be pressed into place, like a truffle in a tray."

Aster shrugged. "I suppose, if you put it like that. Still, think about how lovely it would be to hold a baby of your own. The little dresses. The tiny little shoes." She held out thumb and forefinger. "But I think maybe I've used up my three wishes. What about you, Mira? What would you wish for?"

Mira sketched a curlicue in the dust on the balustrade. Alone of the people within the city walls she'd encountered a djinn. She thought of the pavilion and carpet in the middle of the desert. Perhaps the dishes were already filled with sand. Perhaps the awning had already tattered in the heat. And how many other such djinn-summoned pavilions existed out there, buried under sand?

"First," she said, "no walls. I'd bring down the walls, even if it let the demons back in." She ignored Aster's sucked breath. "Second, stories. I'd bring back the fairytales, and the bookshops to hold them." She looked down into her tea.

"And third?"

"Third," Mira said, "I'd have a house with an herb garden and a purple parlor. And maybe little gold stars painted on the purple."

"Purple parlor! Gold stars! Oh, you *are* strange." Aster grinned. "And what else would be in your purple house?"

"So, lots of dark polished furniture," Mira went on, gazing up into the nook of cloudless sky beyond the balcony. "And a sideboard with crystals, you know. Crystals and spheres, all bright and glittery against the walls. Big windows overlooking the river, with no bars or anything to hide the view, and white lacy curtains that blow in the breeze … And a cat, of course. A cat with a necklace of snail shells and different-colored eyes."

She looked down, blinking, then looked up. Aster was staring at her.

"Is this an actual room?" Aster asked. "Is this where you live, Mira?"

Mira laughed. "It's where I'd like to live," she said.

"But the cat."

Mira looked at her.

"You said you wanted a cat, with different-colored eyes."

"Gold and blue. Well, a kind of gray-blue. Like a storm cloud. Like shadows on the river."

"But cats … You know cats are …"

"Cats are what?" Mira asked, and as she said it she realized with a start that she hadn't seen a single cat in this city, even down by the shore, even at the fishmongers'. Plenty of rats, a few dogs on leashes, but no cats.

"Cats are forbidden," Aster said quietly.

IX

THE HIGH PRIEST

On Monday morning, Rosa was waiting for Mira in front of the chocolaterie. The grate was still locked, and as soon as she saw Mira she took a step forward, fingers fluttering.

"What is it?" Mira asked. "Is it your mother?"

Rosa shook her head. "No. No, it's Aster." She seized Mira's hands. "It's Aster. She's sick. My mother's there, helping out. She said … she said to fetch you."

"But what about the doctor?"

"He was at the apartment yesterday. He's coming again this morning. But she's getting worse."

"What does she have?"

"The ash fever. She's so weak."

Mira felt frost branching in her belly. Her father's sister had died of the ash fever, and she remembered the last days when every breath was a mountain. She tugged her hands out of Rosa's and stepped back. "I can't," she whispered. "I can't … I'm not—"

"Mira." Rosa stepped forward again. "Aster's going to die. Are you able to do anything?"

Mira blinked. Then she nodded. "Open up the store," she said.

"There's no time. Mira—"

"Open it. I need something."

So Rosa unlocked the grate and tugged it up until she could unlock the door. Mira slipped in and went to the kitchen. From the shelves she plucked two bottles, dropped them into the pocket of her dress, and hurried out again, the bottles clinking like windchimes.

"Where are you going?" Rosa said. "The apartment's this way."

"I have to fetch something," Mira called over her shoulder. She started running, clutching the bottles through her dress.

The ash sickness had swept through her town in the south from time to time. It didn't seem to affect the youngest children; more women came down with it than men. During outbreaks, girls would arrive at Mrs. Zaccaroth's door, summoning her to their houses. She'd send them ahead and tell them to boil a kettle, and would go out to gather herbs, placing them in her reticule. Mira had accompanied her on two occasions, and watched Mrs.

Zaccaroth's cures, which involved not only potions but stories and songs, soups and steam baths. Three pages of the magical cookbook were devoted to the ash sickness, with dozens of suggestions in various hands filling the margins. Some witches suggested the patient did better in a sitting position; some recommended the patient lie facedown for a quarter of every hour. They proposed a great variety of potions. The remedies they all agreed on, however, were a tisane of aniseed and marshmallow root, and breathing steam infused with juniper. Mrs. Zaccaroth had added, in her spiky copperplate, a calming charm—more of a nursery rhyme or a lullaby than a magical spell.

Early in her wanderings through the city, Mira had walked to the northernmost of the three bridges, which was narrower and less trafficked than the other two. From its apex, as was her wont, she sat on the balustrade swinging her legs and looking down at the water. And she'd seen, on the western shore, tucked against the last arch, a little stand of plants with velvet leaves and pale mauve flowers.

It took her half an hour to get to the third bridge. Ignoring the ball-throwing boys who shouted at her, she climbed over the low wall bordering the river and clambered down to the shoreline. Ankle-deep in muck, she tugged up one mallow after another, their stems thick and pliant, roots like splayed fingers. When she had an armful, she climbed up to the street once more. The boys were now standing in a row along the wall, watching her. She stuck out her tongue at them and hurried back along the river, past the island. Crossing the southernmost bridge, she angled toward the city walls, to the thin street where Aster lived.

The doctor was a tall, bent man with rectangular spectacles and a halfmoon bloodstain on the cuff of his white shirt. His carefully side-slicked hair was gashed with slivers of scalp. He paid no attention to Mira when she slipped into the house with muddy feet and an armful of muddy plants; didn't even glance at her. He was drying his hands on a towel, which he handed to Aster's mother, then set about placing his instruments in his leather bag—each had its slot.

"Her blood is still too thick," he said. "Too thick and too dark. I will come tomorrow and release more. In the meantime, she should drink wine to build her strength. Wine and white bread." He snapped the clasps shut, nodded at Aster's father, who was sitting in a corner chair, and strode out the front door. They could hear his shoes clacking in the hallway.

"Mira." The grandmother stepped forward.

"How is she?"

The old woman shook her head, eyebrows tangling with each other.

"Could I see her?"

"Of course." She pointed.

Mira handed her the armful of marshmallows, which were dripping muck on the carpet. "Here," she said. "Put these in the kitchen. And boil a kettle."

They'd moved Aster to her parents' bed. She seemed smaller. Her eyes were closed and hooped in ash-colored bruises; her hair had lost its bounce and lay in lank loops across her cheek and forehead. Tamped to her inner arm was a wad of cotton with a scarlet heart. Mira could hear her struggles to breathe.

Sitting on the edge of the mattress, she took Aster's damp, limp hand and gave it a squeeze. Aster's head shifted on the pillow. Her eyes opened to bloodshot slits.

"Mira," she whispered, and started coughing. Each cough made her wince. Mira listened to the rattling pockets of trapped phlegm.

Healing, Mrs. Zaccaroth had told her, was, like much of witchcraft, a matter of balance. The most effective potion, if it was not accompanied by a friendly touch, a well-told tale, or even a bowl of good soup, might fail to stem the illness. The most skillful healers recognized this, and they would often spend the night at a patient's bedside. However, unlike many of the doctors, they were also adept at recognizing when the spirit was ready to depart; when delaying death would only prolong the pain.

The kettle sang, and Mira stood. Aster's mother was standing in a corner by the door, face a labyrinth of worry and weariness. She was muttering a Bible verse and had almost twisted off the top button of her dress.

"While I prepare a tea, can you change her nightdress and the sheets and pillowcases?" Mira said. "That will make her more comfortable."

The mother nodded, relieved to have something to do.

In the kitchen, Mira stood with her back to the wall, eyes scanning the ceiling. She pulled from her pocket the bottles of aniseed and juniper, and placed them on the counter. Then she set about peeling the roots of the marshmallows, releasing a bland, slightly earthy scent. She chopped them into pale segments and set them in a bowl to soak.

Tipping a dozen juniper berries into a saucepan, she filled it with water from the kettle and, like a slap from a satin glove, a bracing scent entered the room. She carried the saucepan into the bedroom and set it on the bedside table.

"Oh my," the grandmother said. "That wakes you up, doesn't it?"

"What—" Aster coughed. "What's—"

"It will help you," Mira said. "Do you think you could sit up? Just for a bit? I'll hold you."

Aster closed her eyes. "I'll try," she said, and even whispered the words seemed to cause her pain.

Mira helped her sit and put her feet over the edge of the bed. Sweat spangled Aster's forehead like crumbs of quartz.

"You're going to cough more," Mira said. "But it will open things up. Are you ready?"

Aster nodded.

Mira pulled the counterpane from the bed and flung it over Aster's head so it made a tent over her and the bowl. Immediately, within the shroud, Aster began coughing and gasping. Mira sat beside her, one arm around her shoulders, the other steadying the table. "Good," she said. "It needs to come out."

After a couple of minutes, the coughing subsided, and Aster's breathing already seemed freer. Mira tugged off the counterpane and Aster sat back, pink-faced and drenched. Mira patted her face with a corner of the counterpane and helped her sit up against the headboard.

Going to the kitchen, she strained the glutinous liquid from the bowl of marshmallow root, added aniseed and honey, and poured it into a mug. She carried the mug into the bedroom. "Here," she said. "This will help. Sip it slowly."

It took Aster half an hour to drink the tea, between spasms of coughing, during which Mira held the mug.

"All right," Mira said when the mug was empty. "Now it's time to rest." She drew the curtains and helped Aster slide down under the sheets. Stroking her damp hand, she half sang, half chanted Mrs. Zaccaroth's calming charm.

> *"By water's edge, where dreams are born,*
> *By moss and pebble, foam and thorn,*
> *Beneath the curly leaves of storm,*
> *The river flows forever on.*

"And so we sing a river song,
Flowing on, forever on,
Carrying the dreams along
Until they founder in the dawn.

"By serpent's hiss and jackal's moan,
Where crickets creak and bullfrogs groan,
Where spider spins her web alone,
The river flows forever on.

"And so we sing a river song,
Flowing on, forever on,
Carrying the dreams along
Until they flicker in the dawn.

"By house of brick and tile and stone,
By church and steeple, hearth and home,
By dust and rubble, skull and bone,
The river flows forever on.

"And so we sing a river song,
Flowing on, forever on,
Carrying the dreams along
Until they flower in the dawn."

As she sang, she felt Aster's hand go heavy; her breathing eased. Mira released her hand and stood. Tiptoeing out of the room, she pulled the door till it was ajar.

"She's asleep," she whispered to the grandmother. "Let her rest. When she wakes up, we'll do more steam, more tea. And, if she's strong enough, some soup."

"What was that song?" the grandmother asked. Her voice had lost its sandpaper and had a wispy, wistful quality. "The little song you sang."

"Oh, just a lullaby."

"I seemed to remember it from somewhere. 'So we sing a river song, flowing on ...' Can't remember where."

"I'm going to make some soup," Mira said.

* * *

Aster woke again in late afternoon, still warm, but Mira thought the fever was lower. She had Aster breathe more steam and drink another cup of tea, and then fed her a mug of soup, spoon by slow spoon, while the mother stood in a corner by the door, whispering prayers. Once Aster's brothers peeked in, their expressions more curious than concerned. The grandmother swiftly ushered them out again.

"The doctor said she should take wine," Aster's father said from the doorway.

Mira shook her head. "Too strong," she said. "Maybe in a day or two, to help her sleep, but now she needs soup. Soup and tea."

Mira spent that night on a chair beside Aster's bed, dozing with her chin on her chest. Once in the night she woke from a dream that she was standing in a field of bones. Before her was a low hill, and beyond it a starless sky. On the hill stood a figure in a pale nightdress, and as Mira watched she turned. Sitting up, heart in her head, Mira reached out and gripped Aster's hand. In a low voice she sang the charm, not to calm her this time, but to call her; to call her down from that hill. Aster's fingers, which had been chilly, grew warm. After a while, Mira slept again.

She woke to a gush of light and a clatter. Jerking her head up, she realized morning had broken and the doctor was in the room—he'd thrown open the curtains and was standing at the foot of the bed. The clatter was his gleaming fleam in a kidney-shaped enamel pan.

"Well, let's see how the patient is this morning," he said.

Kneading a crick in her neck, Mira watched as he bent over the bed. He touched Aster's forehead, listened to her heartbeats and breathing, then straightened. His lips worked as he tried to suppress his triumph. He turned to Aster's mother and father, both squeezed into the doorway.

"My treatments have proven efficacious," he said. "She is showing significant improvement. The fever is down, and her lungs are much clearer." He reached into the basin and picked up the fleam. Mira knew he was going to take more of Aster's blood, and knew it would weaken her. Crafting a small spell with her left hand, she cast it surreptitiously, and the doctor cleared his throat. Dropping the fleam into the pan once more, he placed both in his bag and snapped it closed.

"Aren't you going to release her blood?" Aster's father said. "Yesterday you said it was too thick."

The doctor looked out the window and shook his head slightly.

"That will not be necessary," he said. Frowning, he tapped his rectangular spectacles into place. Then he picked up his bag, and a moment later was clacking out of the room.

Mira turned to Aster and stroked the hair away from her forehead. "You're getting better," she said. Aster nodded, and the ghost of her dimple flickered in her cheek. Mira stood and drew the curtains. "Let her rest," she told Aster's mother and grandmother. "When she wakes up, more tea, more steam, more soup. I'll go to the chocolaterie now, but I'll come by this afternoon to see how she's doing."

* * *

After that, Aster improved rapidly. In two days her cough was gone. Her appetite returned, and she was able to eat a poached egg and toast. The following Saturday, as Rosa and Mira were having a midmorning cup of tea, the front bell jangled, and a moment later Aster came through the kitchen door. She was thinner, still pale, but the ashen hoops were gone from around her eyes and the bounce had returned to her hair. She leaned in the doorway and smiled at them. "I know, I know. I should still be resting," she said. "But it was such a pretty day out, and I really feel so much better."

"Come sit," said Mira. "I'll get you a cup of tea." As she turned to the stove, she listened to Aster's breathing. Her lungs were clearer, but she could still hear tiny sighs and whistles, like distant waterbirds.

Mira came back with a cup of tea, and Aster sipped. "Do you think I could have a chocolate? Just one?" she said.

Mira grinned. "Of course. I've been doing a little experimenting. These are lavender marshmallow."

Aster selected one and ate it with her eyes closed. "Unbelievable," she said. "It's like eating a cloud." She opened her eyes. "Mother says you didn't leave my side. She says you spent the night by my bed, reading and singing to me."

"Just one night," Mira said.

"I don't know how I can repay you."

"Seeing you enjoy a truffle is all the payment I need."

"But where did you learn all of that?"

"All of what?"

"You know: making the teas, singing the songs. Grandmother said it was like the old times. Like the old healers."

"I was wondering the same thing," Rosa said. "How did you know just what to take from the shelves? And those plants you brought in. How did you know where to find them? It's uncanny."

Mira, trapped, stared into her teacup. She shook her head slowly. "I can't say," she said softly.

"It's a secret," Aster said.

"No. Not a secret, but ... well, it's like making chocolates. A mixture of knowledge and intuition. You figure out what works. I'm glad you're feeling better. I'm glad I could help."

"I saw you in one of my dreams," Aster said. "You were standing in a field, singing, and you held out your hand. Your face ... your face was like a fire. Like a flame in the darkness." She gave an involuntary shiver. "Listen, we're going to the big cathedral tomorrow to give thanks for my recovery. All of us—Rosa too. Mother wants you to come. I know you don't go to church, but you'll come for me, won't you? Please?" She reached across the marble and tucked her sticky fingers into Mira's palm.

Mira looked up at the round steam-filmed pane in the door. Refusal would mark her even more starkly. A drop slid, etching a meandering iridescent path. "I'll come," she said softly.

* * *

The next day, she arrived at the cathedral a good half hour early and loitered beneath a fig tree in the courtyard. She hadn't come to this space since the first evening in the city, and once again was struck by the leaden circles of power that emanated from the enormous structure. As the chanting of the priests swelled from the black maw, families began arriving, the faces of the boys shiny from scrubbing, the girls' hair neatly bound. And Mira realized she should have stolen a fresh set of clothes—there were freckles of chocolate on the hem of her dress and butter stains on her sleeves, and her headscarf was fraying at one corner. It couldn't be helped, though.

Rosa arrived, late as usual, just as the chimes were beating ten, followed a few steps behind by her balding little husband and Aster and her family, Aster striking in a frock and headscarf of dark blue, the boys with hair impeccably parted and tamped.

"Come!" Aster exclaimed, reaching for Mira's hand. "The mass is about to begin."

Though every instinct tugged her back, Mira went with them into the cathedral, into the heart of the city's dreadful power, its leaden weight pressing on her shoulders. The holy stench carried her back to the church in her town: hair oil, incense, urine, soap ...

But the interior was vast; much larger than she'd anticipated: tremendous stems of polished black rock rising to a peak far above.

She squeezed onto a pew beside Aster and looked around. They were a third of the way down the aisle. Stained-glass windows as tall as houses lined the walls. Unlike those of the church in her town, these were jewel-bright, casting moments of stunning cherry, sunflower, kingfisher blue across cheeks and forearms. A hundred feet up, sparrows flickered, leaving whorled wakes in the tinted incense. In the distance, on a dais, the black-clad priests moved, bearing crosses and censers. Nine high-backed chairs stood behind the altar, set before a vast crimson curtain embroidered with gold crosses. Eight of the priests were swaying and droning as they bustled about, assisted by a dozen altar boys in spotless robes. How good they must be, Mira thought—how decent, obedient, steadfast—to serve in the central cathedral in a city this size.

The ninth priest, who wore a taller, more elaborate hat, sat on the middle chair, scanning the congregation, and Mira realized with a lurch of horror that he was the priest who had overseen the burning before the convent. His eyes were shadowed. On his lap he held the short black staff, which he caressed incessantly as his eyes roamed. Despite the salt in his beard, he didn't seem old, though he certainly wasn't young either. His head swiveled slowly side to side, scanning, and a chill shook her, so violently that Aster put a hand on her knee and gave her an inquiring glance. Mira summoned a wavering smile, but slid lower on the bench, resisting the urge to dash down the aisle. Though she knew it was reckless to use magic in this space, she quickly crafted a small deflecting spell from Mrs. Zaccaroth's cookbook, casting it with a little twist of her hands and a whisper she hoped Aster would interpret as a prayer. At the moment the spell took hold, she felt the priest's gaze stutter slightly. His head moved more swiftly across the crowd, but the spell was sound: his eyes slipped across her and passed on.

The droning music of the priests came to an end and the whole congregation sang a hymn from the familiar burgundy book, Aster holding it out so Mira and Rosa could see. There was a scripture reading from an enormous Bible on a stand, another hymn, another reading, and then the ninth priest rose for the first time. He wasn't tall or short, thin or fat; just a medium-size man with a trimmed beard and immense power. He moved without haste to the lectern and looked across the crowd, and again Mira felt a slight stammer as his gaze slipped across her spellcast chrysalis. His power was breathtaking, like a fist, like a heel. A power utterly unlike that of Mrs. Zaccaroth or Mother Gotha—his flame, if he chose to summon it, would be pure, white, steady, keen as a blade.

He placed his hands on either side of the lectern. Silence fell.

"Dearly beloved," he said, his voice an iron bell. "Dearly beloved, I greet you in the name of all that is holy. We sit here within these sanctified walls, within this sanctified city, whose foundations are formed of prayer, whose walls are mortared with prayer, whose doorways are fortified with prayer. You are in a sanctuary; a sanctuary so secure that it may seem as you prepare your meals and sing your children to sleep and walk to your places of work that peace reigns across the world. And yet we know from the scripture readings we heard today that demons run rampant beyond these defenses. They are seeking entrance; they are prying at the doors, at the windows, at the walls of your hearts and minds. Some of you have seen them, perhaps; some of you have felt their claws in your dreams. They are knocking at the gates of your thoughts."

A sigh rippled across the congregation. Once again he scanned the rows, his head moving slowly right to left, left to right. "I can feel them," he said, voice rising slightly. "Even within these walls I can feel them trying to enter. But they cannot. They are thwarted. They are held by your prayers, your vigilance.

"I hear the muttering among the youth, among the housewives. Yes, I hear your muttering, even at night, even in your homes, when you imagine you are in private. Muttering that the walls are oppressive, that the locks and shutters are oppressive, that the headscarves are oppressive. You desire freedom—that is what you mutter when you think no one is listening. When you think you are beyond earshot of a priest, of a holy man or a woman of the orders. You desire release. Release us from this oppression, you say. Tear down the walls, shatter the shutters, rip the headscarves from your hair, let your hair loose, let it down. This is what I hear you saying. But that is what they are waiting for ..."

Again he paused, scanning the congregation, and Mira could sense his unease—he was searching; he knew there was a morsel of recalcitrance among the lapping waves of upturned faces.

"Yes, that is what they are waiting for," he said. "They are waiting for that chink, for that crack, so they can pounce. And once they are within, it is all but impossible to turn them back. Even as I speak, priests and sisters of the orders are laboring in other rooms across the city, toiling to cast out demons from the breasts of the young, from the minds of the wayward."

Mira was accustomed to daydreaming during services, her

thoughts flitting about like the lofty sparrows, but this priest with the elaborate hat seized her attention and she couldn't shake free. His voice was a net, binding them, securing them. No snores rose here, and even the restlessness of the children was tamed.

The sermon lasted the better part of an hour, and ended with another admonition that the demons were attempting to breach the walls. He led the congregation in an antiphonal prayer, which Mira realized after a few phrases was a spell, designed to bring the audience under his power. As soon as she understood this, she ceased reciting, closing her eyes until the chant was over. The high priest returned to his chair at the center of the nine. They sang another hymn, and it was time for communion.

Now, as the first rows filed forward to receive the bread and wine, Mira found herself in a predicament. She knew she couldn't approach the priest—up close, her spell of concealment would splinter. He would recognize her; he would know what she was, even as she knew what he was. But neither could she stay seated— that would mark her out just as surely. Her heart knocked in her throat and she clenched her hands between her knees, trying to decide what to do.

The priest intoned the sacred words. The audience sang the hymn of the sacrament, and the rows filed forward, and then it was their turn.

"This is us," Aster whispered, but still she sat. Rosa leaned across Aster and patted Mira's arm, nodding. "Stand up, Mira," she said. Aster pinched Mira's thigh, and she lurched up and stumbled into the aisle, feeling faces turn toward her. For a moment she stood there, a rip in the net, a rock in the river, while the congregants surged around her. And then she knew she had to get out. She turned, burst through the throng, and ran, soles beating on the polished black floor, toward the tall column of daylight at the entrance of the church.

"Close the doors!" the high priest shouted, and the offertory hymn faltered. To either side of her a robed man leaped forward, but they were too late. She was already over the threshold and bounding down the steps, out of the courtyard, dashing along the river like a flake of ash in a gale, ducking into a slot of shadow, through the tangled alleys, and back to the ticking, reeking solitude of the clocktower.

* * *

Most Sunday afternoons she went wandering, but the rest of that day she sat on her clocktower perch, knees clutched to her chest, not daring to brew a cup of tea, not daring to peer over the walls, hardly daring to think. The tremendous force of the high priest's shout remained with her, as if his voice had been a spear and the point was lodged between her shoulder blades. She could feel his mind prying, prowling, even now, probing the crannies of the city for her; but she knew as well that she was hidden. She had successfully concealed herself within the church, and what he'd seen as she darted out the door must have been little more than a silhouette. If she didn't make magic, she might remain hidden.

* * *

Mira was terrified to leave the tower the next morning, but she hadn't eaten anything since breakfast the day before, and besides, it was best to pretend everything was normal. The morning was overcast and malodorous, a lid of fog penning the smoke within the city walls. The tops of the buildings were scuffed with mist, like a charcoal sketch imperfectly erased. Elbows on the balustrade of the bridge, Mira allowed her gaze to founder along with the river into the pallor. Shapes seemed to writhe within the banks of fallen cloud, beckoning at the corners of her vision, but she could never quite catch them.

She lingered a little longer on the bridge than she normally did, and Rosa had already opened up the chocolaterie by the time Mira arrived. She turned from the stove and spread her arms. "Mira! I thought you weren't going to come this morning. What happened yesterday? Why did you run off so suddenly like that?"

Mira pulled one of the stools over to the marble island and sat with her head bowed. "I'm sorry," she said.

"Did you get sick?" Rosa asked. "That's what I told my husband—you must have felt sick all of a sudden."

Mira looked up and nodded slowly. "Yes," she said. "I felt sick. I'm sorry." And it was not far off the truth.

"Oh, my little darling!" Rosa exclaimed. She came round the side of the island and folded Mira into her plump embrace. "And still you came to work today. Aren't you the angel!" She pulled Mira from her bosom and regarded her. "You're pale! But look, today you aren't going to do a thing. You took care of Aster when she was sick; today I'll take care of you. I'll set you up in the corner here with a nice cup of milky tea, and you can just snooze the day away."

And though Mira protested feebly, that's what she ended up doing—curled on the tatterdemalion owl-colored armchair in a corner of the kitchen where Rosa sometimes took a nap on slow afternoons. She sipped tea and ate a slice of buttered toast, and for lunch Rosa made some clear broth with tiny noodles in it. She drifted off in early afternoon, and woke from a nightmare that she was standing on the bridge, as she had been that morning, but now she could see the shapes clearly: hands were emerging from the filthy fog, reaching for her.

The round-paned door banged open and Rosa rushed in. "Mira! I heard you screaming. Are you all right?"

Mira blinked, pressing damp hands to her cheeks. "Bad dream," she murmured.

"Oh, poor child. And you're soaked in sweat. Here, sit up. Think about something pretty—that's what my mother used to say. Still does, in fact. I'll fetch you a glass of water."

Mira took the glass gratefully. She drank and looked up at the ceiling. Something pretty … She thought back to Mrs. Zaccaroth's aerie, chock-full of river light and fairytales, where she'd spend a morning reading on the dusty-rose fainting couch, Mr. Mugwort twitching at her toes, while Mrs. Zaccaroth whistled and clattered away in the kitchen below, making soup or bread or truffles …

Rosa bent to take her empty glass and halted. "What's that?" she asked.

Looking down, Mira realized the gold key on its chain had fallen from her collar and lay on the gray cloth like an ember.

"Oh!" Mira snatched at it, then relaxed. She sat up and held it out on her palm. "Just a keepsake," she said.

"It's beautiful," Rosa said. "What door does it open?"

Mira tucked the key back into her neckline. "I don't know," she said. "I wish I knew."

* * *

Since she'd landed in this city, Mira had sensed eyes—something, someone watching. And she'd recognized that the eyes, or whatever they were, watched for magic; watched for power. For that reason, she'd used magic sparingly here: to sway Rosa's mind, to steal clothes, to conceal herself from the high priest in the cathedral. Even that was probably too much, she now realized. Even those few moments of tampering had alerted the watchers, and they were prying toward her. She could feel them in her dreams, long fingers of light passing over while she cowered.

But nothing happened. She walked from the clocktower to the chocolaterie and back, and no one paid her any more attention than usual. She went on her shopping expeditions, and the shopkeepers and fruit sellers greeted her with the same enthusiasm: "The chocolate girl! What will you have today?" Everything's all right, she told herself. Everything's normal. You're just working yourself into a panic.

Three days passed. Aster didn't come, and Mira didn't ask about her. She made truffles and soups. She drank tea. She went shopping. And nothing happened, though still at night she'd wake with her mouth dry, and was sure she'd been screaming. Nevertheless, she was able to convince herself that the danger was over, that she'd managed to elude the watchers. She allowed herself to relax.

But on the fourth day after the incident in the cathedral, when she arrived at the chocolaterie, Rosa was there before her, and instantly Mira knew something was wrong. Rosa didn't meet her eyes as she bent to unlock the grating, and she glanced down the street as she opened the door.

Once they were inside, she took off her headscarf and set the water to boil as usual, but then sat at the marble island and shook her head slightly.

"What is it?" Mira asked, trying to keep the thrum out of her voice. "Is it your mother?"

"Oh, Mira," Rosa said. "What have you done?" Her voice was hoarse, and she peered at Mira through a toppled scallop of hair. "Oh, Mira, Mira …"

A quiver went up Mira's spine. "What do you mean?" she said. "I haven't done anything. I mean, nothing out of the ordinary. Not that I can think of."

Rosa glanced back at the round pane in the door. "Last night," she said, and stopped. "I shouldn't be telling you this." She was silent for a minute. Then the teapot shrieked, making her jump. She took it off the flame and made the tea. Carrying the cups over to the marble island, she set one beside Mira, and went over to the tray of misshapen truffles they set aside and brought it over and sat popping them into her mouth, one after another, staring at the wall opposite, munching.

As she had the first day in the chocolaterie, Mira reached gently into Rosa's mind and with a charm breathed into her tea was able to prod her into release.

Rosa looked down at the tray of truffles, as if surprised to see them there. The dimples erased, though their ghosts remained: all-but-invisible creases in her cheeks. "You've always been a strange one," she said, glancing at Mira. "I knew. I knew something was different about you from the first day you stepped in, with your wild look and your way of … well, your strange way of knowing. But I'll tell you. You've become a companion, a friend, even, and I'll tell you." She sighed. "Last night, after we'd eaten our supper, after my mother had gone to bed, there was a knock. I didn't know who it could be—no one is out at that hour except doctors and watchmen. I opened the door and … oh, Mira, it was the high priest. The high priest from the cathedral, you know."

Mira's mouth had gone dry. Her teacup trembled as she bent to take a sip, but Rosa, immersed in her story, didn't notice.

"Well, what an honor. What an honor, to have a visit from the high priest! We invited him in and I made him tea and brought out a box of those raspberry-ganache truffles we made last week—my mother adores them—and he sat and talked with my husband for a while. He took a few sips of his tea (which he drinks black, by the way, one sugar), but he didn't touch the truffles. Didn't look at them. He talked with my husband and then, quite suddenly, he turned to me." Rosa lifted her hand to her forehead as though testing for a fever. "He turned to me and asked me about you. He has … he seems so mild, but his eyes are …"

"How did he know who I was?" Mira asked.

"Oh, he didn't. He didn't know your name, I mean. Well, he does now—I told him, of course. He just wanted to know who I'd brought to church that Sunday. It was because you'd run out so suddenly, see? If you'd just stayed … Anyway. He wanted to know who you were. So I told him."

"What did you tell him about me?" Mira asked, pressing once again with her mind.

"Just what you told me: you needed food, you worked for tea and soup and a truffle or two." She gave a thin smile. "Also, of course, that you could perform miracles in the kitchen. And that you helped Aster when she had the ash sickness—gave her teas and sang to her. He seemed quite impressed by that. He wanted to know who your parents were, where you lived, but of course I don't know that, so I couldn't tell him, could I?"

"No," Mira said. "No." She picked up her mug and blew on it and set it down without drinking. The little charm she'd worked to get Rosa to talk had been a mistake, she now realized. She got down from her stool. "I'm heading out," she said, voice steady now. "I'll be gone for a little while."

"Where are you going?" Rosa asked, but Mira shook her head.

She went through the swinging door into the shop, past the glass cabinets of truffles, and out the front door, the tinkle of the bell a sad little farewell melody. For a moment she stood in the doorway, glancing right, then left. Though the street was empty, she had a sudden vision that the hands from her nightmares were crawling toward her across the cobbles like immense gray spiders. She hesitated, but knew she couldn't go back inside. The shop was a trap. She went left, tugging the headscarf over her cheeks, resisting the urge to run, and as she reached the end of the street, drawn by a sound or some other impulse, she turned and looked back.

At the far end, where the street ended in a T, a figure strode around the corner and halted. She would almost have taken him for a silhouette—he wore a black robe and a black hat—but his face was a pale smear, his eyes pockets of shadow.

Even as she turned to flee, she saw his hands rise, the long sleeves like black wings, and invisible chains slipped around her mind, around her ankles. Furious, she beat them back, and was able to take a step, then another, but a second robed figure stepped around the corner and bore down upon her. "Get her mouth!" a voice called, and she swung back, just in time to see a black curtain sweeping over her head: a sack of some soft material, laden with charms and incense. A hand mashed into her lips. Already half shackled by the high priest's curse, she could muster no resistance to this soft cage. Within the fragrant darkness, she felt herself falling, tried and failed to fling out her hands, and her head smacked the cobbles.

* * *

She woke blind, with a headache like a hot tack in her left temple, tapped deeper with each heartbeat. She tried to lift a hand to touch her head, but couldn't shift her arms.

"She's awake," a man's voice said. "Test her bindings."

The voice was a stone cast into the pool of silence, rippling out, diminishing. Footsteps beat toward her, with the same resonant quality—she wondered if her pounding head was tampering with the sound. Someone fumbled and tugged at her wrists and ankles.

"Take it off," the voice said.

And a moment later she was blinking dully in a shaft of ruby light. To either side stone ribs rose, and she realized she was sitting in the center of the cathedral, in the space before the dais. The high priest sat in his chair, holding his short black staff across his body like a bludgeon. The other chairs were empty. Beside her a black-robed man stood. She tried to lift her head to see his face, but twisting her neck amplified the pain, so she sat straight, watching the high priest through the tormented motes in the ruby beam.

The high priest tapped his staff. He stood and came down the steps, halting at the edge of the scarlet islet. For the first time, Mira could see his eyes. Beneath the bristly shelves of his brows they were bits of glass: triangles of broken glass stuck into his skull.

"What have we here?" he murmured. He raised the staff, his lips moving, and she felt clasps tightening around her mind. This was strong magic, but a magic entirely different in flavor and tone from Mrs. Zaccaroth's or even Mother Gotha's.

Mrs. Zaccaroth's magic was like her house and her garden and her recipes: freeform, piecemeal, adapted and adaptable. Mother Gotha's charms had been soft, spreading, amorphous as wool: Mira had sunk within them, floundering. But the clamps the high priest closed on Mira's mind were cold iron: sharp-edged, unyielding. And for a moment she felt utter panic. She scrambled for a spell that might free her, but the iron band would not allow her to craft magic.

Yet somehow, even within her terror, even as the band drew tighter, she recognized that its unyielding nature was both its strength and its weakness. Forcing herself to stay calm, she sensed chinks on either side of the priest's iron clasp where she might form coherent thoughts.

Reaching out with his staff, the high priest tugged the scarf away from Mira's hair.

"A little witch," he said. "A little redhead witch. And how is it we haven't seen you here before, hm? How did you manage to evade the nets?" His glass-shard eyes glittered scarlet in the shaft of light. He took a step back, and they were colorless once more.

He turned to the man beside her. "Go inform the Mother that we have a present for her. We'll be along shortly."

She heard footsteps retreating, and then the snicker of the shutting door.

The high priest stood watching her, holding the smooth black staff across his torso. Mira could feel her cheek twitching with the throb of the headache and tried to hold her head still.

"A little redhead witch. Maybe … what? Thirteen? Fourteen?

That woman, the woman who makes sweetmeats. You told her you needed food. You worked for food. So: no home. Or no home you could go to." His eyes never left her face, and he ran a finger continually along the staff, base to cross, cross to base. "Were you banished from your home, for performing witchcraft perhaps?" His eyebrows bent, arced. "No," he said. "No, I don't think so. We'd have heard of it here. So you've been in hiding. Where? How?"

Mira could feel his prying like cold fingers leafing through the damp folds of her brain, and she squirmed, then forced herself to remain still. The pain spasmed in her temples.

The high priest was silent so long that the ruby beam slipped over the toes of his shoes. When next he spoke, his tone had shifted. It was less ruminative: he was now speaking to her rather than to himself. Still his finger ran along the shaft.

"It must have been difficult," he said. "Out on the streets, with no one to help. Hungry. Lonely. If you'd come to us, to the church, we would have given you food, found you a place to stay. You know that, don't you?"

Mira closed her eyes and breathed.

"We are here to help," he said. "To assist those less fortunate. The waifs. The vagabonds. The urchins. Those without family. And in return, we ask only for honesty. For acceptance. You can't receive a gift with a fist, can you? No. No, of course not. You must open your hand." He demonstrated, lifting his right hand from the staff. "Only with an open hand can you receive."

Again he fell silent. Mira opened her eyes. Her head quivered slightly from the strain of countering his will.

The crimson stain crept up the hem of his garment. After a while, without shifting, he gave a laugh, surprisingly genuine, that set the motes swirling. "It has been some time," he said, "quite some time, since I came across strength like yours. Impressive." The laughter lingered at the corners of his mouth, though his eyes remained as sharp as ever. "Oh, we'll break you," he said. "Have no fear of that. We'll break you eventually. You see"—he leaned forward slightly— "joined voices are always stronger. You're alone, without a family, without support. And that will be your undoing."

Mira wondered if she could tug the shaft from his hand, send it toppling to the floor. Perhaps it would shatter. But as soon as she began to press, the high priest shook his head. "No," he said. "None of that. It won't work in this space." And the bands squeezed so tightly against her mind that she let out a whimper.

"Ah, so you do have a voice." His smile was not unkind, and the band loosened. "Now, no more of that, please, and we'll all do very well." He held the staff upright between them, and for the first time Mira understood its purpose: he was able to somehow channel his power through it. Similar to the way Mrs. Zaccaroth's corroded mirror and mineral spheres let her mind get loose, the length of polished black stone allowed the priest to focus his strength.

"You will not obey now," he said. "I recognize that. But after you have been broken you will obey. And then you will know that we are not harsh masters; no, we are not tyrants. But we cannot allow the demons back into our city. We cannot."

She heard the door of the cathedral open, and the high priest raised his head. He nodded.

Footsteps approached. And then the hood dropped over her eyes once more.

X

THE CONVENT OF THE SISTERS OF THE LIGHT

Reverberating fragments of moans and sighs. Nine blades of light pulsed with her pounding head. She squeezed her eyes closed and they vanished. Opened them. Nine shapes smeared against the dark. Gingerly she stretched her limbs and tested the cords of her neck, gathering her surroundings.

She was sitting on the clammy floor of a cell. In the wall opposite was a low iron door with a palm-size grate near the top. Above the lintel the nine shapes hovered, and she twisted to see the barred window a dozen feet above her head. But as she twisted she yelped: her bruised temple had touched the stone.

After a while, she crawled over to the door, pulled herself to her feet, and peered through the grate. She was looking across a narrow corridor at the grate in another iron door. The voices were louder here, though still unintelligible—sobs and scarred songs of ghosts, luminous with a mangled power. They swirled like river currents, like moon shards in her skull, and she realized they were the voices of incarcerated girls. Like Mrs. Zaccaroth and Mother Gotha before her, she was an inmate in the Convent of the Sisters of the Light. She put a hand to her breast. The key was gone.

"Hello?" she called cautiously, relieved to find her tongue free. There was no reply, and the grate across from her remained dark.

She knew even before she set her mind to them that the locks were sealed with binding spells; nevertheless, she pressed at the doorlatch, urging. It was no use—the locks did not even rattle. If she could get up to the window, though, even to look out upon the world … She ran her hands over the stone, but it was slick with damp.

Returning to her corner, Mira gave a bitter chuckle that rattled around the walls and up through the lofty window. Briefly she wondered why they hadn't chained the voices of the imprisoned girls, and then she knew—they were listening. They were listening to the screams, the moans, the songs, the pleas, the confessions.

Time was the rising and falling, dimming and brightening of the nine shapes of light on the dark, damp stone. Once in a while a chance breeze wafted the chimes of the clocktower through the lofty window, but they were too faint and fractured to decipher the hour. Night did not diminish the voices of the other girls; if anything, it heightened their anguish. She was unable to keep out the clamor or ignore it, as she had the much louder chimes in the clocktower. The voices reminded her of the voices of the demons, which had also kept her awake night after night, but these were even more horrifying because they were so similar to her own voice—she could sense the warped, twisted power, the agony of thwarted witchery, cauterized spellcraft.

For a day and a night she sat squeezed into a corner of the cell, cursing her ill fortune, cursing this rat-ridden city and its locked doors and walls of black stone, cursing even Aster for getting sick and Rosa for her meek acquiescence to the priest. At last she wondered if she would die here, and she recognized some of the wailing as cries of thirst and hunger. She would not cry. She would not give them the satisfaction of hearing her cry, hearing her plead. She would rather die.

* * *

She entered a zone of hallucinations, in which the stone walls wavered like wet black silk, hands pressing, faces pressing into them, gaping mouths printed. So, when footsteps halted and two blunt shapes appeared beneath the door, she wasn't sure if it was dream or reality. But then the decidedly ordinary scent of soup was in her nostrils, and she blinked and jerked. She crawled across the cold stone and tugged the bowls toward her. Two wooden bowls, one of water, one of thin lentil gruel. Kneeling, she drank the water in one long draft and sat panting, feeling it enter the dry places in her bones, her heart. Then she carefully carried the other bowl back to her corner. She sipped the soup slowly, cherishing the warmth, making it last, and licked out the shallow bowl till it was spotless. The nine shapes of light were high on the wall, tarnishing, diminishing. Soon they would be gone.

Footsteps and a sudden clang on the door, making her drop the bowl. A pause, and the clang again, louder. "Bowls," came a woman's voice, harsh. So Mira gathered up the bowls and slid them under the door. Standing, she peered out the grate, but the woman was gone. Receding footsteps, dull tones of wood on wood. And then the moans rose again.

So began a routine that lasted for days, perhaps weeks. Each evening, bowls of water and soup were slipped under the door, then collected. She was never able to get warm, never able to get clean. She developed a cough. For a few days, she was able to subdue it with chants and charms, but then she grew too weak, and lacked the necessary herbs, the necessary human touch to resist it. The cough grew worse, and she woke one day from hectic dreams and knew she had a fever.

"I'm sick," she called when the woman arrived to collect the bowls. But the woman merely rapped louder. So Mira, coughing, crawled over until she could nudge the bowls out. She tried to crawl back to her corner but didn't make it; she slumped on the damp floor.

She was still in the same position when the banging came again—she had been comatose for a night and a day. This time she was unable to call. Though she was terribly thirsty, she was unable to reach for the bowl of water sliding away from her. She closed her eyes and entered a realm of shadows. Dusty cobblestones. Patterns of bones. A dark staircase. And then, as always, the turning figure in the window …

* * *

She woke into an idyll so easeful she thought it was another dream. She was lying beneath a white counterpane in a white room with white curtains. For a long time she simply lay looking at the curtains, which shifted in a small breeze, pearlescent shadows arcing across their folds. Somewhere, not far away, a girl was singing.

Struggling to sit up, she started coughing again—rich, rib-wracking hacks. The fever was gone, though, and the chill had left her bones.

"Just rest."

Mira turned to see a woman sitting in a chair. She wore a gray robe and a gray headscarf. In her lap was an open book.

The woman looked at Mira with kind, tired eyes. "Would you like some water?" She poured a glassful from a jug on the bedside table and held Mira's head while she drank and coughed and drank again. When the water was gone, the woman dabbed Mira's lips with a cloth and laid her head against the pillow once more. It had been months since she'd slept in a bed with a counterpane and a pillow; it was delicious, but even more than the scented softness she relished the woman's touch and voice.

"Do you think you could take some broth?" the woman asked. "It would help."

Mira nodded.

The woman unlocked the door and the singing ceased. She spoke to someone, and then locked the door again and returned to her reading.

Mira coughed, clearing the rags from her throat. "Could you read to me?" she asked. Her voice, unused for so long, sounded strange.

"Of course." And as the woman read the old words, Mira was wafted back to her house in the town. It was Sunday evening, and her mother was reading from the Bible as Mira embroidered a crow onto calico and Paulus dipped a sesame cookie into a glass of milk and her father snored softly in his armchair ... Old soothing words, like the pebbles by the river shore, polished by the passage of time.

The broth arrived, carried by a girl Mira's age, dressed in brown. She gave Mira a furtive glance as she handed the tray across the threshold.

The woman plumped the pillow against the headboard and helped Mira sit up and placed the tray on her thighs. As Mira sipped the lemony broth, the woman returned to her chair and read on.

Before Mira had finished half the bowl, weariness overcame her. The woman took the tray and Mira slid down onto her left side, embracing the pillow, and entered a sleep blessedly free of dreams.

When she woke, a different sister was sitting in the chair, though she too had an open Bible in her lap.

"Are you feeling any better?" the woman asked softly.

Mira nodded.

The woman closed the Bible and stood. "Would you like some breakfast?"

Mira tried to speak, but had to cough for a minute first. "Breakfast?" she managed at last.

The woman smiled. "You slept for fifteen hours. It's morning."

Mira blinked at her.

"So. Breakfast? Perhaps a boiled egg? Toast?"

Mira nodded, eyes abruptly awash. She was unaccustomed to kindness.

Her coughing finally subsided on the third day. She hadn't been left by herself for a minute of that time—a succession of sisters in gray habits occupied the corner chair, and there always seemed to be a girl outside the door waiting to carry out errands.

That evening, on the arm of the attendant sister, she shuffled out of the room and through a tangle of gray hallways and twisting stairways, past dozens of doors. In front of many of the doors sat brown-garbed girls on stools. A few stole glances at Mira; most kept their heads down. From behind some of the doors Mira heard murmuring, and knew that in these rooms other witches lay convalescing under counterpanes, sipping soup, listening to Bible passages, watching the breezes sway the white curtains. At the end of the hallway a sister sat before a door, and as they approached she stood and gave a single knock. A voice from within summoned them.

The Mother Superior reigned from a corner room. Like a queen termite, though one barren of eggs, she lay on a bed like a barge, reclining on piled pillows, flesh rippling under yards of gray cotton, eyes glossy caramels within the bags of skin. Above the headboard, a candle in a wall sconce wavered before an icon of the Virgin. There was a sour smell; a smell of clogged drains, of dough left too long. On the bedside table lay a box Mira recognized with a jolt: it was from Rosa's Chocolaterie—there was the stylized rosebud embossed into the black lid. Breathing in, Mira caught, beneath the rot, hazelnut, rum, and raisin; one of her own favorites.

A chair stood by the bed, and the Mother twitched a finger, its flesh dented by a ring with a cross of rubies. The sister nudged Mira toward the chair and retreated to the corner by the door.

"You may be wondering why you are here." Mira had expected an adenoidal gasp, but the Mother's voice was surprisingly pretty: warm, smooth, soft as cotton candy. She could taste the power in it.

Mira shook her head.

"You're not wondering?" the Mother said, and though her voice remained warm, her caramel eyes glittered.

"No. I know why I'm here." Mira closed her eyes.

"Why are you here, child?"

"I'm a witch." She opened her eyes in time to see the Mother's lips compress, contorting the flesh of her cheeks.

"You will not use that word again," she said.

Mira nodded wearily.

"Where is your family?" the Mother asked.

Mira shook her head.

"You don't know?"

She sighed. "I know where they are. I can't tell you."

The Mother shifted, sending tremors across the voluminous robe. "Child, this is not a game."

Even as she spoke, Mira felt a finger in her mind, and realized with horror that the woman had been prying the whole time, stealthily as spreading mold. She pressed back. There was a slight tussle and, to Mira's surprise, the Mother's head subsided against her pillow.

"We don't play games here," she said, panting. "We don't play those games."

"All right," Mira said mildly.

"This is serious. This is your life."

"All right," Mira said again. She looked toward the window. The curtains were parted on a view of the courtyard below, where the tapered tower stood, honeysuckle licking up its sides. Wings of char bloomed from the girl-size hollow near the top. Dark pocket of horror. Behind it, the cathedral was sharp as cut black paper against the late-afternoon sky, and beyond that were a few sparkling trapezoids of river and a distant watchtower. She looked back at the Mother.

The Mother tapped lightly at her ruby ring. "What many fail to understand," she said. "What many fail to understand, at least at first, is that they have a choice. You have a choice, child. A choice between chaos and calm, between the light and the dark, between the cold cell and the warm room."

Mira was silent. A great hush had fallen across the world; she couldn't even hear the carts on the cobbles below. The Mother had ceased tapping, and was now pressing her fingers into the flesh of her wrist, fans of bloodless white spreading at the corners of her nails.

Mira stared at the woman's fingers, and that tension seemed to travel along the line of her gaze and into her belly. She couldn't speak. She didn't know what to say, and she was so tired ... so terribly, terribly tired.

"Do you know how to pray?" the woman asked.

Mira nodded mutely.

The Mother glanced at the sister who had brought Mira in, and Mira felt a hand on her upper arm, pulling her to her feet.

"You will come again tomorrow," the Mother said. "In the meantime, pray. Pray as if your life depends on it, child. Because it does. It does."

Back in the white room, the sister tried to talk to her, but Mira didn't answer. She lay with her face turned to the white curtain, watching the shadows curl as it belled and caved. She could, she thought, place a binding spell on the sister and leap out of bed, through the window, plummeting to smash her head on the cobblestones. But not now, not now. The bed was too comfortable and she was too tired. She closed her eyes.

At some point during the night, she woke. The lamp was on, and a different gray-robed woman sat turning the pages.

"Was I screaming?" Mira asked.

"No." The woman gave a narrow, exhausted smile. "No, that was a new girl being brought in."

A chill ran out to her fingertips, tickled the base of her skull. "Where did they take her?"

"To the cells."

"Will they bring her here? I mean, to a room like this?"

"If she repents, yes."

"How many girls are down there in the cells?" Mira whispered.

The woman shook her head.

"A hundred?"

"Oh, many more than that, child. Many more than that."

"And how many has the high priest burned?"

The woman was silent for a while, looking down at the book. Then, in a quieter voice, she said, "Only a handful have chosen the Sentinel. It has proven an effective deterrent."

* * *

The next afternoon, the Mother seemed less angry, less tense. A fresh box of cherry chocolates lay on the bedside table, and a chocolate fingerprint decorated the open prayerbook beside it. "You look better," she said. "How is your cough?"

"Almost gone, I think," Mira said.

"Excellent. You needed what we all need. Rest. Recuperation in the light. Nourishment. And, of course, the nourishing words of the Bible. The sisters tell me you have asked them to read to you."

Mira nodded.

"That is good. You are on the path to healing, to acceptance. And have you been praying, as I asked?" She shifted on the pillow, panting, and as the folds of her neck parted something glinted.

Mira hadn't gotten a look at the object itself, but now she saw, on a swell of flesh, the print of ornate wards, and felt the flames rise to her face.

"Have you been praying, child?" the Mother said again, a little more gruffly.

"No."

The woman's face seemed to harden, as if the folds had turned to marble. "What?" she asked.

"No, I haven't been praying."

The Mother let out a slow, whistling breath through her nose. "You must use this time," she said, and Mira could hear the pulse of swelling anger. "You must use this time to think about your choices. The choices I laid out for you yesterday. Calm or chaos. The light or the dark. The room or the cell."

"I *have* been thinking," Mira said in a small, clear, furious voice, sitting straight in her chair, palms on her knees. She looked out the window at the Sentinel. At this hour, the angle of the light was lower. It reached into the hollow, catching the curve of an iron hoop bedded in the rock. Now she knew what those hoops were for. The curtains belled in a breeze and from the hollow a flake of ash drifted out like a moth wing. "I have been thinking," she repeated. "And I have made my choice. I choose chaos. I choose the dark. I choose to return to the cell."

* * *

Crouched once more in the damp, cold corner, knees clutched to her chest, Mira wept. Facing the Mother, rage had kept her sturdy, but now, recognizing that she had forsaken the counterpane and white curtain and sentenced herself to certain torment and possible doom, she shattered. Yet she also knew she'd made the right decision; the only decision she could have made. She was done with deceit. She'd tried with the priest in her town, had made a genuine effort to say the prayers, to change, to subdue her power, and had failed. No longer would she tread that path.

Unconsciously, Mira raised her hand to her neckline. But the key was gone and, like a fist to the belly, she remembered the Mother was wearing it now. The Mother, fed on Rosa's chocolates, pulsing and panting like a great grub among her pillows, beneath the candle and the icon. Mira gripped her dress in both fists, tugging, feeling the seams begin to strain before she released her hold. Toppling onto her side, she lay curled on the cold stone, her moans a strange animal sound now, a sound beyond weeping. She howled, and knew as she did so why the other girls howled in the cells. They howled because they had lost all reason not to, and it was easier to let it out than keep it in.

In torment, she writhed on the chilly flags. Impossible to get comfortable. Cold, damp, and there was something … something like a pebble pressing into her hip bone. Sitting up, she passed her hand across the floor to sweep away the pebble, but found nothing. Absolutely furious now, she got on her hands and knees and peered in the faulty light for a shadow, a shape, but the floor where she'd been sitting was as smooth as the walls. Letting out a shriek of frustration, Mira knelt and patted herself down, and finally found the offending object, lodged in the pocket of her dress. She held it up between thumb and forefinger.

It was smaller than she'd imagined—in fact, she had a hard time believing an object so small could have caused such discomfort. A dingy, linty little thing she was about to flick away. And then she remembered: it was the pomegranate seed she'd saved in the desert, in the parched oasis. The last seed of the last pomegranate of the five Mother Gotha had given her. And Mira's fury melted abruptly as she thought of old Gotha, solitary in her abbey, surrounded by the clapping and calling of crows, drinking peppermint tea and adding to her seven-year stew, and surely making magic now.

A seed. With her bitten fingernails, Mira scraped up all the grit and slime grouting the stone slabs, gathering it into a pile the size of a walnut. In this meager, malodorous hillock she buried the seed. A single leftover tear fell, salty raindrop. And then she returned to her corner, curled up once more, and this time was able to sleep.

* * *

She woke, mouth dry, heartbeats slow quakes, from one of the enormous dreams of change. A dream such as she hadn't had for well over a year. A dream that reminded her of the incident in Mrs. Zaccaroth's garden, when she'd been ensnared by vines, but in the dream, instead of fighting them, she was dancing with them, tendrils caressing her arms, twining up them into the sky. Sitting up, she blinked and rubbed her eyes. The room was almost entirely dark—even the lofty window snuffed. And then, with a lurch of horror, she saw a faint glimmer on tremendous limbs and sinews. Had she summoned a giant? But the limbs, though they took up most of the cell, did not stir. Slowly Mira stood, squeezed into the corner, and placed her hands on her breastbone as if she could press her heart into subsidence. Then she laughed.

During the night from the pomegranate seed had sprung, silently, with effortless force, a tree. Its trunk took up most of the cell. Seeking light, it had shoved through the bars in the window far above, carrying the iron window frame with it. Magic was no match for vegetable strength.

Without further ado, Mira set a foot and a hand on the tree trunk. It was easy to climb, and within a minute she'd reached the window and squirmed through, into moonlight and open air.

She was perched ten feet above a cobbled alley. There was no one around—she could swing from a branch and let go. Then she'd be free once more. Free to return to her clocktower or roam the streets or even find her way out of the city altogether … And then what? Would she make her way along the river, southward to her home? With nothing to show for it, and the key abandoned? She sighed and turned her eyes upward. The branches sprawled along the walls, enormous spindly fingers clutching the black stone, pomegranates suspended among the leaves like dark ornaments.

Slowly, painstakingly, Mira moved up the trunk, toes clinging to the fissured bark, awed that all this had sprung from that tiny seed … from the seed and her dream. At a fork, she chose the thicker branch and climbed up past slit windows, too narrow to enter. She peered in: rows of bunk beds. Soft forms beneath sheets striped in moonlight. Sniffles and sighs. Straddling a branch, she plucked a pomegranate and peeled and ate it, relishing the tartness after the days of bland lentils, relishing the open air, the smattering of lights in houses across the river, the shrieked whispers of rats and bats. When she was done, she plucked another and stuck it in her pocket.

She moved on, along a branch that grew ever slimmer and began to bow under her weight. Bobbing like a sparrow on a twig, she looked up. The lintel of a window was just out of reach … just … she just had to …

Gauging the branch's spring, she crouched, bounced once, twice, and then, using its energy, leaped, clutched, gripped the black sill. With the last of her strength, she scrabbled and squirmed her way upward until she had her torso over the edge. She glanced down. She was too high. There was no turning back now.

She looked into the room. It was small, with a narrow bed against the right-hand wall, a wooden stand beside it. On the stand were a lamp, a Bible, and a glass of water. Against the left-hand wall was a wardrobe of plain wood, one door half open, though she could make out nothing of the contents. On the bed a figure shifted and sighed and seemed about to sit up, but then subsided, an arm dangling.

For a minute, Mira clung to the sill, willing the sister into a deeper sleep. Then she inched through the window. Noiselessly, making sure her wayward hair didn't brush the woman's hanging fingers, she rolled under the bed, squeezing up against the wall. There she lay, exultant, hands at her breast, gazing up at the bowed slats of the cot, listening to the soft breathing a foot away from her face. In the distance, the clocktower beat thrice.

For two hours she lay there, not daring to sleep, hardly daring to breathe, willing the urge to cough into submission. At five, even as the clocktower was throbbing, a bell sounded somewhere within the convent. The slats above Mira's face bent as the woman yawned and groaned.

Two feet descended, and Mira had a moment of panic as they turned and the woman sank to her knees. Was she going to peer under the bed? Had Mira inadvertently let out a sound? But no, she was kneeling to pray. Mira could make out nothing of the groggy murmuring, interspersed with creaky yawns.

In the midst of her prayers, the door banged open.

"Have you looked out the window?" a voice said.

"What?" The kneeling sister's thighs shifted under her nightdress.

"The window. Look out."

The sister stood. And a moment later: "But how extraordinary. Where did it come from?"

"Magic," the first voice whispered. "Must be. Look, it comes out of one of the dungeon cells."

"You mean … ?"

"Yes. One of the inmates escaped. They're sending a party to search the streets. The Mother's in a panic. Even the priests are involved."

Beneath the bed, Mira grinned.

When the sisters left, she waited a few minutes, until all the footsteps had faded, and then rolled out from under the bed. Quickly she opened the wardrobe doors. Four habits on hangers, like thin gray ghosts. Mira tugged one on. A little long, but it would serve. In a drawer she found a gray headscarf, which she used to bind her hair. There were no spare sandals, though.

Out in the city, Mira had used magic sparingly. It was too dangerous—there were watchers. But the air of this convent was crackling with half-made spells, with furtive witchcraft. A little magic of her own would rouse no suspicions.

First, using a spell of duplication, she crafted an extra gray habit and headscarf, so those she'd stolen would not be missed at first glance. Then, working swiftly but carefully, she wove a spell from deep within Mrs. Zaccaroth's cookbook. True invisibility was all but impossible, Mrs. Zaccaroth had told her; however, it was possible to weave a fabric of deception around an object such that it would resemble something else to a casual observer. Mira didn't want to disappear; she wanted a passing sister to imagine she was one of their own. Though she was weary after the interrupted night and the climb, it was delightful to work magic once more, with small motions of hand and heart.

A moment later a new sister, barefoot, slender, in a habit a little too long for her, was pacing through the twisted corridors of the Convent of the Sisters of the Light.

* * *

A house of prayers and sighs, magic and madness. A house of gray walls and gray garments, the prayers and sighs like gray dust settling on tiles and windowsills and minds. There were no decorations here, no potted plants, no bookshelves. Only, on certain walls, small icons of the Virgin. And, of course, the Bible in every room. A house of a single book.

Mira moved swiftly, soundlessly through the chilly halls, keeping her head lowered when she passed a sister; the novices automatically averted their eyes. The sisters murmured as they passed, so Mira did as well: "In his light," "In his light." And as she murmured she shored up her spell of concealment, easing it into the phrase, like slipping a veil of gauze between her and the woman.

Concealed by spell and disguise, she passed down to the lower stories. One floor below was the hallway of white rooms where girls were brought to convalesce as she had been. Dozens of rooms, and outside each, on a stool, sat a brown-clad novice with a Bible on her lap and a glass of water beside her. As Mira walked down the hall, she heard from behind certain doors sighs and murmurs, and knew a sister was in conversation with a young witch, taming her, tuning the cords of her heart, tamping her mind into a mold.

One floor below that were the great dormitories where the girls slept: rooms of bunk beds, all immaculately made, the pillowcases smoothed, the top sheets turned back over thin gray blankets.

Beneath each set of beds were two chests. Mira lifted the lid of one. It was just a third full: neatly folded garments, a Bible, a box of toiletries. The wooden floorboards were laddered with light from the tall windows. One rung was truncated, and Mira turned to see a branch of the pomegranate tree wavering in the bright air. She grinned.

One floor below the dormitories were chambers filled with rustles and twitters and the occasional sharp voice. The door of one room stood ajar, and Mira glanced in to see shrouded heads bent over wooden desks, pens pecking, scratching. A sister stood at a lectern, droning from a Bible. Dictation. On the board behind her, in a spiky hand that reminded Mira of Mrs. Zaccaroth's, were a dozen difficult words, in a tidy row descending from the top left corner. The rest of the board was cloudy with erasures, but near the bottom Mira could just make out beneath an eddy of chalk dust a bird with raised wings. She wondered who'd drawn it—the sister in a moment of whimsy or one of the girls in a moment of mischief.

The center of the ground floor was an immaculate reception area, with a dove-gray carpet and cushioned armchairs and cross-stitched verses on the walls. To one side of the reception was the refectory: rows of wooden tables and benches, and beyond those a set of double doors with misted panes from which emerged a clamor and clang and an odor of scorched lentils. On the other side was a chapel a little smaller than the church in Mira's town. Even the chapel was austere: a cross of plain wood on the wall above the altar, pews without cushions, the wood polished to a gleam by countless cotton-clad backsides. As she stood in the aisle, she had the strangest notion that faint voices rose from the pews or the altar or from behind the gray curtain, as if the ghosts of all the prayers and catechisms and homilies lingered in this room, gabbling softly to each other.

A bell beat somewhere within the convent, and a minute later the novices pattered down the stairs and into the refectory, chirruping like a vast flock of sparrows. Mira followed and stood against the wall, watching them gather behind the benches. When they were all in place, they bowed their heads and there was a moment of sighs and coughs. Then a sister said a short prayer and the girls took their seats. The scullery doors banged open and out came girls bearing trays of bowls and round loaves of bread. As the novices picked up their spoons and set to, Mira saw surreptitious nods toward the windows and heard from beneath the veils the words "tree," "escape," "magic," and she struggled to suppress a grin.

Mira was by this time starving—the climb in the night and the thrill of exploring the convent and the labor of keeping up the spell of concealment had given her an appetite. She wondered if she could just squeeze onto a bench and tug a bowl toward her. If she kept her head down ... But even as she pondered this she noticed among the hundreds of faces one turned toward her. A parched, pale face with eyes of dawn green. The girl's lips were parted and she frowned, then leaned to her neighbor, eyes still on Mira. Panic rose like stormwater in Mira's chest. Tugging the wings of her headscarf about her face, she fled the refectory and scampered up the stairs. Her heart was going and she berated herself—she must remember that she was in a house of witches here, and even a well-crafted spell might be countered by someone with innate power and clear sight.

She moved up past the empty classrooms and the dormitory and the hallway of white rooms, into the honeycomb of chambers where the sisters lived. Outside one of the rooms was a tray. Mira snatched from it a crust of bread and a cold chicken wing. She devoured this skimpy meal, supplemented with the pomegranate she'd plucked, in a broom closet, seated on an upturned pail, surrounded by damp mops and wrung rags.

As she ate, she remembered that Mother Gotha had used a broom as camouflage to explore the convent, and then remembered Mother Gotha's description of Sister Agate's library—in the tallest tower, she'd said. Mira wondered if the library was still there. Closing her eyes, she tried to picture the exterior of the convent. The tallest tower, it seemed to her, had been on the left side as she faced the entrance, and there was an incongruous flash of silver in her memory, like mica frozen in quartz. She sucked the last shreds of flesh from the wing and tucked the bones, along with the pomegranate peel, into a corner by a mop. Going to the door, she listened at the hinges till she was certain no footsteps pattered in the hallway, and stepped out.

Swiftly, while the placement of the tower was still fresh in her mind, she tried to make her way toward that corner of the building. But now a strange befuddlement set in. As if trapped in a dream, she kept finding herself climbing the same short staircase, opening the same door with a faded gray number nine at eyelevel. For what seemed half the afternoon, she wandered fruitlessly in that labyrinth. Finally, after opening door number nine for the fourth time, she closed it and stood with her back to a wall, eyes shut. She shook her head, grinding it against the masonry to clear the fug. A spell was in place here, she realized, not directed specifically at her, but working on her nonetheless. A deftly crafted spell of concealment, secrecy, subterfuge. It was impossible to think her way through it, impossible to see the pattern, but she realized she should be able to unravel the spell simply by recognizing it, and by going against her instincts.

Retracing her steps, she listened to the little voice, the subtle urge telling her to take this turn, to go down this short staircase, and, though it required an effort that drew a gasp from her lips, she was able to press against that inclination and turn left rather than right, up rather than down. After a few minutes of this curiously taxing labor, she found herself moving up a tightly coiled staircase she hadn't encountered before. The enchantment was powerful here: she could feel it through the curved wall and the bowed stone steps. Rounding a turn, she came upon an ancient wooden door, slightly ajar. With a trembling hand, Mira reached out and gave a single knock.

"Come in," said a voice so cracked and worn it might have been the voice of the door itself.

XI

TEA WITH A MAGPIE

Mira stepped into a chamber as lovely and cozy as a fairytale illustration. Octagonal, with walls and floor and peaked ceiling of polished stone. In two of the walls were arched windows, open to breezes and the lemonade afternoon sunlight. The other five were mahogany shelving, filled with books that made her mouth water: she recognized the whimsical lettering and gold chasing of fairytales; the larger leatherbound volumes she guessed contained witchcraft. Among the books were many small bright objects: copper coins and broken glass, bone buttons, brass pins, and even a crushed foil wrapper that might have come from Rosa's Chocolaterie. In front of one window was a little three-tiered fountain of blue-glazed porcelain, the cascading droplets casting morsels of iridescence about the room, creating a tender wavering music. A room cradled in magic, scented with magic.

In front of the other window, in a rocking chair, sat the oldest woman Mira had ever seen. She wore the gray habit of the sisters, though her head was bare. In her hands were silver knitting needles, and on the floor between the rocking-chair runners lay two baskets, one filled with flame-colored fluff that reminded Mira of something she couldn't immediately bring to mind, the other with a colossal coil of flame-colored cord. The woman's skin was tissue paper that had been crumpled and trodden, marred with overlapping ovals and speckles of muddy color, but the crimped eyelids were portals to cloudless sky. On the windowsill beside her perched a magpie dressed in smart black and white, who watched Mira's entrance with an eye like an oiled pebble. His feathers rattled slightly in a breeze.

"Welcome," the woman said in a voice as ravaged as her face, and she held out a hand. "Welcome, my dear. I have been waiting many years for your arrival."

"Sister Agate?" Mira said hesitantly, stepping forward and taking her hand, like gripping a twig broom.

"Yes, I am Sister Agate. And this is Malachi." With a knitting needle she scratched the magpie's head; he leaned into the pressure and uttered his name in a growly voice, watching Mira all the while.

"Oh, he talks!" Mira exclaimed. "And isn't he handsome!"

The magpie ruffled his neck feathers and whirred softly. Magpie greeting, perhaps.

"I'm pleased to meet you both. My name is Mira."

"You are new here," Sister Agate said, tipping her head in a manner not unlike the bird's. "You are not from the city."

Mira nodded.

"And younger than I'd anticipated. Fourteen?"

"Almost fifteen. But how did you know I would come?"

Sister Agate shook her head. "I didn't."

"But you said—"

"Well, I didn't know *you* would come, young Mira. However, I knew my spells wouldn't hold forever. Someday a witch would find her way to my hidden tower. How did you manage it?"

"Oh, your spells were beautifully made," Mira said. "Really artistic—like lace laid over my mind. Like a net of spun silver. I certainly wouldn't have found the tower if I hadn't known it was here. But you see, someone told me about your library. So I tried to find it. And I realized after a while that I was being nudged this way or that, upstairs or downstairs. Nudged in the opposite direction I wanted to go. So I just went the wrong way each time. Deliberately chose the wrong way, if that makes sense."

"The wrong way. Yes. Clever girl. And strong." She rocked a little faster. "But who told you about the library?"

"A woman I met on my journey."

"Ah, I see. A journey. And a journey means a story. And a story requires tea." With a silver knitting needle, Sister Agate tapped a teakettle on a single-burner stove beside her rocking chair. "If you would be so good as to fill this kettle from the fountain there."

Mira did as she asked, dipping the kettle into the lowest basin of the fountain and setting it on the stove. "Do you have matches?" she asked, looking around.

"Matches, my dear?"

Mira giggled. She'd spent so long concealing her magic that she'd forgotten she could make fire. With a fingersnap she lit the flame.

On one of the lower shelves, nestled among the books, were a jar of honey and two lemons on a saucer and spoons and several chipped teacups and a wooden box of tea leaves. Kneeling, Mira prepared the tea. Then she pulled up a stool at Sister Agate's feet and leaned back against a shelf. She sipped a little too avidly, burning her tongue, and sighed blissfully.

"All right," she said, cradling the cup in her lap. She closed her eyes. "My journey. Let's see. Where should I start?"

"Start at the beginning, of course."

"The beginning. Yes. Well, like you said, I'm not from this city. I was born in a town in the south. A town along the river ..." As Mira spoke, Sister Agate's knitting and rocking slowed; she almost seemed to fall asleep, but her head nodded slightly from time to time. It took longer than Mira had anticipated to tell her tale, and in the telling she saw echoes and sparkles she wouldn't have noticed if they hadn't been placed side by side, strung together like beads on a necklace. And she saw as well the gaps in the necklace, or beads that didn't quite fit the pattern: it wasn't complete; it was still in the making. When at last Mira described the pomegranate seed that had grown into a tree, just last night, and released her from her confinement, Sister Agate opened her eyes.

"So that's what it was," she said.

Mira and Malachi both cocked their heads.

"I felt something growing," Sister Agate explained. "Somewhere in here." She put a knuckle on her breastbone. "At first I thought it was heartburn, but then I saw the sisters and priests scurrying about in the streets this morning and I knew something had happened."

The tea was long gone and Mira's cup was cold. The sun wobbled precariously on one of the watchtowers.

"Thank you, Mira," Sister Agate said. "A tale of power and courage and cunning, told well and thoroughly. Though, as I expect you recognize, it is unfinished, a tale still in the telling. I am pleased to learn that Mamie Zaccaroth crafted a life for herself." ("Mamie," Mira whispered delightedly.) "I often recall her solemn, green-eyed gaze. There seemed no limit to the knowledge she could acquire. In that respect she was like my fountain—you could just keep filling her up. Young Gotha spelled disaster for this library, but I am comforted that she discovered her calling in the end. And, of course, her gift of a pomegranate provided the seed that allowed you to escape your confinement." A smile creased her eyelids like rice paper. "Now, one tale, I feel, deserves another. I am guessing you would like to hear my story. Perhaps with another cup of tea?"

"Oh, yes please!" Mira jumped up and filled the kettle and lit the stove once more with a fingersnap.

When they had fresh cups, Sister Agate began rocking and knitting, the knock of the needles like a pulse beneath her words, keeping time, and Mira had the sensation that she was in fact knitting time with her silver needles even as the cogs and coils in the clocktower created time, clicking it out, doling it out.

"Imagine a town," Sister Agate began, "a town along the river where the air shimmers with illusions and crackles with enchantments. A town where magic is not only permitted but nurtured and celebrated. A town with more fairytales than prayerbooks, more bookshops than churches, more witches than priests, filled with ferrets and magpies, cats and owls. A town that sprawls like ivy, a labyrinth of alleyways and unruly gardens, trees taking hands across the cobbles like dancers, flowers falling on the cobbles like a fragrant rain. And in every winding alley a witch's shop, a list of her services in the window. Herbariums selling all manner of philter and powder. Healers. Fortune tellers. Witches who specialize in childbirth, in love potions, in spells of protection. A town filled with florists and chocolateries and shops selling recorders and violins. And, more strangely perhaps, a town where witches go to church and priests have their fortunes told."

"Is this the town you come from?" Mira asked. As Sister Agate spoke, hope had kindled in her belly that there was a place for her, for her kind—a place where she might live unencumbered, without secrecy, practicing magic as freely as bakers and brickmakers practiced their arts.

"It vanished long before my time," Sister Agate said. "This city of black walls, of locks and towers and armored doors, is built on the bones and ashes of that town of witches and enchantments. But the streets and alleys of this city twist so because they are laid over that earlier tangle."

"Why did it vanish?" Mira asked, crestfallen.

"The fear. It rose, as it always does, from imbalance. From a priest trying to chase away the shadows. Trying to erase the darkness. Trying to purify with light. But there is no light without shadow, and imbalance engenders monsters. So the demons entered the city."

"Where do they come from, the demons?" Mira asked.

"From the other side."

"The priest in my town said the boundary has grown thin, the seams are fraying. Are the demons always there, lurking on the other side, waiting to attack?"

"No, I do not believe they are always present. They are created by imbalance. They have risen and been quelled, many times, over the centuries. They will rise again in this city."

"What happened after the demons arrived?"

"The priests erected the Sentinel, which at that time they called the pyre. And then, of course, came the walls and the locks, and this institution, which is a cage, a prison, an asylum for girls with the power. They believe that by subduing the witches they can vanquish the demons. And it works, of course. It works for a time, though it creates its own horror. But unless the imbalance is corrected, the demons will rise again. As they have risen in your town."

"So you think the demons rose in my town because of some imbalance?"

"Certainly."

"Do you know what caused it?"

"I do not. But I suspect your journey is at some level a quest to uncover the cause."

"All right. Go on, please."

"One by one, over the centuries, the bookshops went out of business, until a single bookshop remained. I was the proprietor of the last bookshop in this city, which I inherited from my grandmother. It was tucked away in a dead-end alley, half-forgotten, with no sign above the door, no display in the curtained window. Some days half a dozen customers came in; some days only one or two. They'd find me in my rocking chair, knitting or reading, with Moshi, my fat gray cat, dozing on my lap, and a cup of tea steaming beside me. Some of the customers said they came in just for the perfume of lemony tea and old books and the beeswax I used to polish the leather bindings.

"On the shelves were Bibles and storybooks, prayerbooks and cookbooks, hymnals and nursery rhymes. But if you went to a certain shelf along the back wall and reached beneath it, you would find a brass knob. Press this while muttering an opening charm, and the entire bookcase would swing out on hinges, revealing a second room. This one was filled with books of spellcraft and witch's recipes and the forbidden fairytales. And in this room, after midnight, I held classes in the magical arts. Bookshops have always been schools for witches."

"I heard about your bookshop," Mira said. "From a woman in town. The grandmother of a friend. She used to go there when she was a child."

"Oh, it's gone … long gone," Sister Agate said. "But the books from the secret chamber have survived." She lifted a hand from her needles and made a circle in the air.

"What happened to your bookshop?" Mira asked.

"The authorities had been growing stricter, more oppressive, and the influence of the church was rising. There was a crackdown on what they called decadence. Storybooks, pretty clothes, musical instruments, even sweetmeats were abruptly suppressed or outlawed. It was a terrible time. Smoke in the sky, stones in the streets, drowned cats in the river. Suspicion everywhere, destroying families, ripping wife from husband, daughter from father. Religious vigilantes swept through the city, confiscating flowered dresses, watercolors, violins. They built a great bonfire of books in the cathedral square, and citizens brought their fairytales and nursery rhymes and herbals and flung them into the fire, cheering as the flames soared.

"That was the end of my bookshop, though the contents of the hidden chamber survived. I was brought to this convent and caged, even as you were. When I gained my freedom from the cells, I became an apprentice to the old librarian. At that time, this room was an austere place, filled with dry religious texts. Nevertheless, books are books, and the Bible is a fairytale if you read it right. When the old librarian died, I took her place. Then I made the library into a chamber of magic. I bestowed library privileges on a select few, refusing entrance to all others, and through contacts on the outside I brought in the books from the hidden chamber in the bookshop, where they had remained untouched for years.

"Thus I managed to repel all but the most promising young witches, the girls whose powers would not be quelled. To those I devoted endless hours, and under the pretext of holding Bible studies we practiced magic in the evenings after vespers and deep into the nights. Some of those students, when they were ready, I sent out into the world. Mamie Zaccaroth was one, perhaps the brightest spark to pass through these doors.

"Young Gotha, of course, brought an end to all that. It was my own fault. I recognized at once the power she possessed, but she also had a capacity for cruelty that frightened me. I had made up my mind to wait a year before approaching her, hoping the convent would blunt her sharp edges in that time. Alas, that decision was my undoing. She discovered my little coven and went to the Mother and betrayed us. The girls under my tutelage—six at the time—were broken. Three died. Three lost their minds ..." She ceased knitting, crossed the needles in her lap, and looked out the window. Dusk had settled like ash.

"What about you, though?" Mira asked. "How did you survive?"

Sister Agate turned back into the room. "They came for me, of course. But my power was stronger than theirs. I had been a student and active practitioner of magic for many years, and I bound their limbs and sealed their lips and curdled their thoughts. And then I became a ghost."

Mira sucked in her breath, and Sister Agate cackled. "Not a real ghost, dearie. I'm flesh and blood, despite my age." She tapped a knuckle with a needle. "No, I mean I became invisible to those in the convent. I placed spells of concealment about my person, and stayed in this house, in the forgotten spaces, until the hullaballoo subsided. I overheard them talking—they thought I'd escaped the convent, gone out into the city."

"And the library? How did it survive?"

"Well, they locked it up, naturally. The Mother was terrified that the books would prove too tempting to anyone tasked to remove them. So she ordered the room locked, and personally sealed the door. It took me a while, but one day I realized that by sealing it they had provided my means of escape. I broke the seal and entered. Everything was just as I'd left it—not a book out of place. Working for a night and a day, I crafted the most elaborate spell I'd ever attempted. A spell that essentially made the room invisible and diverted prying eyes, prying minds. I built my own cage. And eventually the library became rumor, then legend, and was forgotten. Though I believe some of the girls still tell tales of an old mad sister locked away in an upper room, making magic. For half a century I have sat here, reading fairytales and drinking tea and knitting, whiling away the time till someone unraveled my spell. Waiting for you, young Mira. For you and your tale."

"How do you get food?" Mira asked.

"I find I need less as I grow older. I drink tea, and Malachi brings me a crust of bread from time to time, or a walnut, or a berry, and often a trinket." She scratched the magpie's head gently. The bird tipped his head and said his name in a guttural, perfectly comprehensible voice. "Malachi also brings me the special fleece I knit into this cord." She reached into the basket beside her and lifted a few fine strands.

Mira leaned forward. "It's … What is that?" she asked.

Sister Agate twisted the strands around a finger. "When the girls take the vow to become novices," she said, "their hair is shorn. Malachi steals those trimmings, and I use them to feed my needles." She sat back, rocking. "Now, speaking of tales and trinkets, let me see your key. The gold key you carry."

"Well, that's just the problem," Mira said, spreading her hands. "That's why I'm still here in the convent. The Mother took it. It's around her neck. And you know her door is guarded at all times, by spellcraft as well as by a sister."

"Ah." Sister Agate closed her eyes and ceased rocking for so long Mira thought she'd fallen asleep. Finally her knitting needles started clicking again, slowly at first, then picking up the tempo. "Some sisters in this house have a streak of cruelty," she said. "The power over the young, and their frustration, become weapons. They turn vicious. But the Mother is not one of those. She was never cruel. In her, the thwarted power became appetite. Greed. She ate herself into immobility, and still she eats. And as well as a weakness for sweet things, she has a weakness for pretty things, for glitter and sparkle, just like Malachi here." She tapped the magpie's beak and he whirred softly. "Your key must have struck her fancy."

"So is there no way to get it back?" Mira asked.

"The Mother's magic is strong, and her door, as you noted, is guarded day and night," Sister Agate said.

Mira nodded with a rueful sigh.

"Her door is guarded," Sister Agate repeated, "but her window is not. She likes the fresh air. It helps her breathe." She held out her arm, and Malachi bounced onto it, head tipping this way and that. She leaned toward him and blew softly into the feathers over his ear. "Listen. We need help. This girl needs your help." The magpie angled his head so an obsidian eye was on Mira. "We need something from the Mother," Sister Agate said. "A gold key. It's around the Mother's neck. Can you fetch it for us?"

Malachi tipped his head inquisitively.

"Wait," Mira said.

The old witch and the magpie cocked their heads at her.

Mira got up and walked around the room, scanning the magpie's gifts. She picked up a wishbone, a snail shell, a broken hairpin, and set them down. Finally she found a little brass hinge, perhaps from a small cabinet or jewelry box. "This will do," she said. Returning to her chair, she held the hinge in her outstretched palm and closed her eyes. She took a moment to recall the spell she had read in Mrs. Zaccaroth's cookbook, how many months ago. Sighing, she said the words and felt the tiny shiver on her skin, as if an insect had adjusted its wings. She opened her eyes. In her palm lay the gold key. She held it out, and the magpie hopped along Sister Agate's forearm and bent his fat beak toward it. "Gold. Mother," he said, and Mira nodded. She closed her hand, opened it, and the brass hinge lay in her palm once more. She put it back on the shelf.

Malachi bounced onto the windowsill and, with a rustle and a caw, melted into the licorice night.

Not ten heartbeats later there was a shriek and a shout: "Catch it!" And then, with a flurry, the magpie was on the sill again. In his beak was the gold key; the ends of the broken chain dangled.

Mira clapped her hands. "Oh, well done!" she exclaimed. Malachi hopped onto her lap—he was lighter than she'd imagined—and dropped the key into her palm, then hopped over to the windowsill again.

Mira turned the key, rubbing her thumb across the familiar shape. Then she laughed.

"What is it?" Sister Agate asked.

"I've been so focused on getting my key back that I haven't thought beyond this moment," Mira said. "But here I am, trapped in the tallest tower in a locked convent in a walled city. And I still don't know what door it opens. The door I've been seeking for months. Do you know? Can you tell me?" She held out the key, hoping desperately that somewhere among these books of magic the knowledge was stored.

Sister Agate rocked. "I cannot tell you where the door is," she said.

"I know," Mira said sadly. "No one can." And she put the key in her pocket.

"I cannot tell you where the door is," Sister Agate repeated, "but I know the way you must go."

Mira watched her. The tea in her belly had turned to ice. "Which way do I have to go?" she asked in a small voice.

"You know the way, child. You must face your fear."

Mira looked into the night. Something glimmered out there—starshine on water, perhaps, or a candle in a distant window. "No," she said.

Sister Agate said nothing. She rocked, and her needles glinted, and her eyes glinted as well, watching Mira.

"Anyway, I can't get out of here, so it doesn't matter," Mira said hopefully.

"I can give you the means to escape the convent," said Sister Agate. Crooking a finger, she tugged up a loop of the flame-colored cord. "I'll tie one end to the arm of my chair here," she said.

"Is it strong enough?" Mira asked. The cord seemed awfully frail, and now that she had a way out, she found she wanted nothing more than to be caged in this octagonal library with its pretty books and magpie-gathered trinkets and blue-glazed fountain and cups of lemony tea.

"With every click of my needles I weave in a thread of power," said the old woman. "This cord could hold a carthorse, to say nothing of a wisp like you."

Mira nodded, suddenly weary. "What if I slip?" she said. "What if I lose my grip?"

"You climbed up the tree," Sister Agate told her. "Descending will be easier."

Mira gave a longing look at the shelves. "Oh, how I'd love to spend a week here, a month, a year, chatting and drinking tea and reading the books. All the books."

"The night is still young," Sister Agate said, smiling. "Ideally, you will depart after midnight, when there are fewer eyes at windows. So choose a book, young Mira. Choose a book to read and make yourself another cup of tea and help yourself to hazelnuts from the bowl over there. I'll let you know when it's time to leave."

Mira stood and did what she had longed to do since she'd entered this room: she went to the shelves, running her fingers along the bindings, tipping down book after book, muttering the titles, leafing through the opening pages. Books of charms, books of potions, books of recipes. She knew she should use her time in this treasury to gain greater knowledge, to add more spells and recipes to her collection, but her eyes and hands were drawn irresistibly to the books of fairytales, with their fanciful gold lettering, the embossed images on the covers. She found one called *Black Cats and Pomegranates*, illustrated with sprightly etchings, and this she carried to her stool. Leaning back against the wall, she opened the book.

The endpapers were silhouetted cats in all manner of contorted shape, interspersed with segmented pomegranates. She came to the table of contents and ran her finger down the titles. Sister Agate ceased rocking and leaned. "Ah," she said. "Try 'The Devil's Wife.' One of my favorites. Would you care to read it aloud?"

"Oh, I'd love to!" said Mira.

As she began to read, Malachi hopped from the windowsill onto Sister Agate's lap, then onto the arm of the rocking chair, and finally, to Mira's delight, onto her shoulder, chin feathers tickling her ear, head angled to see the illustrations.

The Devil's Wife

Once there was a girl whose house stood on the border of fairyland. She was forbidden to walk in that direction but often, on rainy days, she'd kneel on the window seat in her bedroom and look out past the herb garden and the low stone wall and the meadow of wildflowers to the shimmering place where fairyland began.

"What would happen if I went there?" the girl asked her mother one day, but her mother shook her head and pressed a finger to the girl's lips, so the girl knew she should never speak of it. Still, she gazed out the window of her bedroom on rainy days and wondered. But she might never have strayed in that direction if her mother hadn't died when the girl was eleven years old.

The girl's father took a new wife, a slovenly woman who lay all day on the sofa in the parlor. The first thing she did was throw out all the books in the house. "You won't have time to read anyway," she said, and she ordered the girl to mop the floors and make the meals and scrub the pots and pans. The only respite from the scolding and ordering about was once a day when the girl's stepmother sent her to the village market. The girl tied on a red headscarf and took a basket and walked along the path to the market, where she lingered as long as she dared, enjoying the sun on her forearms and the friendly smiles of the vendors. She bought potatoes and carrots and onions and fish, and she always saved for last her visit to the fruit seller, an old woman with marvelous wares. People came from miles around to buy her plump persimmons and enormous strawberries and, especially, her golden apples, which were crisp and juicy and had just the right balance of sweet and tart.

One day, the girl burned the breakfast porridge, which put the stepmother in an especially foul mood. "Go to the market," she told the girl. "And when you come back, you are to scrub all the walls, inside and out. And the windows. I want the whole house spick and span by nightfall."

The girl tied on her red headscarf and took the basket from the kitchen and walked sadly to market. She bought the items her stepmother had ordered and then went to the old fruit seller, who crouched among her overloaded trays like a dragon in its treasure hoard. The old woman looked up at the girl and put a crooked finger alongside her crooked nose.

"Something ails you today," she said. "Tell me your sorrows."

So the girl told her that she'd burned the porridge and would now have to wash the whole house, inside and out. "Even the windows!" she said. "And you know how hard *they* are to get clean."

"I do. I do indeed," said the old fruit seller. "You're in a bad way, dearie, but I believe I have just the remedy." Reaching behind her, she plucked from a basket one of her famous apples—the largest the girl had ever seen, as stunning and golden as the sun—and held it out. "Now, this is not for you," she said. "Nor is it for your stepmother. No, this is a present for the devil's wife."

"The devil's wife!" exclaimed the girl. "But how will I find her? Where does she live?"

"She lives in fairyland, of course."

"Oh. Well, I'm not allowed to go there."

"Of course you aren't. But you will."

"Isn't it dangerous?"

"Naturally. Like all adventures, it is dangerous. But the alternative, as you know, is washing windows, inside and out."

So the girl took the apple. She returned home and placed the items from the market, all but the apple, on the kitchen counter. Then, ignoring her stepmother's calls, she went out the back door, through the herb garden, over the wall, across the meadow, and into fairyland.

It wasn't much different from the world she'd left. There were the same flowers and trees and bees and butterflies, though everything seemed to shimmer slightly as if it were sprinkled with sugar or as if she viewed it through a dusty mirror.

After an hour (though time was uncertain in that land, and it may have been much longer or much shorter), she came upon a crow sitting on a low branch, and she asked the crow where the devil's wife lived.

"Oh, you don't want to go there!" the crow cried. "She's a wicked woman."

"But I've got a present for her," the girl said, patting the basket.

"Well, in that case," said the crow, "walk straight on till you see three hills. The devil's wife lives beneath the middle hill. But listen, before you go, take one of my tail feathers."

"What will I do with it?" the girl asked.

"If you hold it up to the wind, it might carry you away," the crow told her.

So the girl plucked a black feather from the crow's tail and tucked it into her hair beneath her red scarf and, having thanked the crow, she walked on.

After a mile (though distances were uncertain in that land, and it may have been much more or much less), she saw before her three low hills, and smoke seeped from a door in the base of the middle hill.

Walking up to the door, the girl knocked, and a moment later the door opened and the devil's wife looked out. She was tall, with red hair and green eyes like a cat's.

"What are you doing here?" she asked the girl.

"I brought you a present," the girl said. Reaching into her basket, she took out the golden apple. And in that land of shimmer and uncertainty, the apple seemed even larger and more vivid than it had in the village marketplace.

"Oh, isn't it beautiful!" the devil's wife exclaimed. She took the apple and rubbed it against her hip till it gleamed. "I'll make this into a pie for my husband."

Just then the ground shook and the doorframe trembled. "And there's my husband now," the devil's wife said. "Quick, come into my kitchen and I'll hide you in a pot."

So the girl followed the woman into the house, and the woman picked her up and dropped her into an enormous pot and put a lid on it. Just in time, too, because her husband marched into the kitchen, banging the walls.

"What's that I smell?" he shouted.

Heart pounding, the girl cracked the lid and saw an enormous black-bearded man standing in the middle of the kitchen. He held a club in one hand and a knife in the other, and he was dressed from head to toe in the skins of his enemies.

"I got a present today," his wife said sweetly. "A gift from the land of the mortals." And she held up the golden apple, which in that dim room under the hill seemed to give off a light of its own. "Now, you go put your feet up and I'll make you a nice apple pie."

So the devil went into the parlor and took off his massive boots, and soon he was snoring, his hairy feet up on a stool.

As the girl watched from beneath the lifted lid, the devil's wife took down an old cookbook from a shelf and leafed through it. Seeing the pages, the girl realized that this was no ordinary cookbook: it contained not only recipes for the kitchen but magical spells and fairytales. And more than anything, the girl craved the book, for she'd been deprived of stories ever since her stepmother had arrived.

The devil's wife came to a recipe for apple pie, and she made the crust and sliced the apple and mixed it with flour and butter and cloves and cinnamon and nutmeg and sugar and salt, and she arranged the apple slices in the crust and put the pie in the oven. Soon it was bubbling, and oh, it smelled good! The devil's wife peeked into the parlor where her husband sat snoring. Then she took the lid off the pot and lifted the girl out and told her it was safe to go.

The girl was just tiptoeing out of the kitchen when she heard the oven door open. Turning, the girl saw that the devil's wife was bent over, peering at the pie. And while she was thus distracted, the girl snatched the cookbook from the counter and dashed down the hallway. Behind her, the oven door slammed, and the devil's wife shouted, "Stop, thief!"

There was a sudden roar: the devil had woken from his nap. Glancing back, the girl saw him pounding toward her, brandishing the club in one hairy fist and the knife in the other.

Just in time, she made it out the door. Plucking the crow's feather from beneath her scarf, she held it to the wind, and a moment later was high in the sky, while below her the devil stamped and shouted and his wife shrieked.

When the girl returned from fairyland, her stepmother came to the door. "Where did you get to, you lazy child?" she asked. "You haven't even started on the walls and windows. And you forgot the potatoes. I specifically told you to buy potatoes, and you forgot."

"I have something much better than potatoes," the girl said. Opening the cookbook, she found a spell that sealed her stepmother's lips till she could find a kind word to say. Then, in blissful silence, the girl carried the cookbook into the kitchen and set about making a pie.

* * *

Sister Agate ceased rocking, tucked the silver knitting needles into the basket of yarn, and turned to the slot of window. Only a sparse sprinkle of lights now, where an insomniac sat up over a cup of warm milk or a mother tended a colicky baby. The streetlamps on the bridges were strings of pearls on the dusky throat of the river. "That was lovely," she said. "You read very well. But now, my dear, it is time."

Mira sighed. She closed the book, and the magpie nibbled at her earlobe, tugging gently on the thin gold hoop.

"Would you like one of my earrings, Mr. Malachi?" Mira asked. She popped it out and he accepted it with a dainty twist of his head. A single sweep of his wings took him to a shelf, where he set the earring on a coin. Mira stood and replaced the book in its slot.

When she turned, Sister Agate was tying a knot around the arm of her chair. "Two half hitches," she muttered. "That should hold." She tugged at the cord with her rickety hands and nodded. Reaching into the basket at her feet, she lifted the whole thick bundle of coiled cord and tossed it through the window. It whispered as it went, and then with a twang was taut between chair and sill.

Going to the window, Mira leaned out.

"Did it reach the bottom?" Sister Agate asked.

"I can't tell," Mira said, pulling her head back in. "It's too dark." She sat on the windowsill, looking into the room, trying and failing to summon a smile. "Thank you," she whispered. "I don't know if I'll see you again."

"You won't. But it has been a pleasure, a great pleasure, to encounter a girl with such courage, such strength, such a lovely reading voice. And now, my dear, it is time to go."

Mira leaned forward and gripped Sister Agate's hand, eyes squeezed closed. Then, before she lost her resolve, she turned the slender red-gold cord twice around her left wrist, swiveled, and eased herself over the sill and into the night.

XII

THE RIVER DOOR

Sister Agate was right: once she learned to trust the cord, descending was easier than climbing. Placing her soles on the stone, she walked herself down the wall, past the Mother's open window, past the smaller windows of the sisters' rooms and the tall slits of the novices' dormitories and the wider windows of the refectory, past the armored slots of the prisoners' cells, and then she was down. The cord dangled within a foot of the cobblestones. Taking the tasseled end, like gripping a fellow redhead's ponytail, Mira flicked her wrist and watched the curve waver lightly up the wall. A moment later, the cord began to vanish upward.

She turned and leaned against the stone. A witch abroad in the night city. Clutching the key through the cloth of her dress to shore up her courage, she darted across the street, into a shadowed alley.

At night, the houses seemed taller, the rivulets of sky thinner. She was aware of a thousand tiny rustles and squeaks, from every direction, and caught the occasional dim glint of an eye on a window ledge, the twitch of a pale tail in a gutter. Even in this midnight city inhabited by rats, Mira was thrilled to be outside once more, breathing untrammeled air. Be a rat, she told herself. You're just a rat. She stepped furtively through the shadows, pulling her gray headscarf close. At every intersection she paused, eyes twitching, and then scampered lightly across, dollop of antic shadow on the cobblestones. Maybe a fat rat. Maybe a trick of the light.

Only once did she deviate from her path. She realized she was just a block from Rosa's Chocolaterie, and had a sudden craving to see it again—she wouldn't go in, but surely it couldn't hurt to peek through the glass at the nuggets in their foil nests. But when she came to the street, she almost walked past the chocolaterie; what had been the chocolaterie. She backtracked and clutched the grate. Beyond the iron lattice the glass was smashed, and smithereens of the dollhouses and treasure chests Rosa had used to display her wares lay under a moth pelt of dust. It must have been ransacked soon after Mira's abduction. Sniffing, she caught the faintest filaments of almond and cinnamon, twined with rat urine, char, mold. She shouldn't have come. Swiftly she turned and walked back down the street.

In a few minutes she reached the bridge that led to the southern end of the island. The river, unconcerned, slobbered contentedly at the piers. Scant teaspoonfuls of light on the water at this hour. She inhaled the familiar deep-green odor. "Old friend," she whispered.

There were three lit windows on the island side. One dimmed at regular intervals and she heard a faint wail: a mother pacing with a child. The rest were unwavering.

Lamps arced across the bridge like blossoms on stone stems, leaving not a smidgen of cover. She had three options, she realized: take her chances and stroll across, use magic to snuff the lamps, or use magic to conceal herself. Every choice seemed haloed in danger. She breathed, closed her eyes a moment, opened them. With a low chant, she slowly swept her right hand along the river shore, south to north. As if they were candle flames, the lamps on the three bridges flickered and went out. In the abrupt darkness, Mira ran across the bridge. As she neared the far side, there was a shout to her right—a man's voice. She dashed into an alley, turned, and released her hold on the spell. The lamps blinked on again, and the voice that had shouted gave a call she told herself was the all-clear.

Turning right, she moved through the wider streets at the southern end of the island until she came to the tree-lined square.

The cathedral loomed, a cliff against the sky. Standing in the parcel of denser shadow beneath one of the figs that flanked the courtyard, she could feel the leaden net of holy sorcery spreading from this source—the net she'd sensed the first day in the city, fitted precisely over the walls. She was suddenly choked with terror, and had to fight to keep from turning and running back along the island to the lofty seclusion of the clocktower, where she had her thin mat and the blue fairytale book from Rosa's mother and her collection of lightning stones and a stashed tin of almonds and raisins and dark-chocolate nibs.

The cathedral backed up against the water, even as the church in her town had. She walked around it, left to right, scanning the windows for a moment of color, but they were as dark as the leading between the shapes of glass. On the right side, a house was tethered to the cathedral by a covered walkway. A house no larger than the one Mira had grown up in. One upper window gleamed in the walls of black stone. She was about to step toward the house when she heard a low snuffle. In the dark portico, she now saw, a slumped figure slumbered, head swaddled in a scarf, spear angled between his thighs. Watchman.

Leaning back against the wall of the cathedral, Mira closed her eyes. In a voice less than a whisper, with minimal gestures, she crafted the spell of farsight from Mrs. Zaccaroth's cookbook, dabbed spittle at the corners of her eyes, and pressed her palms into her sockets. She wasn't certain it would work—she didn't know if she had the necessary connection—but as she lowered her palms, the spangles diminished and she was looking down at an open book. The lines were slightly fogged, and it was a moment before she realized it was a book of magic. Along the top margin, a hand gripped a black object; a spare hand with hair lapping over the knuckles. The object seemed familiar, but it wasn't till the gaze shifted slightly that she recognized it as the high priest's staff. She focused on the writing. Though it was magical, it was nothing like the chaos of Mrs. Zaccaroth's cookbook, with its plentiful asides and queries and alterations. These texts were framed as prayers; like those in the prayerbooks on the backs of the pews. They used the cadences of prayers and had the shape of prayers, but they were spells, girded with iron bands of power. She was reading a binding spell. A spell that could be fitted to the bounds of a house or a city, ensuring the inhabitants remained within its thrall. The language was heavy, without delicacy or prettiness, but oh it was strong—strong as arches, strong as oak beams. As with the priest's power, however, she recognized that its rigidity was also its weakness. There were cracks around the edges; cracks that allowed a girl like her to sneak through the streets at night, to sneak even into the high priest's private room and peer from his eyes.

The gaze lifted suddenly from the page and darted around the room. An austere interior: a lamp, four shelves filled with the drab plumage of religious titles, a narrow bed, neatly made, an iron cross on the wall above it. Then the gaze rose and moved to the window, and in a moment of supreme strangeness, Mira was peering through the parted curtains at her own gray-shrouded figure leaning against the wall of the cathedral. Slighter than she would have imagined: ghost in the night.

Swiftly she tugged herself out of the spell and rounded the corner of the cathedral, out of sight of the high priest's house. She was breathing hard and had to will herself to unclench her hands. Her nails had pitted her palms.

Going to the great arched doors of the cathedral, she placed her hands on them. Locked, of course, but not with spells; they had never imagined they'd have to keep a witch out of church. Muttering, she slid her left palm across the wood and heard the enormous bolt rasp back. She pushed the leaf open, stepped inside, shot the bolt home.

A strange beauty at this hour: the stained-glass images shades of pearl and moonbeam, the ceiling lost. Not a rustle, not a flicker. Somewhere the sparrows slept. She went up the long aisle and across the nave, where a small wooden chair stood, cords knotted to its legs. She walked to the dais, up four steps, moved around the lectern, and climbed into the high-backed chair at the center of the nine. And she realized as soon as she sat on that throne, feet dangling, palms on the armrests, that she was at the very core of the city here; at the center of power. Closing her eyes, she could sense the streets and bridges and alleys branching like arteries from this dark heart. Below the dais, the roots of the cathedral sank deep, deep, under river seep and silt and sand, to black bedrock.

Opening her eyes, she kindled a mauve light on her finger, which was now as bright and sharp-edged as Mrs. Zaccaroth's green light had been. The light traced faint lines up the closest stone ribs, though it couldn't penetrate the farthest reaches or the ceiling. For a long time she sat on this seat of power, waiting, listening. After a while, for something to do, she hopped down and lifted the thick Bible from the lectern and returned to the high priest's chair. Placing the Bible on the seat, she clambered up beside it and hauled it onto her lap.

It was a gorgeous old book bound in chased goatskin, with illuminated capitals and stately lines of text. She turned to the opening pages. The Bible is a fairytale if you read it right, Sister Agate had said, and she saw now how true that was. "Old friend," she whispered, as she had whispered to the river, and she traced a capital with a finger. Her fingertip came away gilded. Rubbing the gold onto her wrist, she began reading. A river, a garden, a tree … And, with ferocious pleasure, she saw that these were like the polished stones by the river shore, like the baubles on Mrs. Zaccaroth's mantel, like the magpie-gathered trinkets on Sister Agate's bookshelves. She could pick them up, flip them over, rearrange them as she pleased.

She was still reading, immersed in her purple cocoon, when there was a footfall to her left. She looked up.

The high priest, in his black vestments now, though his head was bare, strode down the southern transept to the dais. He gripped the black staff in both hands.

"You," he said, and though he'd made no motion she could see, the cathedral was suddenly ablaze with light, every lamp burning.

"You should not be here. I should have been more vigilant." Once again Mira could taste the power in his voice, bitter as iron.

Mira set the book aside, watching him. She liked being perched above him on this throne. Pulling off her headscarf, she shook her curls free. "My name is Mira," she said.

"Mira. Good." He took a step closer and brought the black staff up to his chest, held horizontally, like a barrier, like a banister. "You've had your little adventure," he said. "And now it's time to leave. I see I was wrong to try to contain you. This time I'll let you go free. Back to your home. Back to your mother."

She watched him.

"Mira," he said. "Young Mira …"

"Don't take another step," she warned.

"Or what?" He laughed, a sonorous baritone that tapped each wall and subsided. "You forget that this is my place. My palace of power. You are an intruder, and a girl." Spreading his arms, he half-closed his eyes and began to mutter a prayer. A prayer that was a spell to stifle her, to bind her.

Mira felt the fury rising, chaotic. With intense focus, she cradled it, channeled it. Closing her eyes, she reached deep, deeper than she ever had. When she'd turned her house around on her thirteenth birthday, she'd done it in her sleep, the power released by her dream. Now, thanks to Mrs. Zaccaroth's tutelage and months of practice, she could access that power at any time, could harness it, hone it, shape it.

As if they were harp strings, the tapered ribs of the cathedral twanged, and somewhere near the entrance an icon smashed to the floor. She opened her eyes. The priest's face had gone the color of eggshells. He put out a hand to steady himself. And in that instant, with a gesture of her left hand as though she were strewing salt across fresh truffles, Mira flung his staff to the flags, where it shattered into a thousand black triangles.

"I turned my house around," she said. "I made a journey through the desert. I grew a tree to escape my cell and stole my key back from the Mother. I can bring this cathedral to the ground."

The priest stared, mouth a black slot in his granite beard. He rubbed his trembling palms on his robe. "So you are not from this city," he said slowly, forcing his voice into submission. "You arrived here from the desert. From the south."

"Yes."

"From Gotha's sanctuary, I presume."

"No. I met her. I met Mother Gotha, and released her from her long years of servitude. But I come from farther south. From the town beyond the cataracts. Sit," she told him.

He took a step toward her, but she shook her head. "No. There, on the chair where you tie up the girls."

So the high priest crunched through the black fragments of his staff to the small chair and sat. It seemed to have cost him a tremendous effort, and his head slumped slightly. She could hear his breathing.

Curling her fingers around the arms of the throne, she leaned forward. "Somewhere else in this city," she said in a clear, angry voice, "in another palace of power, a thousand girls scream in cold cells beneath the earth. They scream because it's easier to let it out than to keep it in. They scream because that's the only way they'll be heard. For many, it's already too late. Their minds are torn, and they'll never be whole. Some are able to stifle their magic. To stifle the best, the prettiest part of themselves, becoming dim gray ghosts roaming dim gray halls. Their power curdles; they use it to torment the novices. I was one of the prisoners in those cells. For how long? I lost count of the days. You crouch in a corner on the damp stone, coughing, shivering. Your only companions the screams and the nine shapes of light from the high barred window. Your power stolen from you. Once a day thin soup in a wooden bowl. You long for madness. You long for death. Yes, you long even for the pyre. For the flame."

He was starting to get his breath back. Now he looked up slowly. "We are not overly dissimilar, you and I," he said. "I too grew up angry and full of pent-up power. My family's apartment was near the western wall of the city, and I was furious that it concealed the horizon. I was furious that I had to open my bedroom curtains onto black rock. I too thought the walls should come down, the doors should be flung open. But then I entered the seminary and learned the terrible history of this city. From my teachers and from the old books, I learned of the demons, which is why the walls were erected. You who are young have no knowledge of those creatures. But in the books I learned of the destruction they caused. Entering the city every night. Running through the streets, ranting. Stealing children. Stealing babies from mothers, snatching little girls from open windows. Forcing the city to live in terror. But for centuries we have had no demons in this city. We have kept the demons at bay by walls and watchtowers, locked doors and locked hearts, prayers and vigilance. We cannot allow the demons to return, to breach our barricades. We cannot. And so we confine the girls, those with tendencies toward sorcery. We confine them and turn them to the light."

"But now one has gotten loose." She grinned. And again, reaching deep, she made the temple thrum. This time one of the stained-glass windows came down like a tumbling rainbow. The moon glimmered where it had stood, and a cool wind swept the chamber, laden with the deep-green scent of the river.

He clutched the edge of the chair, knuckles leached of color. After a few seconds of hard breathing, he gasped, "If you bring the church down, girl, we will both be killed."

"Yes. Is that what you want?"

He shook his head.

"Neither do I. But I'll do it if I have to. Do you understand?"

He nodded, head bowed. "You don't know," he said, and she heard genuine anguish in his voice. "You do not know how many years of toil have gone into keeping this city safe. And not simply mortaring the walls, armoring the doors and windows, building the watchtowers. No, I refer to the centuries of prayer, laying down words like stones, layer upon layer. Prayers that keep the citizens safe in their houses at night, the children safe in their beds."

"And now a little redhead witch has come to undo all that work with a snap of her grubby fingers," Mira said. She held up her left hand, poised.

"Don't destroy everything we've built," the priest said. "I beseech you. Turn away from this path of destruction. Come to the light, Mira. Return to the light."

"No thank you. I prefer the darkness."

He was silent for a long time. Once his fingers moved to his lap, as if to take hold of the phantom staff; then he lowered his hand once more.

"What do you want?" he asked finally.

"Here's what I want. I want you to go to the Convent of the Sisters of the Light. I want you to release the girls."

"And if I refuse?"

"You know what will happen. I'm not afraid."

He leaned back. "You are releasing chaos," he said. "Mayhem."

"Yes. Embroidery. Chocolates. Fairytales. Magic. Chaos and mayhem. But so pretty. So delicious. It's only evil if you try to chain it, you know." Even from her perch, she could see his heartbeats quivering in his head. "I'll stay here," she told him.

"How will you know if I've succeeded?"

"I will be watching through your eyes."

"Watching ... So that was ... ?"

"Yes."

He stared at her. "How did you become so strong?"

"I had a good teacher."

He nodded. For another minute he sat, staring at the fragments of his shattered staff. Then, placing his palms on his knees, he pressed himself to his feet. Shoulders bowed as if he bore the weight of the altar itself, he made his way down the aisle, out the door. He didn't look back.

Closing her eyes, she crafted once more the spell of farsight, and then was with him, out in the dark streets. His journey shorter than hers, as he had no need for furtiveness or detours to shattered storefronts. He strode across the lighted bridge, down the center of the streets, and in a few minutes was at the door of the convent. He knocked. And a moment later the door opened.

Mira maintained the spell, keeping watch, until the girls emerged dazed from doorway and chamber and cell, some shouting, some weeping, but most just turning in circles, looking around, looking at the sky, looking at each other. Tethered to the high priest's gaze, Mira couldn't scan the faces to her satisfaction, but surely Rosa's daughter was among the freed girls. In an hour or so, she imagined, she hoped, there would be a knock at Rosa's door. And then a breakfast such as there had never been in that home. A breakfast with tea and chocolates, stories and kisses, laughter and tears.

Releasing her hold on the spell, Mira hopped down from the high priest's chair. She was halfway down the aisle when she turned, one hand on the sticky back of a pew. All her life she had desired to peer behind the curtain. And here she was, alone in the great cathedral.

She walked back to the dais, up the steps, past the row of nine chairs, to where the great velvet curtains hung. Curtains she'd been trying to open, it seemed, her whole life. Their ripples like a sumptuous crimson cataract. She laid her hands on the thick folds, prying till she found the gap, and slipped between them.

She found herself in a cluttered room. On a table in the center, two rats lifted their noses from scraps of communion bread, whiskers twitching, then bounded off the table and scurried away. Mira looked around. Chalice, censer, half-empty bottle of wine. Boxes of prayerbooks and hymnals in a corner. Folded robes. A leaning stack of dusty icons. And, at the far end, a low door of plain wood set into the black stone.

Stepping up to the door, she tried the knob. Locked, and

impervious to her opening spell. She stood back, then stepped forward once more. Taking the gold key from her pocket, she placed it in the hole. It fit. She glanced back once at the small, cluttered room, the shaggy backs of the velvet curtains, and then turned the key.

And she had a strange sensation as she did so that it was not the key that turned but the world around it: the door, the cathedral, the city itself …

* * *

As she'd expected, stone steps descended to the river, which slopped quietly at the lowest, combing and recombing the weeds. But, raising her eyes, she realized with a shock that the far shore was not the anticipated bank of black walls and shuttered windows, but a thickening of the darkness across a wide expanse of water, too dim and distant to make out clearly. And the light had a curious texture: the light just before dawn, perhaps, or just after twilight. Low clouds coiled like pent smoke.

Mira descended the steps, and as she reached the waterline looked to her right and saw what she hadn't noticed at first. Bobbing in the water was a small fishing boat, sail wrapped against the mast. In the stern, one hand on the tiller, sat a youth with hair like a spray of bracken.

She walked along the step toward the boat, then halted. "Tolly!" she exclaimed. "But how strange. What are you doing here?"

"Mira," he said. In the half-light she couldn't see his expression. "Mira. At last."

"Oh. Your voice," she said. "It's changed."

"Yes. Get in. Come."

"But why are you here? How did you get here?"

"I've come to take you to the other side. Get in." He stood, gripping the mast, and held out his hand. He was taller than she remembered, his shoulders wider.

So she stepped onto the triangular bow seat, and then into the inch of bilgewater. A net lay bunched under the middle seat, the blown-glass floats glimmering among the cords as if Tolly had been fishing the stars from the sky.

With an oar, he pushed off from the slick steps and, balancing like a dancer, unleashed the triangular sail. It flapped ineffectually for a minute, until he tied the tail to a ring in the gunwale and shoved the tiller to the left. With a snap, the sail belled, revealing its haphazard quilt of patches, and the little boat was cutting through the waves, trailing a pale plume. The river slapped at the sides and Mira licked the cold droplets from her lips.

Sitting in the prow and clutching the gunwales, she scanned the receding shore. A silhouette she knew: the church, the layered houses, the smokestack of the brick kiln, and, a little apart, the Sentinel.

"So ... so I'm home," she said, still uncertain.

Tolly nodded, though his eyes were on the water beyond her. "You're home, Mira. Where did you go? Where have you been all this time?" She was still unaccustomed to his new deep voice.

"Such a long journey," she said. "Such a long, strange journey."

"They had a funeral for you."

"What?"

"They thought you'd died. They thought the demons had taken you."

"Well. No."

"I didn't go to the funeral. I never believed them. I'd seen you walk along the river that afternoon. And that night I looked out my window to the north and saw the face of the Sentinel on fire. No one else saw it, but somehow I was sure it was you and I always said you'd come back."

"And you were waiting for me by the steps. How did you know?"

Tolly tugged at the string of the sail and, with a deft flip of his fingers, retied it more loosely. The boat settled into a slightly different rhythm. He sat back, forearm draped over the tiller. "Twice," he said. "Twice, when I've been out on the river, a fish has spoken to me." He glanced shyly at her, but she said nothing. "You're the only one who would believe me," he said. "If I tried to tell someone else, the other fishermen ..."

"I believe you," she said softly.

"The first time I didn't believe it myself. A fish swam up as I was readying the net. It didn't look any different from the others, but it put its head out of the water and spoke. It said ... well, it knew your name, Mira. It told me to catch it and take it to you. So I did. I thought I might be going crazy."

"You weren't going crazy," Mira told him. "And the second time?"

"The second time was yesterday evening. Again, in the center of the river, a fish swam up and spoke to me. And this time it told me to wait for you by the church steps. It told me you needed to go to the far shore. So I brought the boat to the steps. I waited for hours.

And just as I was about to give up and go home, the back door of the church opened and you came down the steps, barefoot and wearing … what is that? I wasn't even sure it was you at first."

Mira looked down and fingered the gray habit. "I stole it," she said.

"From who?"

"That's part of the tale," she said. "A tale you've had a role in, actually. You see, that first fish who spoke to you—this is what it brought me." She held out the gold key in the palm of her hand. "It was my birthday present, but I didn't want it. I tried to throw it away. I did throw it away, as far out into the river as I could, but the fish brought it back. So then I knew I had to make the journey. To find the door it opened."

"What door does it open?"

She pointed over his shoulder. "That one. The river door in the back of the church. The one you saw me come through."

"So you were in the church the whole time?"

She laughed. "No. And the door I opened with the key was not in the church. Well, not in this church."

"I don't understand."

"I'm not sure I do," she said.

For a minute they were silent as the little craft cut through the dark water. Creak of mast, flap of sail, gulp of waves at the boards.

"You seem different," Tolly said at last, and she could hear the hesitancy.

"I've been gone for a while."

"I mean, yes, you're taller. A bit taller. But also …"

"What?"

"Stronger. And not as …"

"Not as spiky?"

He nodded.

"I guess I don't have to be. Not as much, anyway. Someday I'll make you a cup of tea and tell you the whole story, all right? From the beginning. But …" She lifted a hand. They were almost at the shore.

"Where am I taking you?" he asked. "What's over there?"

"I don't know." She swiveled so her hair was blown back across her cheeks. The dark line of the shore was thicker, more defined, and she had a strange sensation she'd approached it before.

"Are you scared?" Tolly asked.

"A little. Yes."

"Do you want me to—"

"You can't, Tolly."

"All right."

A dark city lay before them, and she saw now that it was an echo of the other shore, with the same church and houses and smokestack, but all in ruins. No trees grew here, no river bracken, no flowers. The windows and doorways were vacant, the roofs caved. And she knew that the strange half-light was the light of this land: the light just before dawn, just after dusk, that would never brighten to day or deepen to night. She shivered and wrapped her hands around her arms.

Tolly tugged the tiller, angling the boat to the stony shore, and as he did so he released the sail. Abruptly listless, the boat sidled groaning into the gravel and rocked there. They sat, looking into the dim land. A land without light or wind or movement.

Tolly stood and gripped the mast and held out his hand. Ignoring it, she stepped out.

"Mira."

She didn't turn. "Don't wait for me."

"Will you be safe?"

"Don't wait for me, all right? Go back across the river." But her voice seemed to fall at her feet like a flake of ash.

She set out along the shoreline of that shadowy land, heading toward the town. She didn't look back. Though she was walking along a stony shore much like the one she'd frequented in the town, these stones seemed less substantial, as if they were dim blown eggshells. Her vision strangely curtailed, as if she peered through a mist. But there was no mist in this land, just a thickening of the twilight here and there—the shadows congealing, or the tangible eroding.

After a while, with a lurch that was both hope and horror, she heard a sound. Someone was singing a song she almost recognized; a song like an upside-down lullaby, sung in a silvery whisper that drew a tendril across her nape. A little later she saw a solitary demon crouching on the shore. He was trying to stack stones while he sang his backward song, and as she watched the little cairn toppled. He started stacking the stones again with fingers that in the sourceless light looked to be scarcely more than bones. There seemed no reason to hide, not in this land, so she kept walking toward him, and after she'd taken a few steps he raised his head. For a moment he crouched there, head cocked, watching her approach with enormous eyes in a face that was far too thin. Then he stood on narrow legs, the knees knots. He wore a necklace of pierced pebbles and the tattered remnants of an altar boy's robe, the fabric held together by the embroidery; through the rents she could see his crosshatched ribs.

"Paulus?" she said. She held out her hand, not afraid now, not at all afraid, and the demon looked at her. Then he walked up and took her hand. His touch was more delicate than she'd imagined: fingertips of dust or down. "You *are* Paulus," she said, but he made no sound; only looked at her with his luminous eyes. Without a word, he turned and led her up the stony shore, away from the dark river. A path she knew. A path she'd never walked.

"Where are you taking me?" she asked. Her voice sounded strangely flat, echoless.

The small demon pointed a tapered, silvery finger toward the derelict town. He might have whispered something in his thin voice, or it might have been his soles on the stones.

As they approached the town, she had a sensation that the streets were coming into focus, as though she were lifting the translucent sheet of paper from an engraving in an old book. Rubble and bones on the cobbles. Slants of dust that would never blow away. Windows like empty eyes.

Demons stood from bowls of dust or games of bones or emerged from dark doorways, and came to her. There were many more than she'd imagined. They wore necklaces and bracelets of pierced teeth or bones. Some wore rags of old clothes, but most wore nothing at all, and they cast no shadows under the starless sky. They whispered and touched her hands and her arms. Their touch was delicate as moths and, looking down, she saw that her fingers as well seemed to have less substance in this place. She could understand nothing of their whispers.

"Where are you taking me?" she asked again, and they pointed. Dark streets, dark houses. There was no wind to sweep the dust from the corners.

After a while they turned a corner, and she saw what she had least expected. Like a petal in ash, a light was on in the window of a house at the end of the street. The whispers of the demons rose like brushed sand, died away. They led her to the doorstep of the house with the lighted window and released her hands. Some walked away. Others stood watching her, among them the demon who might be Paulus, who was surely Paulus, in his tattered altar boy's robe.

For a moment she stood on the dark threshold. A threshold she knew, had always known. A moment that had been a node, a knot, a hinge. She went in, through a dark hall, up a flight of stairs. Stairs she'd climbed in countless dreams, in another lifetime.

At the top of the stairs a door stood ajar. Mira approached the angled rind of light, and knew before she entered what she would see. A tall woman in a dress of iridescent shadows stood at the window, one slender hand on the sill. Her hair was a thundercloud, loose on her shoulders, and she turned, as she had turned before, countless times, in Mrs. Zaccaroth's corroded mirror, in bits of broken glass and crystal balls, in dreams. But this time Mira would not wake up; she would remain within the glass, within the dream.

The woman turned. Her face was thin and white, though this was not the silvery pallor of demons. This was the whiteness of madness, and within it dark eyes simmered, pools of mad power. A face Mira knew. A face she'd always known.

The woman's head tilted, eyes narrowed as if trying to disentangle Mira from the shadows. Her expression shifted.

"It's ... Is it ... Can it be?" She raised a hand—whether in welcome or defense Mira could not tell.

She stepped through the doorway. "I'm Mira," she said softly.

The woman froze, hand still raised. Then she came swiftly forward, shadowy dress shimmering like oil on water, like the iridescence of a dove's throat, and laid her hand on Mira's cheek. Not the evanescent touch of a demon Mira had feared; the fingers were cool but solid. "Mira," the woman said. "At last, at last. My child. My daughter. Oh, but you're so tall. Taller than I'd ever imagined. And so pretty. Your hair ..." She reached out both hands and gripped Mira's shoulders.

Mira took a step back, pulling out of the woman's grasp. Something was stuck in her throat. At last she got out: "Daughter?" Her heart, which had been strangely sedate since she'd entered this land, was abruptly a bonfire.

The woman nodded, her mad, eager eyes never leaving Mira's face, hands half raised. "Yes. You are my daughter. My long-lost daughter. And I am your mother."

Mira shook her head. "No." She lifted a trembling finger to the window. "My mother ... My mother ..."

"The woman who raised you is not the woman who gave birth to you. It's strange, I know. So strange. But it's the truth. You found me at last. Oh, you found me at last! I am your mother, the one who gave birth to you. The one who gave you your name. Mira. Mira, my child."

Mira wanted to be anywhere else: to turn and run; to dash down the stairs, out into the dark town. And then what? To cast herself into the dark waves? To sit stacking stones by the shore? To make patterns with bones in the dust?

"Come, my Mira. Come, sit. I'll explain."

For the first time, Mira looked around the room. Dust in the corners. The light came from a single candle whose flame did not waver, and she knew it was a candle that would never burn down in this land, kept alight by the woman's power. On the wall above the candle was a clock without hands. An empty picture frame. A cracked mirror reflecting nothing but shadows. And in the center of the floor two derelict armchairs.

"I wish I could offer you tea or … or some delicacy," the woman said. "But there is only dust in this place. Dust and bones."

"It's all right," Mira said. And she realized she wasn't hungry or thirsty, and knew she never would be as long as she stayed in this dry land. She sat.

The woman sat across from her, leaned toward Mira as if to touch her knee, then sat back, hands grappling with each other. She shook her head slightly. "You're so pretty," she said. "So tall and pretty. I can't stop looking at you."

"Tell me," Mira said.

"Have they told you nothing, then? Nothing at all?"

Mira shook her head.

"Of course they didn't," the woman said. "Of course they didn't. They needed to keep the secret." She put her hands to her white cheeks. "How long has it been? Time is erased in this land."

"I'm nearly fifteen," Mira said.

"Fifteen years. So long? I would not have believed it, yet here you are."

"Tell me," Mira said. "What happened?"

The woman composed her white hands in the shimmering shadows of her lap. "They took you away from me. I was young. Not much older than you. A young witch, wild. Red hair like yours, Mira, my Mira, though I sacrificed that, as you see." She lifted a hand and touched her storm-cloud hair. "I didn't want the power, but who decides? I had the power. When I was a child, I would leave the house at night. My parents would try to keep me in, but what are locks to a witch? Walls, locks, doors … 'Stay inside,' they'd say. 'Stay inside and play.' And I'd say, 'What is inside and what is outside?' And a second later I'd be standing out in the rain, in my nightdress, laughing at their horrified faces through the window. Then I'd run through the streets, shrieking.

The priest tried to tame me but I'd knock his hat off or his robe would come undone, so he let me go. Finally one day I found my way to the house of the woman who lived on the outskirts of the town. They'd warned me about her, but I couldn't stay away. And she became my teacher. Mrs. Zaccaroth, with her green eyes and outlandish hats and love of chocolates. Oh, it was so lovely to find someone who understood. For three years I studied with her, learning fairytales and cookery and the dark arts, turning the pages of her enormous spellbook. But then ..."

"What happened?" Mira asked gently.

"Well, I longed for a daughter. And a witch, as you know, generally gets what she wants. So, nine months later, you arrived. My beautiful baby girl. I was so happy to hold you, my Mira. To hold you and call you by your name. You were just a little slip of a thing. A little white kitten, but with red curls already, damp on your scalp. And the same bright eyes." Again she reached a hand, let it fall. "They allowed me to keep you for a week. The loveliest week of my life. I sang you lullabies. I told you fairytales. You never cried. Just watched me with those eyes. The same eyes. The same vivid look. You never cried until they took you away."

"Who?" Mira asked. "Who took me away?"

"The priest, of course. The church. I tried to stop them. I used my powers, but it was no use. I heard your strong voice, wailing, fading. And then I was alone in the room. Milk staining my nightgown. I thought they would bring you back. I thought I could have you back. I was wrong. I should have known. But you came back at last, my Mira. My daughter. You found me at last. How did you do it? How did you cross the river, all on your own?"

"Not on my own," Mira said. "I had help. But first, I need to know. What did you do after they took me away?"

The woman sat very straight, hands in her lap. For the first time her eyes left Mira's face and she glanced out the window. A smile flickered on her pale lips. "I did something wicked," she said. "But I had no choice, do you see? They left me no choice. Lying there alone in that locked room, I crafted a spell from my anger and my sorrow and my pain. A spell they had never imagined anyone of sound mind would make. But I was not of sound mind. No, I was not of sound mind, and I'd had a good teacher.

"The spell at the end of Mrs. Zaccaroth's cookbook remained unfinished, and Mrs. Zaccaroth told me this was intentional. It was too dangerous to complete. But I completed it. Alone in that room I crafted a spell of annihilation. A spell that would turn the worlds inside out and carry me to this dark shore. And here I have remained. But not alone. No, not alone. Because, you see, I have become a fisherwoman. I brew my nets of storm and hurl them across the river, filled with my chattering lovelies and their bitten fingernails, to haunt the streets and gather my catch. My harvest. They stole my child. I steal theirs. Yes, I steal theirs." Her voice, which had risen almost to a shriek, fell to a whisper. Leaning across the space between the armchairs, she scrabbled, and Mira felt her mother's claws digging into her wrists. "But I never caught you in my nets, Mira, though I scoured my catch every day. Even so, you came back to your mother on your own, so tall and strong and pretty. I won't let you go. They can't take you this time. They can't reach you here. At last you're mine. Mine, mine, mine."

Mira shook her hands free and stood and went to the window, rubbing her wrists. Putting a hand on the lintel, she looked out into the dim street. The demons had wandered away, all but the small demon that might be Paulus. He crouched on the cobbles, crooning, drawing in the dust with a slender glimmering finger. Beyond the ruins lay the river, the far shore lost in darkness. And she felt a sudden panic. She was too far away. She had come too far.

"All the tears," she murmured.

"What? What did you say?"

Mira turned back into the room and sat on the windowsill. In the derelict armchair her mother sat white-faced, eyes enormous, hands twisting in her lap like pale elvers in shallows. And she saw now why she knew the face, why she had always known the face: it was her own. The same dainty chin, the eyebrows like dragonfly wings. The same curly hair, though the color had long ago leached to ashes. But this was a face sculpted by torment, by sorrow and madness. "The river is all the tears of the mothers whose children are gone," Mira said. "Whose children were stolen in the night. On the other side of the river, the nights are filled with weeping. And here the demons eat dust and play with stones and bones and sing backward lullabies and nursery rhymes, trying to remember. And they can't even remember their names."

"They taste despair. They will taste despair, even as I have," the woman said, Mira's white-faced mother, frantic, gripping handfuls of her shadowy garment, which rustled softly like charred paper.

"They have tasted despair," Mira said. "For fifteen years they have tasted despair. Fifteen years of mourning and weeping, Mother. It's enough."

"No."

Mira watched her, tenderness and sorrow and anger churning like stormwater within her breast. "Listen," she said. "I'm going to give you a gift. The gift of my tale, which is finally whole. And then I'm going to release you."

"Release me?"

"Yes. Release you from these chains of anger and revenge. I am going to release you as I have been releasing others on this journey. Djinn, abbess, priest. The thousand caged witches of the walled city in the north. And then we'll leave this town of shadows and dust and go back across the river, to the land of the living."

The woman stared.

"It will be fine," Mira said. "We don't need to stay in the town. Perhaps we can go south along the river. We can find a place to live. A way to live."

"Oh child, have you not understood?"

"Understood what?"

"When I crafted the spell of annihilation, I locked the door. That is the bargain. There is no return."

Mira looked at her in horror. "Then … then we'll find a way to live here," she said, choking. "I'll stay here with you. But first, you'll have to set the children free."

The woman's mad eyes were pools of oil where twin candle flames burned. Mira left the window and returned to the armchair. Reaching across the space, she lifted her mother's white hand, stroked it, held it, let it go.

"Here is a story," she said, sitting straight-backed, hands in her lap. "A fairytale for you. A fairytale you helped write; a fairytale you're a part of.

"Once upon a time, in a town beside the river, a young redhaired witch longed for a child. Now, witches generally get what they desire, and nine months later she gave birth to a redhaired daughter. But the church in the town was terrified of magic, and so her daughter was taken from her. Stolen from her. They thought they were doing the right thing. They thought that by stealing the child they could quench the magic. But they hadn't reckoned on the woman's power, on the force of a woman's anger.

"The witch went mad. Casting a spell with the strength of an earthquake, she turned the worlds inside out and crossed the river to the dry land. And there—here—in a room with a cracked mirror and a stopped clock and an empty picture frame, by the light of the sole candle in this land, she brewed storms fashioned from fury, sending them from shore to shore to net the children, and then sending the children themselves, demons now, to dance and shriek through the streets, causing havoc, driving the townsfolk mad with fear.

"Meanwhile, the witch's redhaired daughter grew up, wild and willful, in the house of her aunt, her mother's sister. Like her mother, the girl had enormous power, and because that power was suppressed it released itself in dreams. Her childhood was filled with tantrums and mayhem. Flowers on fire. Falling icons. Shattering crockery. She was banished from the church for trying to pull the curtain aside. And through her negligence, her brother—no, not her brother; her cousin—was stolen by the demons.

"On the morning of her thirteenth birthday, the girl woke from one of the dreams of change to find her house was backward. Picked up, turned around, set back down, without so much as a whisper. She went out the back door, which was now the front door, and walked down to the river. The light was strange—the light just before dawn or just after twilight. And as she sat there on the shore, the waves rushed up and brought her a key. A pretty little gold key." Mira fished the key from her pocket and held it out. Her mother reached out a white finger and touched it.

"Yes. Go on."

So Mira went on, telling her mother the story of her life since the arrival of the key, which gained both strangeness and solidity in the telling. How she'd found her way to Mrs. Zaccaroth's house above the river. How she'd seen this room, this very window, in Mrs. Zaccaroth's corroded mirror and, terrified, had tried to run, had tried to throw away the key and reject her task. And how the key had returned to her in the belly of a fish. The first fish that spoke to the fisherboy Tolly in the middle of the river.

She told of her months with the old witch, learning to make chocolates and soups, picking herbs in the garden. Reading fairytales in the aerie with Mr. Mugwort at her feet, acquiring the foundations of the magical arts and the spells contained in the great book of recipes. And then she told of the storm that smashed the aerie, that killed Mr. Mugwort and nearly killed Mrs. Zaccaroth. The storm that forced Mira to leave the town.

She told of the long night in the Sentinel, keeping the demons at bay with curtains of fire, and then of the journey north along the river, and the encounters with Mother Gotha and the djinn, and the months in the walled city of locked doors. A city from which the young witches were banished, imprisoned in chilly cells beneath the earth. A city without cats or fairytales, trapped under the leaden lid of the church. But in that city was a single chocolate shop, where she found the space to spread her wings a little.

"The girl was not vigilant enough, however. She made a friend—the niece of the owner of the chocolate shop. Her friend got the ash sickness, and the girl used her powers to heal her. But that gesture would be her undoing. The high priest captured her, and she herself was imprisoned in a cell beneath the convent.

"Then the girl entered despair. She was caged not only by walls, but by the stifling magic of the church. They stole the key; they almost stole her mind. But she didn't give in, tempting though it was. And one night she discovered in her pocket a pomegranate seed. The last seed of the last pomegranate Mother Gotha had given her, to sustain her on her journey into the desert. She planted the seed and watered it with a tear. During the night, it grew into a tree, bursting through the window into the moonlight, sprawling up the walls of the convent. And so the girl escaped, but not into the city. No, she knew she had to retrieve the key, so she climbed the pomegranate tree and entered the convent once more.

"Using her powers, she found a hidden library at the top of the convent where an old, old woman sat rocking and knitting, a magpie beside her. This was Sister Agate, who had been Mrs. Zaccaroth's first teacher. With the help of Sister Agate and the magpie, the girl got her key back. And then she descended from the tower and walked toward her fear. Clutching her heart, clutching her key, she confronted the high priest in the cathedral. She smashed his black staff and caused the foundations of the cathedral to tremble and forced him to go to the convent and release the inmates.

"The girl walked down the aisle of the church. She was walking away. She was going to find her way out of the city. But then she realized that her desire was behind her. Her whole life she'd been trying to peer behind the curtain, and now at last she was alone in the cathedral. She turned. Behind the curtain she found a little room, and in the far wall, there it was. A little door in the back of the church. It was locked, but of course she had a key. So the girl put the gold key in the lock and turned it … and stepped out, perhaps the strangest of all the strange things that had happened, into her own town. Where Tolly the fisherboy was waiting for her in his boat, to bring her to this shore."

She sat back and spread her hands, palms up. "And here I am, in this dark land, beyond day and night, beyond hunger and thirst, beyond time. Alone in a room with a mother I never knew I had."

The white-faced woman stared at her, lips twisting, a spark wavering in each eye. Slowly she raised her hands, and Mira knew she was going to craft a spell, a spell to chain her daughter, to bind her daughter to her will, and knew that here, in this land, she would not be able to counter it. But, arms aloft, the woman hesitated, and then she immersed her hands in her gray hair like lightning returning to storm clouds, and closed her eyes. "I don't know how to let go," she said, her voice almost as silvery and whispery as the voices of the demons. "I've been holding on to my anger all these years, and I don't know how to release it. Can you help me, my daughter, my Mira? Can you help me to let go?"

Mira smiled sadly. "You don't have to let go," she said. "You don't have to let go, Mother. All you have to do is blow out the candle and walk away."

The woman opened her eyes. And her face seemed to soften, the fires quelled. "Yes," she said quietly. "I see that now. And it will be a relief. A release. But oh, I'm glad I saw you first, my Mira. My beautiful, powerful daughter. I'm glad that at last I got to see you and touch you and hear your tale." She sighed and lifted a hand. Mira took it. No clutching this time; no claws. Just a gentle contact, cool as a shadow. With an elegant movement, hair sweeping forward like wings, the woman leaned and blew out the candle. "All right," she said. "We can go now."

In darkness they walked down the stairs and out the door. The demon that was Paulus looked up from the dust where he crouched, crooning, and as they walked through the streets the other demons looked up from their bowls of dust and games of bones and with glimmering eyes watched them pass.

Out beyond the last houses mother and daughter went, hand in hand. They stepped past gaping doors and vacant windows, moving always upward, away from the river, and walked on through fields of dust and bone. The fields came to an end. Ahead of them was a low, dry hill, a hill of bones beneath a starless sky.

"Mira." Her mother turned and gave her a last embrace. She placed a hand on Mira's cheek. Then, tearless, she turned and walked on alone, a tall woman, unbowed. Mira watched as she came to the top of the low hill, and without a backward glance passed beyond it.

Mira turned and walked back across the barren fields into the ruined town. Silent now, emptied of demons. She walked through the dusty streets, past the abandoned bones, the stacked stones. No footprints save her own. No tears save her own, the only rain that land had ever known.

At the shore, she sat on the cairn Paulus had made and wept. An exile in a barren land. She could imagine no spell that might carry her back to the land of the living.

* * *

After a while, through the fence of her fingers, she saw a shape, and roughly brushed the veil of tears away. A pale triangle on the water, so vague and distant she thought at first it might be a trick of the light. But it came closer and, hope like a twig in her throat, she leaped to her feet. "Tolly!" she cried as the boat swung in to shore. "I told you not to wait."

He stood and gripped the mast and reached out a hand. "I disobeyed," he said, grinning, as she stepped into the bilgewater. "I stayed for a long time, a long, long time, but you didn't come. So I sailed back. But when I was halfway across, a great whispering went by, like a thousand invisible birds rushing past. And then, as if you were sitting beside me in the boat, I heard you crying. So I turned around."

"Oh, Tolly. Thank you. Thank you." And she had to keep herself from leaping the length of the boat and flinging her arms around his sunburned neck.

He trimmed the sail and they set off once more across the dark river.

"So … So did you … ?" he asked.

"It's done, Tolly." She pulled the key from her pocket and, with a flick of her wrist, tossed it into the river. Little sip, and it was gone.

"Will it come back to you again?"

"No. Not this time. It's over. The journey is over."

XIII

WITCH

A year later, the young witch stood on the threshold of her cliffside house, beneath an arbor of scarlet roses. She was wearing an emerald dress embroidered with white leaves and stars, and she held a saucer with a porcelain teacup and two truffles: cherry and chili, saffron and cinnamon. "What a pretty day!" she exclaimed. A white cat with eyes like storm clouds and a necklace of shells turned once through her ankles and stepped out. It toppled and squirmed, belly up, on a warm flagstone. The witch sat on the threshold and drank her tea and ate her truffles, watching the butterflies. Then, setting the cup and saucer on the stone, she wound through the neat, irregular beds of thyme and lavender, where bumblebees trundled their portly torsos blossom to blossom. She went past the laden pomegranate tree to the door in the stone wall. Unlocking the door, she followed the cat alongside the wall, trailing her fingers over the rough stone, and then down the steep path to the river. The shore was empty this morning, and the cat, whose name was Miss Amethyst, went looking for crabs. The witch tipped a crate over and sat staring out at the unstitched sunlight, waves simmering around her toes. She picked up a handful of stones and flicked them one by one into the water. Not far; just giving her fingers something to do so her mind could float.

She had come back to a town so full of rejoicing the townspeople scarcely noticed the return of the wayward redhead. The children had not aged during their incarceration in the dry land and seemed to have little memory of their time under the enchantment. They were frail and pale and timorous, taking pleasure in small everyday things: in apples and sunlight and their own shadows on the cobblestones. In sipping hot chocolate and sitting on their mothers' laps and listening to stories and songs, and their parents were only too happy to indulge them.

The day after Mira got back, she walked up to Mrs. Zaccaroth's house. The outer wall was encircled now by a dense tapestry of vines that writhed menacingly at her approach, and she had to use a spell to uncover the door and another spell to unlock it. The house was derelict, the garden a frolicking jungle. One window in the purple parlor had blown open, allowing the rain to enter;

mushrooms had sprouted on the carpet. But the interior had not been ransacked by human hands. The spellcast wall of vines had kept intruders out, as had the rumors of witchcraft, the memories of curses.

Mrs. Zaccaroth's skeleton lay on the bed beneath a sheet tattered into stained lace. On the side table a book open to a certain fairytale. A teacup with a dead bee in a sediment of brown dust. Lamenting, Mira buried the bones of her teacher in the backyard, beside the catmint bush under which Mr. Mugwort lay. On Mrs. Zaccaroth's grave, in memory of her tart green eyes, she planted a lemon seedling.

And then she set about putting the house to rights. It was in dreadful shape. Ants had gotten into the sugar in the kitchen and mice had gnawed through the sacks of flour and chocolate, so most of the foodstuffs had to be thrown out. She tossed the carpet and curtains and doilies and the old mattress through the window into the river. Stripping the parlor sofa and chairs to the frames, she reupholstered them in patchwork sailcloth, which she embroidered here and there with cats and pomegranates, candlesticks and crossbones, gold keys and magpies and roses.

Most of the spices were still good in their corked bottles. The stone spheres and crystal clusters on the mantel were of course unaltered under their pelt of dust, and the books Mira had rescued were dry, if warped. The ancient cookbook of witchcraft still lay on the top shelf in the kitchen.

Mira came every day, working from midmorning to suppertime. She dusted and swept and scrubbed and mopped. With Tolly's help, she rebuilt the aerie using boards scavenged from abandoned fishing boats, on some of which were scraps of paint and scraps of names. The curved walls gave the house a curiously windswept look. She made new bookshelves from orange crates, fitting them to the angles. The windows, though, she had to barter for: a charm against gout for the old glazier, plus a tray of truffles for his wife.

Tolly helped Mira carry her mattress from the backward house in the town, and the morning after the first night in her new house, as she was sitting on the doorstep with a cup of tea between her fingers, a cat arrived. A white cat with one tattered ear and eyes like cloudy gemstones. It stepped carefully along the stone wall and then hopped down to investigate.

"I've got a bit of lamb I was going to use for a stew," Mira told the cat, scratching its skull. "But we can share. Come."

Some mornings Tolly would come by with a fish for her and one for Miss Amethyst, and Mira would let him in with a grin and they'd sit in the purple parlor and drink tea and eat truffles. And, while Amethyst twitched in her lap, Mira would tell him tales of djinns in deserts and witches in ruined abbeys, of marvelous chocolate shops and talking magpies in distant cities, and he never knew if they were real or gathered from her fairytale books. In the evenings, housewives came to her for potions and charms, and sometimes she went to their houses to tend to the sick. But most of her days she spent alone, making chocolates and soups and spells, tending to her herb garden, reading tales and sipping tea in the aerie while Amethyst slumbered at her toes, and that was what she liked best.

Mira flicked the last stone into the river. Leaving the cat to chase dragonflies, she walked up the low hill, through the river bracken, along the thin path flanked by wildflowers, into town. She was going to the market, as she did most days, but this morning she didn't immediately head down the main street past the church. Instead, she turned left and walked up a lane where she knew the shape of every cobblestone.

The door of the backward house was ajar, and for a minute she stood on the threshold, watching her aunt and Paulus at work in the kitchen. They were making cookies, tapping the balls of dough into a saucer of sesame seeds, setting them in rows on a tray.

Though Mira hadn't made a sound, her aunt suddenly looked sharply around.

"Mira!" she exclaimed. "I thought I felt someone in the doorway."

Paulus gestured with floury hands. "The first batch is almost ready," he said. "You're just in time." Fringe of soft black hair falling over his eyes, he bent to take the tray out of the oven. "They're hot," he said. "I'll put some on a plate for you."

Mira took the plate of cookies and went to sit on the steps. Her aunt joined her, groaning and grimacing as she settled on the bricks.

"I'll come in a bit," Paulus called. "I just have to get these into the oven."

"He's getting to be quite the cook," her aunt said.

Mira blew on a cookie and, too soon, took a bite, burning her tongue. "Delicious!" she called back into the house, and Paulus grinned.

"He'll never be as good as you, though," her aunt said softly. "You have the touch. You always had the touch."

Mira put a palm on the warmed brick between them. The back steps, which were now the front steps. "I could turn the house back around, you know," she said. "If you like."

"Oh, I know," her aunt said. "But I've grown used to it. And besides, we'd have to rearrange all the furniture."

Mira laughed. She ate another cookie, and this time it was just the right temperature. She let her gaze wander down the twisting cobblestone street, past the last houses and the stony shore. Paulus was clattering in the kitchen, humming one of his little songs; somewhere in another street, children were laughing.

The river at this hour was a torrent of sunlight, the far shore drowned in sparkle. She wondered if the gold key still lay out there in the cool green depths, buried to the grip in silt. Or perhaps it had already moved on, in the belly of a fish, or in the pocket of some other redhaired girl who'd received an unexpected birthday present.

Acknowledgments

I would like to thank the following people for assistance during the writing of this novel: Edward Miller, Leocadia Miller Wanjira, Erica Cavanagh, Michael Courtney, Isabel Samatar, and Sofia Samatar.

Thanks as well to Sofia at Elsewhen Press for her attentive editing, and to Peter Buck for deftly shepherding the book through the publication process.

Several early chapters were written in Tatiana Caruso's eponymous café in Ventura, California, and her generous spirit and potent espressos cast a spell over the book.

Special thanks to Gail Ambrosius, who cast a professional eye over the chocolate-making sections. Her extraordinary creations are available at gailambrosius.com.

I found *Cunningham's Encyclopedia of Magical Herbs* by Scott Cunningham useful in researching the medicinal and magical uses of plants.

An early version of chapter six, "The Last Djinn," appeared in the *Journal of Mennonite Writing* 2, no. 1 (2019). An early version of the story "The Blue Girl" from chapter eight appeared in the June 15, 2014, issue of the *Ventura Country Reporter*.

Elsewhen Press

delivering outstanding new talents in speculative fiction

Visit the Elsewhen Press website at elsewhen.press for the latest information on all of our titles, authors and events; to read our blog; find out where to buy our books and ebooks; or to place an order.

Sign up for the Elsewhen Press InFlight Newsletter at elsewhen.press/newsletter

The Vanished Mage

Penelope Hill and J. A. Mortimore

A vanished mage…

A missing diamond…

The game is afoot.

"From Broderick, Prince of Asconar, Earl of Carlshore and Thorn, Duke of Wicksborough, Baron of Highbury and Warden of Dershanmoor, to My Lady Parisan, King's Investigator, greetings. It has been brought to my attention that a certain Reinwald, Master Historian, noted Archmagus and tutor to our court in this city of Nemithia, has this day failed to report to the duties awaiting him. I do ask you, as my father's most loyal servant, to seek the cause of this laxity and bring word of the mage to me, so that my concerns as to his safety be allayed."

The herald delivered the message word-perfect to The Lady Parisan, Baroness of Orandy, Knight of the Diamond Circle and Sworn Paladin to Our Lady of the Sighs. Parisan's companion, Foorourow Miar Raar Ramoura, Prince of Ilsfacar, (Foo to his friends) thought it a rather mundane assignment, but nevertheless together they ventured to the Archmagus' imposing home to seek him. It turned out to be the start of an adventure to solve a mystery wrapped in an enigma bound by a conundrum and secured by a puzzle. All because of a missing diamond with a solar system at its core.

Authors Penelope Hill and J. A. Mortimore have effortlessly melded a Holmesian investigative duo, a richly detailed city where they encounter both nobility and seedier denizens, swashbuckling action, and magic that is palpable and, at times, awesome.

ISBN: 9781915304186 (epub, kindle) / 9781915304087 (212pp paperback)

Visit bit.ly/TheVanishedMage

AN ORCHID IN MY BELLY BUTTON

KATY WIMHURST

Offbeat short stories that explore our fragile world

These stories savour the surreal, flirt with magical realism, dabble with dystopia. A boy sees the ghosts of dead crabs. A girl with a fox tail is bullied. A disenchanted woman sprouts orchids from her belly button. Fashion models pursue the trend of having plants as hair. Electronic goods amassing all over London herald an apocalypse. Darkness and wonder, the strange and the ordinary, interweave to offer an environmental and social portrait of our times. Guaranteed to evoke a response, whether a giggle, a gasp, or a nervous gulp, these stories will stay with you, enriching your perception of the world.

Surreal, absurdist, magical realist; Katy Wimhurst writes speculative fiction that meditates on our reality. Although bleak themes are examined – dystopian futures, the climate crisis, bullying – a quirky imagination and wry humour lift the tales above the 'realm of grim'.

ISBN: 9781915304797 (epub, kindle) / 9781915304698 (160pp paperback)

Visit bit.ly/AnOrchidInMyBellyButton

ABOUT KEITH MILLER

Keith Miller is an American citizen, but was born in Tanzania and has spent most of his life in East and North Africa. He is the author of the novels *The Book of Flying*, *The Book on Fire*, and *The Sins of Angels*, as well as translations of Arthur Rimbaud's *The Illuminations* and Charles Baudelaire's *The Flowers of Evil*. He and his wife, writer Sofia Samatar, currently live in Virginia's Shenandoah Valley. They have two children.